Brothers and sisters, I do not consider myself yet to have taken hold of it. But one thing I do: Forgetting what is behind and straining toward what is ahead, I press on toward the goal to win the prize for which God has called me heavenward in Christ Jesus.

—Philippians 3:13–14 (NIV)

MYSTERIES *of* BLACKBERRY VALLEY

Where There's Smoke
The Key Question
Seeds of Suspicion
A Likely Story
Out of the Depths
Run for the Roses

MYSTERIES *of* BLACKBERRY VALLEY

Run for the Roses

CATE NOLAN

A Gift from Guideposts

Thank you for your purchase! We want to express our gratitude for your support with a special gift just for you.

Dive into *Spirit Lifters*, a complimentary e-book that will fortify your faith, offering solace during challenging moments. Its 31 carefully selected scripture verses will soothe and uplift your soul.

Please use the QR code or go to **guideposts.org/spiritlifters** to download.

Mysteries of Blackberry Valley is a trademark of Guideposts.

Published by Guideposts
100 Reserve Road, Suite E200
Danbury, CT 06810
Guideposts.org

Copyright © 2025 by Guideposts. All rights reserved. This book, or parts thereof, may not be reproduced, stored in a retrieval system, or transmitted in any form or by any means, electronic, mechanical, photocopying, recording, or otherwise, without the written permission of the publisher.

This is a work of fiction. Apart from actual historical people and events that may figure into the fiction narrative, all other names, characters, businesses, and events are the creation of the author's imagination and any resemblance to actual persons, living or dead, or events is coincidental. Every attempt has been made to credit the sources of copyrighted material used in this book. If any such acknowledgment has been inadvertently omitted or miscredited, receipt of such information would be appreciated.

Scripture references are from the following sources: *The Holy Bible, King James Version* (KJV). *The Holy Bible, New International Version* (NIV). Copyright © 1973, 1978, 1984, 2011 by Biblica, Inc. Used by permission of Zondervan. All rights reserved worldwide. www.zondervan.com.

Cover and interior design by Müllerhaus
Cover illustration by Bob Kayganich at Illustration Online LLC.
Typeset by Aptara, Inc.

ISBN 978-1-961442-96-2 (hardcover)
ISBN 978-1-961442-97-9 (softcover)
ISBN 978-1-961442-98-6 (epub)

Printed and bound in the United States of America
$PrintCode

Chapter One

Sunlight dappled the back roads of Blackberry Valley, Kentucky, as a gentle breeze made the colorful leaves dance overhead. Endless pastures of rippling grasses spread out beneath a clear blue sky, and not a cloud was in sight on this glorious November morning.

Hannah Prentiss took a deep breath of the unusually warm autumn air blowing through her open window as she guided her green Subaru Outback along the narrow country road.

She tucked a wayward strand of blond hair behind her ear and smiled over at her friend, Lacy Minyard. "Doesn't the air smell delicious? I missed the changing seasons when I was in LA. We had some fall colors, but nothing like this. I'll never regret coming home to Kentucky."

Lacy patted the scarf she'd tied around her reddish-brown hair. "You look happier and more settled every day that you're here. I'll say it again. I'm glad you came home. I missed you."

Hannah released a happy sigh. "You know that feeling when you're absolutely sure you made the right choice because all the pieces simply fall into place?"

Lacy smiled dreamily. "That's how I felt when Neil proposed."

Hannah shook off the twinge she felt at Lacy's words. Someday, if it was God's will, she'd have that kind of love, but for now she was content to run her restaurant.

Content. That was exactly how she felt in Blackberry Valley. She had a business she loved, a community of people who had welcomed her with open arms, good friends to spend her time with—including a certain handsome fire chief—and even the occasional mystery to keep things interesting. Life was good.

"I think you take the next turn up on the right," Lacy said.

"Thanks."

Lacy was playing navigator as they headed to an estate sale Hannah had seen advertised in the *Blackberry Valley Chronicle*, promising a sample of Old Kentucky history. Hannah was always on the alert for local artifacts she could use to decorate her restaurant or the apartment she lived in above it. This habit she'd developed was probably a residual sting from the newspaper's first review of the Hot Spot, which had called the decor *generic*. Thanks to Fire Chief Liam Berthold and his grandfather, that description no longer suited the restaurant, but their contributions had triggered Hannah's interest in memorabilia.

She and Lacy had left early, hoping to be among the first to arrive. Hannah expected to make it back in plenty of time for the dinner rush, but she knew the Hot Spot was in good hands if they were delayed.

"You should slow down," Lacy warned. "With all these overgrown bushes it might be hard to see—"

Lacy's words were interrupted by a streak of brown and white darting into the road ahead of them. Hannah slammed on the brakes and skidded to a halt scant inches from a dog.

Hannah's heart pounded inside her rib cage. She leaned her forehead against the steering wheel and whispered a prayer of thanks. When her pulse calmed, she lifted her head and turned to her friend. "That was a close call. Are you okay?"

"Fine." Lacy watched the dog, who ran in circles on the road ahead, barking at them. "I think he's trying to tell us something. Like he wants us to follow him."

"I think you're right," Hannah said slowly. "Are you game?"

"We'd better. He risked his life to get our attention."

Hannah eased up on the brakes and let the car inch forward. "Okay, pup. Lead the way."

They followed the dog around the turn they'd been planning to take anyway, where the bright red ESTATE SALE SATURDAY sign marked the entrance to a rutted dirt road.

Hannah was grateful for the excellent suspension on her car. Based on its condition, this road wasn't frequently traveled. That didn't bother the dog though. He raced ahead, glancing back every so often to make sure they were behind him.

A few minutes later, she saw a large yellow farmhouse off to the right, and then the lane ended in a yard with a barn directly ahead. The dog dashed to the barn and pranced impatiently as he waited for Hannah to park.

"I guess this is the place," Lacy said. "And he seems friendly enough."

Bold banners advertising the estate sale were draped across the entry to the barn, but the women didn't need those to know where to go. The dog made it clear when he ran straight for it.

Hannah and Lacy climbed from the car and made their way toward the wide barn doors. The dog came up to them, tail wagging as he nuzzled Hannah's jean-clad legs. She ran her hand through his soft fur and felt a collar. He was healthy and clearly well cared for, but when she slipped her hand beneath the leather band, he tugged free and nudged her forward. Obviously, he was still eager for them to keep moving.

"Hello?" Hannah called as she stepped out of the sunshine and into the dim interior of the barn. Near the entrance, dust motes drifted in the air above stacked bales of hay. Ahead, a wide aisle separated two rows of stalls. "Is anyone here?"

"Help. Back here." The feeble call was barely audible in the large space.

The dog barked again and ran toward the voice.

"We're coming," Lacy called. "Keep talking if you can, so we can follow the sound of your voice."

"Or we can just listen for the dog," Hannah added as he continued to bark excitedly.

"I'm behind the stalls, by the tack room."

The voice sounded relieved, and Hannah shared the feeling. How fortunate that they'd chosen to follow the dog.

Lacy hurried down the aisle between the rows of stalls filled with furniture, knickknacks, and antiques of all kinds, but Hannah had to force herself to keep moving. Her ten-year-old self would have been starry-eyed and daydreaming of all these stalls filled with horses instead, and to be truthful, her adult self was inclined to do the same. But someone needed their help.

"Over here." An arm waved in the air, and Hannah hurried forward to find a young woman lying prone on the scattered hay.

Lacy knelt beside her. "Are you badly hurt? Do we need to call an ambulance?"

"No, I think I'll be okay once I get some ice on my ankle. I just can't get free."

Hannah could see her leg trapped beneath a large box. A stepladder rested on its side a short distance away. "What happened?" she asked as she struggled to lift the heavy box.

"I was nearly done setting up the sale when I saw that box on a shelf above the door to the tack room. I could see some sort of trophy sticking out, and I wondered what else was inside. I got my hand on it, but then I lost my footing. When I grabbed at the edge, it tumbled down on me and knocked me off the ladder." She made a face as she gestured to her leg. "Obviously, it was foolish to try it on my own. I'm Sylvia Parsons," she added. "How did you find me? Are you early for the sale?"

Hannah and Lacy introduced themselves. "Your dog came and got us," Hannah added. "He ran all the way out to the road."

The woman's jaw dropped in surprise. "He did all that?"

"He did," Lacy replied. "Nearly got himself killed running in front of the car. Lucky for him, my friend's brakes and reflexes are good. He must really love you."

Sylvia raised her hands. "He's not mine. I never saw him before today. He sniffed around the barn all morning while I worked on setting up for the sale. He disappeared when I fell, and I thought the commotion scared him. It's amazing that he went to get help."

"You must have been so scared," Lacy said, giving Sylvia's hand a gentle squeeze.

"I wasn't too worried. I figured someone would show up for the sale sooner or later," Sylvia said. "And if not, I trusted God would provide."

Lacy laughed. "I guess He provided via a four-legged creature. I wonder what your rescuer's name is."

"He has a collar," Hannah said. "I was able to grasp it earlier, but he managed to pull away before I could see if there was a tag."

"There isn't," Sylvia said. "I checked that when he came to visit me. Maybe it broke off and got lost. What a mystery. I wonder who he belongs to. He must be someone's pet, given how friendly and healthy he is."

Hannah's gaze caught Lacy's as she heard the word *mystery*. *Here we go again.*

They knelt behind Sylvia, one on either side, and helped to lift her until she could balance on her good foot. With Hannah and Lacy supporting her, she managed to hop over and settle on a nearby hay bale.

"I can't believe I did this," Sylvia said ruefully. "Yesterday there were four big strong men here moving everything from the house to the barn, but no, I have to wait until I'm all alone."

"I can take a look at your ankle if you want," Lacy offered. "I live on a farm and have tended to more than my share of injuries. Mostly on goats and horses, of course, but some humans too." She chuckled.

Sylvia nodded. "Thank you. It might be worse than I thought. There should be some ice in the house, since the electricity is still on and the owners didn't want to sell the refrigerator. I hate to ask, but—"

"Say no more," Hannah interrupted. "I'll grab the first aid kit from my car and then go find some ice. Is there someone we can call for you?"

Sylvia shook her head. "I'm here to supervise the estate sale for my firm. I'm staying at the Blackberry Inn. I don't know anyone in town."

"Well, now you know us," Hannah reassured her. "Don't you worry."

Hannah retrieved the first aid kit and left it with Lacy before heading to the house. It felt odd walking into someone else's home, even though she knew the owners were no longer there. It was an estate sale, after all. As she walked through the empty rooms, she couldn't help but wonder about the people who'd once made this their home. Who had they been? Why was there no one left?

Hannah opened the freezer, and the burst of cold air cooled her curiosity enough that she could laugh at herself. Coming back to Blackberry Valley had not only allowed the business side of her personality to emerge, but the instinct that had made her love mysteries seemed to be thriving here too. Every time she turned around, she found something new to investigate.

She had to admit that it was sure making her life here an adventure.

By the time Hannah returned with ice, Lacy had pronounced Sylvia's ankle badly bruised. They set her up by the makeshift cash register and volunteered to help however they could. Hannah called the Hot Spot and explained the situation to Elaine Wilby. Her capable hostess promised to take over if she wasn't back by dinner.

Hannah had already hung up before it dawned on her that Elaine might know the people who'd left this estate. Her family had owned the King Farm in the valley for more than a hundred years. Maybe Elaine would even know who owned the dog.

People were beginning to trickle into the barn by then, eager to search for treasure. Remembering the box they'd left on the ground, Hannah hurried back to move it out of the way. The trophy that had caught Sylvia's eye had fallen out. Hannah picked it up, and a thrill went through her as she held the golden cup. It was a first-place trophy for a horse race. For a moment she was ten again and dreaming of riding. She'd had a few lessons as a child and had read every horse book on the Blackberry Valley Library shelves. She smiled, remembering those happy days.

A peek into the box revealed more trophies and racing memorabilia. On a whim, she dragged the box over to ask Sylvia if she could purchase the contents. She'd come for artifacts for the Hot Spot after all. These weren't quite on theme for the converted firehouse, but she couldn't resist.

Once her purchase was settled, Hannah shoved the box under a table against the wall and got to work. She and Lacy were soon caught up in the excitement of the estate sale. By midafternoon, when the flow of customers dwindled, they were all exhausted. Lacy flopped down on a hay bale beside Sylvia, but Hannah had something else in mind.

"Sylvia, that box that fell on you—should we look at it together? I've been dying of curiosity all day to know what I bought."

"Let's," Sylvia agreed. "Better be something good to make up for all the trouble it's caused."

Hannah got down on her knees and tugged the box from under the table. The dog, who had vanished for most of the day, came up beside her and sniffed at the cardboard. "What do you think, pup? Is there something good inside?"

The dog yipped, and the three women burst into laughter.

Hannah settled cross-legged on the hay and opened the box. The first thing she pulled out was the golden trophy she'd set on top. "I'll bet this is what made the box topple over onto you. It's really heavy." She hoisted the trophy so Sylvia could see.

The woman squinted and read the label out loud. "'First Place, Kentucky's Angel, May 4, 1963.' I wonder who that was. Or rather, whose horse."

Hannah gently set the trophy aside and pulled out another, smaller trophy, topped with a golden horse. "This one's for Kentucky's Angel too, from a year earlier." She dug back into the box, removing an assortment of ribbons, racing programs, and finally, at the bottom, a photo album with *Kentucky's Angel* embossed on the front. Hannah flipped open the book and found page after page of dried flowers. "Whoa. These look like they're from the garlands that get draped over first-place horses, like in the Kentucky Derby."

"That's a lot of wins." Lacy took out her phone, tapped on the screen a few times, and let out a low whistle. "I haven't read the whole thing, but listen to this. 'Police have still uncovered no clues as to the whereabouts of Kentucky's Angel or her jockey, Mickey Dawes. The pair disappeared on the eve of what was expected to be the champion filly's run for the roses.'"

Sylvia gasped, and Hannah sank back against the box, a stunned expression on her face as she gazed at the memorabilia strewn before her. The dog nudged her leg, and a smile slowly spread over Hannah's face. "Sounds like we have two new mysteries to solve. Who owns this dog?" She patted the pup then lifted the trophy. "And what happened to Kentucky's Angel and Mickey Dawes?"

Chapter Two

The November sun was low in the sky, and a chilly wind had replaced the morning breeze by the time Hannah and Lacy finished repacking the box, neatly stacking programs on top of the album and nestling the trophies more securely against the side. Hannah stood and brushed stray bits of hay off her jeans as they got ready to leave.

She started to hoist the box, but as she got it settled in her arms, she caught a glimpse of Sylvia struggling to stand. After exchanging a glance with Lacy, Hannah set the box back down and walked over to the young woman.

"Sylvia, there's no way you can drive yourself back to the inn. Why don't you leave your car here and come back with us? I'm dropping Lacy at her farm, but then I can take you straight to your room."

Visible relief washed over the injured woman's face, but she protested anyway. "I can't put you to that much trouble." She looked back at the house. "Maybe I should just stay here for the night."

Lacy linked her arm through Sylvia's. "There is no way we are leaving you here alone. Hannah and I will worry about you all night. If you don't want to stay at the Blackberry Inn, you can stay with me on my farm. I'm sure my husband, Neil, won't mind. He owns the bookstore in town."

"Legend & Key? Oh, that's a lovely store. I stopped in there as soon as I settled in my room yesterday. I always bring a book to read, but I finished the last one on the plane."

Hannah laughed. "You fell in with the right people. We love to read. Though Lacy loves puzzles more."

Lacy's face split into a grin. "We're having a puzzle night at my house on Monday. You should join us."

Sylvia smiled back at her. "Thanks. That sounds like fun. If I'm still in town, maybe I will."

Hannah looked down at Sylvia's swollen ankle that couldn't bear weight. "My unprofessional diagnosis—a puzzle night with your leg elevated is just what the doctor would order. But seriously, if your ankle isn't better by morning, call me and I'll take you to our local doctor for a checkup."

Tears sparkled in Sylvia's eyes. "You ladies are too sweet. I don't know how I would have managed without your help."

"We're happy we were there," Hannah assured her. "If you were planning to stay in Blackberry Valley, you'd learn quickly that there are no strangers in this town. Only friends you haven't met yet. I know it's a cliché, but it's true here."

"And now we're friends you *have* met. So let's get moving," Lacy prompted. "I'm starving."

Hannah and Sylvia laughed. "That's a good thing for you," Hannah whispered. "Lacy's a great cook—especially when she's hungry."

Hannah ran ahead to pull her car up to the barn door so Sylvia wouldn't have to walk very far. While Lacy took the keys and locked up the barn and house, Hannah helped Sylvia get settled in the back seat and then placed the heavy box in the rear compartment. She wasn't going to chance a trophy rolling out and hitting anyone. But as she got behind the wheel, she couldn't stop thinking about the missing horse and jockey, and everything they'd found in the box.

Once Lacy had climbed in beside her, Hannah started back down the road. "Sylvia, I hope this won't breach any kind of confidentiality agreement, but do you have any information about who that box could have belonged to? Do you know who owned this farm?"

Sylvia heaved a frustrated sigh. "I really don't, honestly. My boss handles that part of the arrangements. I just do the on-site work. Sometimes the owners are present, but most of the time they're not. I think it's probably too sad for any remaining family members to have to watch their family history be sold off."

"That's so hard," Lacy said. "My farm has been in my family for generations, and I expect to pass it on to my own children someday. How tragic it would be to have no family left to take over."

Sylvia nodded. "Sometimes there's no one left, but sometimes it's finances. Sadly, we often have family members fighting because they feel no connection to the property and just want the money. Then we sell everything and divide it up according to a will."

Sylvia's words turned Hannah's thoughts to her own family home. She couldn't imagine fighting with Drew, her younger brother, over it. They both had such sweet memories of growing up here in Blackberry Valley in that house. Though it had been hard for her father living alone there after her mother's death, he'd come up with the perfect solution by having Uncle Gordon move in with him. Hannah didn't think she could have borne it if her father had sold it instead.

She shook off the thoughts as she focused on the road. Dark fell earlier each day in November, and she had to watch out for deer.

Which reminded her of the last animal she'd had to be wary of on the road. "We forgot the dog. Did you see him as we were leaving?"

"I searched and called for him," Lacy reassured her. "He wasn't there. He probably lives on a neighboring farm and went home after his adventurous day."

Hannah had to settle for that answer, but she made a private vow to call the vet's office tomorrow and ask if they recognized the dog from her description. She needed to make sure he was all right.

Lacy and Sylvia fell to chatting as they drove through the deepening twilight, and Hannah's thoughts returned to the box they'd found. Kentucky's Angel. Her imagination filled with vibrant images of the horse racing to all those victories.

The years fell away as she recalled her dad bringing her to visit his friend at the Keeneland race course. Oh, she'd been horse crazy back then. Apparently, she still was. She had to find out more about Kentucky's Angel. Surely someone around here remembered something.

Maybe when she called the vet, she could ask about the filly too. He might remember hearing about the disappearance and know who to ask about her. The excitement of a new mystery to solve swirled through her head, but she forced herself to focus her attention on the road until they reached Lacy's turnoff.

When Hannah parked at the farmhouse, Lacy swiveled in her seat to face Sylvia. "Did you decide? Will you stay with me for the night?"

Sylvia flushed. "Thank you for the offer, Lacy, but if Hannah doesn't mind dropping me off, I should stay at the inn. I have a conference call with my boss first thing in the morning. I need to get ready for it."

"If you're sure."

Sylvia nodded. "I am. Hopefully I'll see you for puzzle night."

"Good. See you then!" Lacy gave Hannah a wink as she opened the door. "Don't you stay up all night going through that box."

"Who, me?" Hannah feigned confusion. "Why would you think a mysterious horse and rider disappearance, and a box of racing memorabilia, would interest me?" She could barely keep the laughter out of her voice.

"Why indeed? Nothing like that would ever get your attention. What was I thinking?" Lacy shook her head and pushed the car door closed. "Hope you have a good night at the restaurant," she called as she started toward the farmhouse door.

As Lacy disappeared inside, Hannah asked Sylvia, "Do you want to stay back there or move up front?"

"I'm fine back here, as long as you don't mind looking like my chauffeur."

"Not at all." Hannah pretended to doff a cap. "Next stop, Blackberry Inn, the finest place to rest your head in all of Kentucky." Hannah started back down the drive, but then a thought occurred to her. "It might be too late for dinner at the inn, and you're in no shape to go running out for food. Why don't I stop by the Hot Spot and pick up something to go?"

"What's the Hot Spot?"

Hannah grinned. "My farm-to-table restaurant."

"You own a restaurant, and you spent the day helping me?"

"I've got a great staff, and my chef—well, he's a little quirky, but his cooking is amazing. We'll pass the restaurant on the way to your inn. You can pull up the menu on your phone. Let me know what sounds good, and I'll phone it in. Jacob will have it ready by the time we get there."

Hannah smiled, listening to Sylvia's excited commentary as she scrolled through the menu. Nothing made her happier than people appreciating the delicious meals Jacob whipped up. It gave her a sense of satisfaction to know she had created something people loved, and she knew Jacob felt the same. Too bad Sylvia couldn't make it inside to get the full Hot Spot experience.

"It all looks so good. I don't know what to choose."

"I can ask them to do a Firehouse Sampler. Then you get a little bit of everything. How does that sound?"

"Like far more than I deserve for being awkward enough to pull a box down on my ankle."

"We all deserve a treat now and again." Hannah used her hands-free system to call the restaurant.

Elaine picked up, and Hannah smiled at the warm welcome in her voice as she said, "Hello, this is the Hot Spot, Blackberry Valley's hottest restaurant. How can we help you?"

"Hi, Elaine. It's Hannah. I need a favor for a new friend, Sylvia Parsons. She's visiting town and hurt her ankle, so she can't really get around on her own. I'm dropping her off at the inn, but if we don't feed her, she'll have no dinner. Would you have Jacob make up a sampler for her? I'm heading in from Lacy's now, so I can swing by and pick it up."

"Oh, Hannah, what bad luck for her. I'll ask Jacob to put together something extra special."

"Thanks, you're the best. Appreciate it. See you soon."

When Hannah disconnected the call, Sylvia said, "Y'all are far too kind."

"Not at all. It's Blackberry Valley hospitality. Where are you from, Sylvia? I never asked. Is your company local?"

"No, I work for a big auction house in Atlanta. We don't often have business in Kentucky, but someone must have recommended us. I was excited to be the one sent here. I've never been to Kentucky before. I'd planned to do some sightseeing before I head back, but I guess that's out of the question now."

"Then you should extend your stay. Come to puzzle night Monday. If you need a book to read, Neil will be happy to deliver to the inn, or I can ask Evangeline at the library if the bookstore doesn't have what you want. I'm happy to check it out for you."

Sylvia chuckled. "I picked up quite a few from Legend & Key, but I'll let you know if I finish them."

"Atlanta. Hmm," Hannah mused aloud. "I wonder who these owners were that they hired a firm from out of town."

Sylvia laughed. "Lacy wasn't kidding. You do love a mystery, don't you?"

"They seem to keep finding me ever since I moved back here." Hannah pulled her Subaru up in front of the Hot Spot where Elaine was waiting at the curb.

Sylvia peered out the window. "Isn't that a firehouse?"

"It used to be, but the fire department moved to a new building. I renovated this one, and now it's the Hot Spot."

Hannah rolled down the window to greet Elaine. She knew her hostess would be curious to meet Sylvia, so she pressed a button to lower the back window too.

Elaine leaned in. "Hey, I'm Elaine. Chef Jacob packed the best dinner for you. I know you're going to love it. I stuck a menu inside," she added as she handed over the bag and accepted Sylvia's credit card. She dashed inside to run it and was back in a flash. "If you need anything else, just call the number on the menu. Enjoy."

Sylvia seemed completely overwhelmed as she murmured her thanks. "I really appreciate how kind y'all have been to me."

Hannah understood the feeling. She'd been stunned by how welcoming and helpful the people of her hometown had been when she came back to set up the restaurant. She guessed it wasn't the kind of thing a child would have noticed, but as an adult she was so thankful to be part of such a special community. And Elaine was a huge part of it. Her legendary friendliness was what made her such a great hostess for the Hot Spot.

Elaine was turning to go back inside when Hannah remembered the dog. "Hey, Elaine, have you ever seen a stray dog running out by your farm? Long story, but he ran to get help for Sylvia after she fell, and he disappeared again. A mutt. Brown and white fur."

Elaine thought for a moment. "Doesn't sound familiar, but there are a lot of farm dogs roaming out there. Could belong to any of the families. Where were you?"

Sylvia rattled off the address, and Elaine shook her head. "Not familiar with that one. But as I said, he could belong to anyone. I'll keep an eye out when I drive home."

"Thanks. I'll be back as soon as I get Sylvia settled. How are things going?"

Grinning, Elaine said, "The Hot Spot is smoking tonight."

Hannah laughed. There was apparently no end to the puns around her restaurant's location in the old firehouse, but that was fine with her.

She delivered Sylvia to the inn and entrusted her to Sabrina Hill amid a flurry of hugs and promises to check in the next morning. The inn's proprietor was trying to keep the family place running now that her parents had retired and left it in her care, and Hannah suspected she was excited to have a guest from Atlanta. Sylvia would be in good hands.

Within minutes, Hannah was on the way back to her restaurant, but without Sylvia as a distraction, her thoughts started spinning. A mysterious dog and a missing horse and jockey sixty years apart. Could they somehow be connected?

Chapter Three

Saturday dinner was in full swing as Hannah stepped through the door, and her heart lifted as it always did to think this was all hers. Back in Los Angeles, she'd worked in other people's high-end restaurants, catering to celebrity clientele. Having her own place someday had been nothing but a dream. But here in Blackberry Valley, she owned the Hot Spot and was serving the community she loved. Her heart was so full she still had to pinch herself sometimes. Everywhere she looked were people she knew, and they all seemed to be enjoying themselves.

Miriam Spencer's son, Tom, sat at a table with Connie Sanchez's husband, Hal, and Evangeline Cooke's husband, Ted. She chuckled to see them sitting clear on the opposite side of the large room from Miriam, Connie, and Evangeline. The men were probably talking football as usual.

Firefighters Colt Walker and Archer Lestrade occupied a booth, and she could see there was some serious conversation taking place between them. Maybe Archer was planning something special for his girlfriend, Bryn Reynolds.

Too bad Jack Delaney, the editor-in-chief of the *Blackberry Valley Chronicle*, wasn't there. She would have liked to ask if he knew anything about the dog or the horse. She made a mental note to stop by the *Chronicle* on Monday and see what she could find out.

Marshall Fredericks, the local food critic and blogger, was posted at his favorite booth in the corner. She used to get nervous when he showed up, but now she knew he was here to see her server, Raquel Holden, more than to critique anything on the menu. It was sweet that he chose to come here to eat and work on *The Gourmet Guy* just to be near Raquel. They made a cute pair, and Hannah was thrilled to see them enjoying each other's company. She'd make sure Raquel got a break so she could go sit with him for a while.

"Hannah!" Miriam waved her cane. The eighty-five-year-old woman constantly amazed Hannah with her energy and enthusiasm for life. Hannah hoped she had even half that much zest in her spirit when she reached her eighties.

Crossing the room, Hannah said hello to her friends. "I'm sorry I wasn't here when you arrived."

Connie, the church secretary, squeezed over to make room for Hannah. "Will you join us?"

"I would love to," Hannah said, while she remained standing, "but I just got here and I need to check on everything."

Elaine stepped up beside her. "Everything's fine. I'm sure Sylvia isn't the only one who's hungry. Why don't you rest a bit and let me bring you tonight's special? It's a hit. I think Jacob's trying out some ideas for the Thanksgiving menu."

When Hannah's stomach growled softly, the ladies all laughed. "Come join us," Miriam insisted. "We want to hear all about who this Sylvia is."

Though Hannah pretended to glare at Elaine, the hostess merely shrugged and laughed. "What can I say? They heard me talking to you when they arrived."

Hannah shook her head. This, too, was part of small-town life. "Okay, scootch over. Have I got a story for you."

Hours later, Hannah smothered a yawn as she bade goodbye to the last of the diners. In the kitchen, Jacob was shutting down and cleaning up. Raquel made fast work of straightening the tables and wiping things down. Was it possible Raquel had Sunday plans with Marshall? It would be nice to have someone to spend the day with.

Someone like Liam. She'd kept an eye out all evening, but the kind, thoughtful firefighter had never joined his friends. He was probably on duty.

Stretching, Hannah thought of her comfy bed. She wanted nothing more than to curl up and go to sleep. It had been a long day. When she and Lacy started out that morning, she'd had no idea they would have so much happen, topped off by finding a mystery in a box of memorabilia.

She'd completely forgotten about the box. By the time she'd finished telling her church friends the story, the restaurant had gotten so crowded that she'd jumped in to help. The rush had driven her new mystery right out of her mind. Some sleuth she was.

Dylan pushed through the kitchen doors, carrying a tray of teetering glasses. "Dylan," she called—and instantly knew it had been a mistake. He swung toward her, the tray tilted, and the glasses began to slide.

Hannah jumped forward and steadied the tray, deftly shifting it to her own secure grip.

Dylan's face flushed. "I'm sorry."

Hannah immediately sought to reassure him. She had a soft spot for Dylan and had been trying to build his confidence. He'd always been a bit clumsy, but he had such a good and generous heart, and he'd been working and studying so hard. Since their talks about his being more than capable of succeeding at college, his work performance had improved. She didn't want her mistake to set him back. "It was my fault, Dylan. I shouldn't have startled you."

He shuffled his feet. "Did you need something?"

Hannah nodded, hoping her request would make him feel better. "I do. There's a heavy box in the back of my car. Do you think you could carry it upstairs for me? You can leave it on the landing."

"Sure thing, Hannah."

His eagerness to help made her smile. "Thanks, Dylan. The car's unlocked. Be careful with the box though. There are some trophies in there that might fall out."

While Dylan took care of the box, Hannah finished closing the restaurant. By the time she finally locked the door behind everyone and headed up to her apartment, she was ready to collapse from fatigue. It had been such an exciting but exhausting day. Her body wanted to fall into bed, but her mind buzzed with questions about the contents of the box. They'd barely glanced through everything while in the barn. She couldn't wait to examine all the racing programs and look more closely at the album. Maybe a tiny peek tonight would satisfy her curiosity—enough to let her sleep, anyway.

When she reached the landing, Hannah unlocked her door and dragged the box inside. Resisting the urge to dive right in, she went to the kitchen, filled a kettle with water, and set it to boil while she changed into comfy pajamas. Once she had her mug of cinnamon spice tea, she set it on an end table, switched on a lamp, and dragged the box up beside the sofa.

First, she lifted the smaller trophy she'd seen earlier for a closer examination. Its weight was solid in her hands, and she rotated the base, taking it in from all angles. This was no cheap award. The horse was so beautifully molded that she almost expected it to burst from the base and gallop across the room. *Kentucky's Angel* was etched on the base and below it, *August 23, 1962*. Goose bumps rose along her arms as she thought about it. Someone had accepted this trophy for a victory almost thirty years before she'd even been born.

Hannah closed her eyes and let her imagination take her back in time to the summer before she'd turned eleven. That was when her fascination with horses had really begun. Her father's good friend, Owen Murphy—or "Murph" as he was known in racing circles—was working at Keeneland that year, and Hannah and her father visited him almost every weekend.

They'd rise before dawn and head up to Lexington while it was still dark in order to catch the morning workout. While her father and his friend caught up, she would balance on a rung of the fence and watch the horses gallop around the track. She'd especially loved being there when they were doing speed workouts. The horses would surge past her, little more than a blur.

Afterward they would have breakfast in the track kitchen with the riders and trainers. Murph had grown up in western Kentucky and had been around horses all his life. He loved regaling Hannah with his exaggerated stories, and she'd hung on to his every word.

When Hannah thought back on her life, that summer stood out as a highlight. Those times with her father were cherished memories. She'd learned so much about horses from listening to Murph and watching the training. And she'd read every book she could find about the majestic animals. For one blissful summer, she'd planned to grow up to be a jockey. While most kids begged their parents for a dog or cat, she'd begged for a horse for her birthday.

She smiled now, thinking about it. What would they have done with a horse in their backyard? Hannah didn't get the horse, but she did get something special. The morning of her eleventh birthday, her father had suggested a trip. Although she had a party planned for later with her friends, she'd been excited to get up early and drive out to horse country as the sun was rising behind them. The ground was covered with a light frost, but that didn't keep the horses from frolicking in the fields.

Only a few days earlier, for Christmas, she'd received a full set of Walter Farley's *Black Stallion* books. Flame was her favorite horse from the stories. Even all these years later, she remembered the feeling that had come over her while reading about the wild Island Stallion. That birthday morning, she'd been overjoyed to visit real horses again. When she learned that her birthday present was riding lessons come spring, her love affair with horses was sealed.

If her parents had thought that gifting books and lessons would take the place of her own horse, they learned their mistake quickly. Rather than satisfying her yearning for a horse, the books had only fired her up. Hannah smiled at the memory. She was pretty sure her parents had regretted the day they'd introduced her to horses. Maybe that was why her mother had fostered her interest in cooking.

A wave of sadness washed over her as she thought of her lovely, vivacious mother, Frieda. She had been gone eight years, and not a day passed that Hannah didn't think of her. She might have gotten her love of horses from her father, but her love of cooking had been nurtured in her mother's kitchen.

Hannah had such fond memories of watching her mother invent recipes based on the ingredients they had on hand. Sometimes they made a game of it, coming up with truly crazy combinations. Hannah chuckled. Her mom would have loved Jacob and his culinary creativity.

She moved to set the trophy back on the table, but as she shifted it, the light caught something they'd missed in the dim barn lighting. Below the horse's name and the date, there was more engraving on the base, but it was nearly worn away. She brought the trophy closer to the light. It was a little better, but she still couldn't make out the words.

Hannah groaned in frustration. If she could read the rest of the words, they might give her a clue as to how to begin searching for the horse. And she *needed* to find where Kentucky's Angel and her jockey had gone when they went missing all those years ago. It wasn't just any mystery. That horse-crazy little girl still lived inside her, and she demanded answers. And whoever this box belonged to needed it back. No one took that much care with a memory book and then tossed it away carelessly. Hannah felt in her bones that there was more to this story.

And the writing on the trophy might hold a clue if only she could read it.

Suddenly, Hannah remembered a documentary about how researchers tried to read old tombstones by making rubbings using a pencil or crayon over a sheet of paper. It helped to define the indents, making the writing a bit clearer.

Taking the trophy with her, Hannah ran back downstairs to her office, where she grabbed a sheet of copy paper and a couple of pencils. Since the restaurant kitchen had better lighting, she headed there instead of going back upstairs. With all the lights on, she set the trophy on the counter and rested the paper on top of the inscription. Then she rubbed the side edge of the pencil across the paper, slowly increasing the pressure.

When she felt like she'd covered all the writing, she lifted the paper and studied the random, scattered letters. She could make out some—a *C*, an *M*, and an *N*—but not enough to read the full text.

By now, her eyes burned from fatigue and the strain of trying to read the letters, so she cleaned the counter, shut off the lights, and headed back upstairs.

Back in her own apartment, Hannah rested the golden horse on the counter where she could see it and settled back on the sofa, dragging a soft crocheted afghan over her lap. She debated whether to go to bed or delve deeper into the box. She had church in the morning, so the wise decision would be to go to sleep, but the questions swirling in her brain seemed unlikely to allow that. Maybe she'd just flip through the album.

Almost reverently, Hannah slid her finger beneath the album cover and lifted it. The flowers had been pressed with care, and each had a date written beside it. Maybe if she found the date for the trophy in this album, she could research which race used these flowers— the way roses were the flower of the Kentucky Derby and black-eyed Susans draped the winner of the Preakness Stakes.

With that thought in mind, Hannah started thumbing through the pages. The last several pages were empty, which made sense because the final bouquet had a date only weeks before Kentucky's Angel had gone missing. Presumably, if the horse had not disappeared, those pages would also have been filled with more victory bouquets.

Hannah closed the album. She was disappointed that she'd reached a dead end, but she couldn't let that deter her. Someone had taken a great deal of care to preserve these memories, which didn't add up with the box being left in the barn. What had happened to the person who had made this album, and why had the box been abandoned?

Chapter Four

Lexington, Kentucky
June 1955

James "Chaddy" Chadwick Sr. stood in the shadow of the barn, trying to ignore the latest round of fighting between his boss and the reprobate who'd run off with the boss's daughter. He couldn't see them from where he stood, but as head trainer, Chaddy had witnessed plenty of their arguments over the years. He'd made it a habit to stay clear of the fallout.

He watched as a child slipped out of the car and toward the paddock. It was a shame the way this family had fallen apart because a rebellious young woman had chosen to marry a man her father disapproved of. Her father had cut all ties. Now his daughter was dead, and her child was left to the mercies of an unfit father and a proud grandfather who might never get to know the child.

At least the kid had the sense to seek out horses. Horses could soothe the soul like nothing else. Chaddy should know—he'd been training them his entire long life, and now he was raising his grandson to do the same.

The voices from the yard grew louder and more violent, so Chaddy stepped out of the shadows to welcome the kid into his world.

He was still too far away when he saw the kid climb the rail. The pack of horses raced toward the fence, hoofbeats roaring like thunder. Their tails streamed out behind them like banners in the wind as they raced in circles.

One young horse, running a little slower than the others, broke from the pack and cantered up to the railing.

Chaddy held his breath. He trusted his horses, but one never knew what to expect from a child.

But as he drew closer, he overheard a one-sided conversation.

"Hello. You're beautiful. I like watching you run."

The child's voice sounded deliberately low so as not to risk scaring the horse away. The colt came closer to the fence and pushed his nose between the rails.

Chaddy heard more soft words. "I wish I had a carrot or an apple to give you."

Stepping forward, Chaddy also spoke softly, not wanting to spook either the horse or the child. "He likes peppermints." He offered the child one from his pocket.

The kid accepted the candy with a solemn nod.

Chaddy's face relaxed into a smile as he watched the small body lean against the fence and rest a hand on the rail, slowly unfurling fingers for the horse to sniff. The peppermint lay on a perfectly flat palm, and the horse nibbled it up. The kid never flinched.

"How did you know to do that?" Chaddy asked.

"My friend knows about being friends with dogs. He always says that you should let them approach you. I figured horses couldn't be that different."

So focused was he on their interaction that Chaddy scarcely registered the bigger horse that came up beside the colt. But when the larger horse nudged the baby aside, he heard more gentle words.

"You must be the mama horse. I'm not going to hurt your baby. I only wanted to meet him."

The larger horse sniffed suspiciously until Chaddy handed over another peppermint. "You have the same way with horses that your mother had."

The kid went completely still. "You knew my mother?"

"From the day she was born. Your mama loved these horses."

He watched while the kid gazed over the field, eyes never leaving the horses, though Chaddy could see that his words had set thoughts in motion. "Then why did she leave?"

Chaddy sighed softly. Ways of the human heart were not something he understood much about. "Seems she loved your daddy more."

A bellow from the parking lot made Chaddy shake his head. The father, his face beet-red and sweaty, stormed toward the parked car, shouting back at the grandfather.

Resignation settled over the kid's face and tugged at Chaddy's old heart. "I reckon I'd better get going."

Chaddy leaned against the railing to chuck the horse under the chin, but also to murmur an offer. "I reckon so, but you come back anytime you want. You're always welcome here. The horses know a soul they can trust, and they trust you."

The kid dropped down from the fence, avoiding Chaddy's gaze. "Will you tell me about my mother?"

"You betcha."

Chaddy watched as the father bellowed again, and the child ran toward the car, stopping only to turn and wave. Chaddy waved back, but disgust roiled in his gut. Some people didn't deserve children any more than they deserved horses. At least the old man had the ability to keep the kid's father away from the horses.

Chapter Five

Morning sunlight filtering through the living room curtains woke Hannah. She stretched, wondering why she felt so stiff—until she opened her eyes and realized she was on the sofa. She had a vague memory of deciding to close her eyes for a moment while she pondered the mystery, but she must have dozed off. Fortunately, the scrapbook had slid onto the sofa rather than the floor, and a quick examination revealed that nothing had been damaged.

Yawning, Hannah rubbed her eyes and reached for her phone to see what time it was. Seven a.m. Too early to be awake on a Sunday morning after a late night of work, but too late to go to bed before church.

She swung her legs around to the floor and stood. A hot shower and a cup of coffee should revive her enough, and she might even have time to go through some of the racing programs before she had to leave.

As she was choosing a comfortable skirt and a warm sweater, Hannah suddenly thought of Sylvia. Maybe she would like to join them for services. Hannah usually walked the short distance to Grace Community Church, but she could drive to the inn and pick up her new acquaintance.

It felt too early to call, so Hannah texted an invitation before heading to the shower.

She was dressed and sipping her coffee by the time a reply came. If it wasn't too much trouble, Sylvia would love to join.

Hannah smiled. She couldn't wait to introduce her new friend to Pastor Bob Dawson and his wife, Lorelai.

Once she had the arrangements settled, Hannah brought the stack of programs over to her kitchen table. Since she was feeling more alert, she decided to search through them to find one for the date on the trophy, but even caffeinated she found nothing that matched. Maybe she needed to search online, but the race had been so long ago that she wondered whether she would find much. She glanced at the clock. Time to leave. The search would have to wait.

The morning was brisk and sunny as Hannah walked down to her car. It was a perfect day for a horse ride down a long tree-lined lane with leaves glowing red and gold overhead against the blue autumn sky. Even without a horse, the weather was glorious, and she planned to enjoy it while it lasted.

Within minutes she pulled up in front of the inn. Thinking that Sylvia might need help, considering her ankle, Hannah parked and hurried up the path to the Blackberry Inn's entrance. Before she could even knock, the door swung open.

Sabrina Hill greeted her warmly. "Good morning, Hannah. It's wonderful to see you. Please come in. I've been meaning to speak to you about setting up packages so our guests can get a weekend special that includes dinner at the Hot Spot. What do you think? Did you ever do anything like that in LA?"

Hannah was delighted by the innkeeper's enthusiasm. In the time she'd been here, the only real interaction she'd had with Sabrina was when she dropped Sylvia off last night, but since they both ran businesses in Blackberry Valley, it made sense to collaborate. "I've never done that, but it's an intriguing idea, Sabrina. Right now, I'm here to take Sylvia to church, but you should drop by the Hot Spot for dinner some night and we'll talk more about it."

"I'll do that. Poor Sylvia. She's had a rough time of it. I rewrapped the bandage this morning and gave her a cane another guest left behind last year. It's kind of you to step in and help care for her."

Hannah detected a faint undercurrent in Sabrina's voice that she couldn't quite identify. Rumor had it that Sabrina was having her own rough time trying to run the Blackberry Inn after taking over when her parents retired. Maybe she could use some kindness herself. "Would you like to join us for church, Sabrina?" Hannah asked.

Sabrina quickly smothered her surprise at the invitation. "It is so nice of you to think of me, Hannah. Sadly, my Sunday employee gave notice this week, so I've had to fill in. But please give my best to Pastor Bob and his dear wife. Let me go get Sylvia so you're not late."

"I'm right here." Sylvia's cheerful tone greeted Hannah. The woman barely seemed to need the cane as she made her way down the hall, but she still walked with a limp.

"You look so much better this morning. Sabrina must be taking excellent care of you."

"She is," Sylvia said with a smile at the innkeeper.

"I'll see you later for dinner," Sabrina called as they made their way to the car.

Hannah waved back. "See you then."

By the time Hannah drove to church, dropped Sylvia in front, parked the car, and hurried back to the door, they barely had time to slip inside before service started. Hannah loved gathering with friends and family at Grace Community Church, and Pastor Bob always inspired her, but today so many thoughts raced through her head that she feared she would have a hard time staying focused.

However, as soon as Pastor Bob's rich voice began to fill the room, Hannah's mind settled, and she listened carefully as he read the parables from Luke about the shepherd searching for his lost sheep and the woman who had lost a coin.

"Luke tells us, '…there is rejoicing in the presence of the angels of God over one sinner who repents.' Through these parables, he reminds us that no matter how far off track we may roam, Jesus, the Good Shepherd, will not give up on us. He will always guide us back to God."

With Pastor Bob's words filling her mind, Hannah spent the remainder of the service focused on worship. After singing the final lines of the closing hymn, she sat beside Sylvia. "Let's wait for the crowd to thin out before we try to leave. I wouldn't want someone knocking you down in their rush to get to brunch," she teased. They chatted easily until they were interrupted by Allison Prentiss.

"Hey, Hannah." Her sister-in-law leaned in to give Hannah a hug.

"Allison." Hannah stood to accept the hug. "I want you to meet my new friend, Sylvia. She's visiting Blackberry Valley to run the estate sale Lacy and I went to yesterday, but she had an unfortunate accident and is staying another day or two to let her ankle heal before she attempts the drive back to Atlanta."

Turning to Sylvia, Hannah said, "This lovely woman is Allison Prentiss. She married my brother, and they have given me three darling nieces and nephews."

Allison smiled at Sylvia. "I'm sorry you got hurt, but you're in good hands if Hannah befriended you. Hannah, I came to ask if you'll be joining us at your father's place for lunch. Drew and I are hosting. Maeve and Hunter are bringing their gang, and I think Ryder will be there. You should come and bring Sylvia."

Hannah turned to Sylvia, who looked a bit dazed by all the attention. "Do you feel up to it, Sylvia? Allison is an excellent cook, so the food will be great, and I imagine you'll be amused by the antics of her children. But if you're too tired, we can always go back to the inn."

"Y'all are so kind. If you don't mind me tagging along, I'd much rather visit with your family than hang out in my room feeling sorry for myself."

Hannah touched her arm. "You won't have a moment to be sad when you're surrounded by this group. Do you need me to bring anything?" she asked Allison. "Jacob was experimenting last night, and I have some leftovers at the restaurant."

Allison laughed. "I have it covered, but if you're trying to make things disappear, you know my crowd will eat anything."

Hannah grinned. "This was tasty. He did a Thanksgiving twist on a shepherd's pie. I need to come up with a name for it for the menu. So far all I can think of is Fireman's Pie, but maybe if I bring it, the family can help me come up with something better. It's made of ground turkey with a sweet potato topping sprinkled with dried cranberries and drizzled with a maple glaze."

"That sounds amazing."

"It is," Sylvia chimed in. "There was a mini version of it in the sampler you gave me last night, Hannah. It might have been the best thing I've ever eaten."

Hannah soaked in the praise she'd be sure to share with Jacob. It was only a few short months ago that she'd feared her restaurant would take a hit from a depressing review by the resident food critic who, among other complaints, hadn't liked Jacob's sauces. She wasn't too proud to recognize that Marshall had been right about a few things, and each member of her staff had taken the review as a challenge to improve and grow the Hot Spot into a recognized destination for foodies. Marshall had become their number one fan, although that probably had more to do with his affection for her head server, Raquel.

"Let's get going," Sylvia prompted. "My taste buds are already singing for an encore of that Fireman's Pie."

Hannah was laughing as she reached to help Sylvia stand. "I'm rethinking sharing your review with Jacob. I don't know if I should tell him to encourage him, or if your praise will make his head swell."

"Oh, you should definitely tell him," Sylvia gushed. "It was that good."

Chapter Six

After picking up the Fireman's Pie, Hannah drove Sylvia to the house her father shared with his brother. She parked and went around to help Sylvia out. "Welcome to my childhood home."

"This is so lovely." Sylvia's face took on a wistful expression. "I'm a little jealous. I grew up in an Atlanta apartment. We didn't have our own garden except for a small box of herbs on the kitchen windowsill. I always dreamed of living in a place like this."

Hannah put an arm around her shoulder. "It's never too late to move. Honestly, I didn't fully appreciate it while growing up here. But when I was in LA, all I could think of was coming home and starting my own restaurant in my own community."

"I hope I'll have time to visit the Hot Spot before I leave."

"We'll try to make it happen," Hannah promised as she released Sylvia to open the Subaru's back door and pull out the box of food.

They started up the front path, and Sylvia continued her lavish praise of the gardens as they strolled toward the porch.

"Thank you," Hannah said. "My mom and I planted a lot of these when I visited from LA before moving back. Mom's been gone eight years now, but this garden is a constant reminder of her as it changes with every passing season. Dad and I added all these mums when he took down the Halloween decorations this year." She laughed. "Mom loved to decorate for the holidays, but

Dad and Uncle Gordon go all out with the decorations. One year they even created a maze in the backyard with bales of hay and dried cornstalks for the neighborhood kids. It was the talk of Blackberry Valley."

"That sounds like fun, but I love the simplicity of the hanging baskets of fall flowers. I think your mom would be proud of how you've kept up her gardens."

Blinking away tears, Hannah beamed at her new friend. "Thank you. That means more than I can say."

They mounted the steps to the porch, and Hannah opened the front door to sounds of chaos.

"Goodness," Sylvia said. "Is everything all right?"

Hannah laughed. "That's just my family watching Sunday football. They can be a bit enthusiastic." A collective roar from the living room underscored her words.

There were so many family members there that Allison had set up the food buffet style to let people fix a plate and settle where they could. Since Sylvia was leaning on the cane, Hannah walked her through the buffet and held a plate so Sylvia could fill it with a range of goodies.

"Where would you like to sit? There's room in the living room with all the football fans, or you can join the quieter kids in the den. If it's peace you want, Allison and I usually hide in the kitchen."

Sylvia grinned. "I'll sit with the football gang. They remind me of watching with my dad. He used to take me to the college games when I was a teen."

"You'll fit right in then," Hannah responded as she led the way into the living room. "Dad, Uncle Gordon, everyone." She gestured to the nieces and nephews scattered around the floor with plates on their laps. "This is Sylvia. She's my guest, and she's a football fan."

Dad set aside his plate and stood to greet her. "Welcome, Sylvia. I'm Gabriel Prentiss. Any friend of Hannah's is a friend of mine. Actually, that might depend on which team you're rooting for," he teased. "We're all Titans fans."

Everyone laughed at that, and Sylvia had a wicked grin as she replied, "Depends on who they're playing. Dyed-in-the-wool Falcons fan here, but I'm happy to root for the Titans against the Jags."

"Then come on in and make yourself comfortable, Sylvia. The game's a little tight, but maybe you'll bring us luck."

Shaking her head, Hannah set down Sylvia's plate and headed back to the kitchen to get some food for herself. "Allison, you've outdone yourself," she told her sister-in-law. "If Jacob ever needs time off, I know just where to find a substitute."

Allison handed Hannah a plate and reached to wrap an arm around her husband, who had just entered the room for seconds. "Then you'd need us both. We come as a team."

Hannah's wide-eyed expression earned her a friendly elbow from her brother and an explanation from Allison. "He was up before dawn getting this meat in the smoker, and the barbecue sauce is all his."

"Really?"

Hannah picked up a plate and took a tiny forkful of the pulled pork. She took a tentative taste—and a grin burst across her face. "Who taught you to cook?"

"There's room for more than one talented chef in this family." Ever the peacemaker, Allison spoke up in defense of her husband.

"I'll say," Hannah responded as she went back for more. "This is great, Drew. Maybe I need to host guest chefs. Don't tell Jacob I said that."

Her brother laughed and tugged on her hair. "That's blackmail material."

"Jacob knows he has a special place in my heart."

"Speaking of special people, how's our brave fire chief?" Allison donned an innocent expression, but she couldn't hide the twinkle in her eye.

Hannah choked on her mouthful of barbecue. "Sorry, spicy," she muttered when she could finally speak. "I need water."

Allison crossed her arms and shook her head. "Not buying that excuse from the woman whose restaurant has Inferno Chicken Wings on the menu."

"I just serve them. I don't eat them."

"Does Liam?"

"No, he prefers the medium-heat version."

"Gotcha!" Allison crowed.

"He's a regular. I'm bound to notice his preferences," Hannah protested. "He's fine, I guess. We've both been busy with work, but we did get to explore a cave together." Hannah took one look at Allison's reaction and added, "That reminds me. I need to talk to my dad at halftime."

Allison made a face. "Going out with Liam reminds you of your dad?"

"No, you trying to make me say something about Liam reminded me that it was time to make a break for it, and I do need to talk to my dad."

Hannah quickly made her exit with Allison's laughter ringing in her ears, but as she stood in the doorway, she had to admit having Liam here with her family would have made the day even more perfect.

The truth was, she hadn't wanted to open herself to Allison's questions about Liam because she wasn't sure how she felt. Ever since last month when they'd spent time together exploring a cave, she'd been doing her own exploration of her feelings. Did she want to date him? What did he think about the idea? The only thing she really knew for sure was that her feelings were starting to seem like something more than just friendship.

Football still commanded everyone's attention in the living room, but the half was nearly over. Maybe she could ask her dad about his friend before the third quarter.

Wise enough not to interrupt before the whistle, Hannah leaned against the doorframe and soaked in the wonderful atmosphere in the room. Her mother would have been in her element surrounded by all the loving family members. Frieda had been the quintessential hostess. Whether it was family, the church group, or a school fundraiser, her mom had been the one to make sure everyone felt welcome.

Glancing at Sylvia, cheering along with the rest of the family as the Titans scored a touchdown with seconds on the clock, Hannah realized she had walked in her mom's footsteps today by turning Sylvia's misfortune into a fun afternoon.

When the whistle ended the half, everyone rose to go in search of dessert.

Hannah grabbed her father's arm. "Dad, once you get your brownie, can I talk to you for a minute?"

Dad's face puckered into a frown. "Sure, honey. Is something wrong?"

"No, not really." Hannah waved away his concern. "Let's get dessert for us and Sylvia."

Dad looked back at Sylvia, who was in an animated debate with Hannah's cousin, Ryder. "I don't think she's worried about dessert. That woman sure does take her football seriously."

Hannah laughed. "Like you don't."

Dad threw his arm around her shoulder as they walked into the kitchen. "Where did you meet her?"

Leaning into his hug, Hannah grinned up at him. "That's related to what I want to talk to you about."

"Well, now I'm intrigued."

The youngest cousins had gone outside to play in the yard with Dad's border terrier, Zeus. Once they had their treats, Dad led Hannah to the vacated den. "What's up, sweetheart?"

"I'll try to make this fast. I don't want you to miss your game."

He took a seat on the sofa. "I always have time for my girl."

"There's kind of a long story behind this that I'll explain, and I know you must have been pretty young at the time, but do you remember anyone talking about a filly named Kentucky's Angel that disappeared?"

Dad nibbled on his brownie as he mulled over the question. "I don't think so. When did she disappear?"

"May 1963."

He laughed heartily. "Hannah, I wasn't even three years old then. I surely don't remember."

"Are you sure you never heard anyone talking about it? Murph, maybe? It was apparently quite a scandal."

Dad's smile dimmed at the mention of his friend, and Hannah remembered too late that Murph had passed while she was living in Los Angeles. She knew her dad had been sad when Murph took a job that moved him out of Kentucky, but they'd stayed in touch until an accident took Murph's life suddenly. Hannah thought back to the lovely days she had spent with him indulging her horse craziness and smiled softly. "I've been thinking about him a lot since yesterday."

A cheer sounded from the living room. Apparently, the game had resumed. "I can wait and tell you more about it after the game," Hannah offered.

Shaking his head, Dad said, "I can always watch the replay later, but I can't recapture missed time with my daughter. Tell me your story."

"I love you, Dad. I am the luckiest daughter to have you as a father." Hannah launched into the tale. "Lacy and I headed out into the country to an estate sale yesterday. I was looking for trinkets for the Hot Spot."

"Did you find some? Are you thinking you need a new display case for the restaurant?"

"Oh, that's an intriguing idea." She pondered it, considering a possible display of the horse memorabilia. Maybe it would be a good temporary display in May when everyone had Derby fever. It wouldn't hurt to feature more local history than just the firehouse. "Mind if I get back to you on that? I actually need a different kind of help at the moment."

"What's that?"

"Well, as I said, I went looking for trinkets." She paused dramatically. "I found a mystery instead."

Dad groaned good-naturedly. "Not again."

"Yes, again. That's how I met Sylvia." Hannah proceeded to recount the afternoon, ending with her examination of the box and the trophies. "I've had a little time to search the internet. So far I've only found news stories about the disappearance of Kentucky's Angel and her jockey, Mickey Dawes, but then no follow-up."

Dad set aside his brownie. "You're right. Murph would have been the perfect person to ask about this. He was only a few years older than me, but he might have heard stories. If not, he'd have known who to ask."

"Do you know any of his friends from the racing world? Anyone who might remember something?"

"Not really. Even though we visited at the racetrack, our friendship was separate from that world. I met a few people from time to time, but no one whose name I remember." Dad picked up his brownie again and took a bite, chewing while he thought. "Have you considered going to Keeneland? They have a library with incredibly thorough archives. Failing that, I'm sure there must be someone there who remembers the horse, especially if, as you say, she was expected to win the Derby."

"That's a great idea, Dad. I'm also planning to check in with Jack at the *Chronicle* tomorrow and see if the paper ran any stories."

"This may sound like a silly question, but can't Sylvia ask the people whose farm it is? I mean, they might just have overlooked the box."

Hannah sighed. "I did ask her about that, but she didn't know. She promised to check in with her boss, since she didn't even know the property owner's name, but she didn't think it would yield any additional info. Confidentiality agreements and all that. I'm going to check in with Evangeline too. She's helped with a lot of my questions lately."

Dad nodded. "Sounds like you have a plan."

Hannah's thoughts returned to the morning's scripture. In the parable, neither the woman nor the shepherd had given up until they found what they were searching for, and neither would she. "I do, so now you can go watch football again. And Dad?" Hannah hugged him as he got up from the sofa. "Thanks for not asking why I need to find the horse and her rider."

Dad enveloped her in his strong arms. "No question about that, sweetheart. No question at all." As he released her, he winked. "And I have no doubt you will."

Chapter Seven

Hannah had just taken the first sip of her coffee when her phone rang on Monday. "Sylvia, good morning. How are you feeling?"

"Much better. Thank you for asking. My ankle isn't swollen anymore, and I can walk fine, so I'm going to drive home tomorrow. I wanted to call you first and thank you for including me yesterday. I really enjoyed visiting with your family. You were all so welcoming and made a stranger feel like she belonged." Before Hannah could respond, Sylvia continued. "But I also wanted to tell you that I need to go back out to the farm today to retrieve my car and make sure everything is locked up. Sabrina recommended a taxi I can take, but I thought maybe you would like a chance to check around a little more, now that you've had time to look through the box of memorabilia. It's fine if you don't have time though."

"Oh, I would like that. And the Hot Spot is closed today, so I actually can." Hannah had planned to visit the library to seek Evangeline's advice on how to find out who owned the farm, but this would be so much more intriguing. Hannah knew that once Sylvia was gone, so would be her chance to do any sleuthing around the property.

"I'll also need to pack up any of the things that weren't purchased in the estate sale. I'll take an inventory and let my boss decide what to do with them. You don't have to hang around for all of that. I'll be fine on my own."

"I have no plans for the day that can't be easily changed. Why don't I stay with you, and then we can go to puzzle night at Lacy's? If you still want to, that is."

"I'd love that. Do you think Lacy would want to join us?"

"I'm not sure if she'll be able to. Bluegrass Hollow Farm takes up most of Lacy's time. I'm sure she'd love to come if she can, so I'll check."

They made arrangements for Hannah to pick up Sylvia from the inn before Hannah called Lacy. She was delighted to learn that her friend was finishing some chores but should be done in the next half hour. Before she disconnected the call, Hannah had a question. "Any chance Neil's bookstore has some books on horses?"

Lacy laughed merrily. "Of course he does. He has books on everything. What are you looking for?"

"I don't really know." She quickly filled Lacy in on what else she'd found in the box. "It made me reminisce about how much I loved horse stories as a child, so I thought it might be fun to try something involving horses for adult readers."

"I'll ask Neil what his most popular titles are and have him set some aside."

Hannah had a sense of déjà vu as they drove down the lane to the farm, except this time Sylvia was with her and Lacy. "I wonder if that dog will come by to visit us. I've worried about what became of him. Before I picked you both up, I called the vet's office. They didn't know him specifically and said the description could fit any number of dogs. If we see him today, I'll snap a photo so they can put up a flyer in case he's a stray."

"Oh, that would be wonderful," Lacy agreed. "I'd be happy to take him to my farm if we can coax him into the car. That way we'll know he's okay."

There was no sign of the pup when they arrived, so Sylvia unlocked the door to the farmhouse and ushered Hannah and Lacy inside.

"Does this ever feel weird to you, Sylvia?" Hannah asked. "Like you're walking into someone's life?"

Sylvia shrugged. "I know what you mean, and it did feel strange when I began this job, but I've gotten used to it. It's not much different than when someone sells a house. The family was long gone when we came in. They took anything of sentimental value. Whatever they left here is going to consignment or to be discarded. It's just an empty house now."

A wave of sadness washed over Hannah. She understood that Sylvia thought of it in practical terms as her job, but Hannah kept thinking of the person who had left the box behind after all the care they'd poured into the photo album. The thought persisted as she walked through the house that had once been someone's home and wondered about the family that had lived here. Had one of them tucked away that box of trophies? Had one of them been the missing jockey?

Had Kentucky's Angel slept in the stalls of that barn?

"Sylvia, can we look in the barn again?"

"Sure." Sylvia was sorting some dishes, so she handed Hannah the key to the barn padlock. Just as she and Lacy left the house to head for the barn, Lacy's phone rang.

"I have to take this, Hannah. You go on ahead."

Hannah crossed the yard separating the house from the barn. She inserted the key into the lock, threw the doors open wide enough to let in enough light to see, and stepped inside. As she walked down the central corridor, trailing her fingers along the stalls, she imagined the barn as it once might have been—alive with horses and riders and groomers and trainers.

But had this been a training barn? She really had no reason to think so and knew it was unlikely, but she couldn't shake the feeling that Kentucky's Angel had been connected to this building, given the box of her keepsakes. She could almost hear the horse neighing and the young rider, Mickey, encouraging her. But who *was* Mickey?

Her thoughts were interrupted by Lacy at the door. "Find anything?"

"Just more questions. We found the box here. Does that mean Kentucky's Angel trained here? Or was she hidden here? We don't even know why she disappeared or how." Hannah sighed and leaned against one of the stall doors. "Do you think my imagination is running away with me?"

Lacy studied her friend for a long moment. "Probably. But that doesn't mean there wasn't a mystery here. We know for a fact that someone connected to the horse was here. That box of mementos wasn't spun out of your imagination. I guess the real question is whether there is any way for us to find out enough to solve the mystery of where the horse and rider went. But…"

"But what?" Hannah prompted.

Lacy kicked at some straw on the ground. "Maybe you should consider whether they wanted to be found."

"What do you mean?"

Lacy stuck her hands in her jacket pockets. "I mean, maybe there was a scandal. Maybe the jockey doesn't want to be found. If he's even still alive. I mean, this is an estate sale. Maybe it was Mickey's estate. Maybe he's passed away. I don't know. There are so many possibilities."

Hannah nodded in frustration. "There are. It's kind of a good thing and a bad thing. So many possibilities to investigate, but at the same time *so man*y possibilities to investigate. And maybe none of them is the right one. But I'll keep trying. I plan to stop by the library and have Evangeline help me figure out who owns this property."

"Did you ask Elaine?"

"I asked her about the dog, and she didn't recognize him from my description. I haven't seen her again since I went through the box, but I'll ask her tomorrow."

"I hope she has some answers for you." Lacy strolled through the barn, trailing her fingers along the stalls much like Hannah had earlier. When she came to the middle stall, she stopped in her tracks and bent down to examine a metal plate on the door. "Hannah, do you have a cloth of some kind? This looks like a nameplate. It's dirty and tarnished, but I think the first letter is a *K*."

Chapter Eight

Lexington, Kentucky
June 1955

Chaddy was up well before dawn, as usual. The day began early on a horse farm. There were first feeds, quick checks, and stalls to be mucked. As senior trainer, none of that was his direct responsibility, but he oversaw it all. Examining his horses each morning kept him connected and certain they were fit. It also helped him catch potential problems as early as possible.

Today, like every other day the past week, he noticed the kid hovering at the tree line.

Once the morning rounds were done, he strode across the field. "Hello, Mickey."

The kid glanced out from under an oversize cap. "That's not my name."

"Nope, but it will do. Better not to let on your real name. Everybody goes by a nickname on this farm, and we don't want to tip off your grandfather about the identity of his newest hostler."

Mickey's eyes widened. "What do you mean?"

"I mean that anyone who would go to the lengths you have to visit these horses deserves a job here." Chaddy didn't let on that he'd seen the kid arrive before dawn each day on a bicycle that was hidden in the woods on the outskirts of the farm, but he had taken note. The love of horses and racing ran deep in the blood of this family, and the kid shouldn't be denied.

"Why would my grandfather care?"

That was a question Chaddy couldn't answer. He wasn't sure how the old man would react to his daughter's child being in his stables, but he wasn't going to risk Mickey losing a chance to be with the horses. The kid's life was hard enough. If the horses could add joy, Chaddy would make it happen.

But that wasn't an answer for Mickey. "I reckon he still hasn't forgiven your mother for leaving. She was her daddy's girl until she left with your daddy."

As they walked back across the field together, Chaddy heard the kid echo his own thoughts in a mutter. "Bad choice."

He reached down and patted Mickey's head. The kid was dressed in old jeans and a baggy shirt, but there was no disguising the enthusiasm. If Chaddy was reading this right, the kid might have a bright future with the horses as an exercise rider or maybe even rise to trainer one day.

As they approached the paddock, Chaddy beckoned to a boy not much older than Mickey, who was working with one of the yearlings. When he reached them, he stood back so as not to frighten the colt.

Chaddy inclined his head. "This is my grandson, Jamie." He gestured to the child. "Jamie, this is Mickey Dawes. Mickey will be working with us, and I want you to be in charge of training." He patted Mickey's shoulder. "Kid is as green as that colt but has a heart for horses, so you do it right, like I trained you. Starting with how to muck out the stalls. I want Mickey to learn from the best."

Chaddy wasn't sure if he would ever let on to his grandson about the kid's identity, but for now he'd let it be. He didn't miss Jamie's sullen expression at the chore, but as the morning wore on, Chaddy saw his attitude change and watched a friendship begin to form. There was nothing like the love of a horse to unite two souls.

Mickey had a way with the horses that would soften even the hardest of hearts. With time, maybe a mutual love of horses would even breach the divide with the kid's grandfather. Until that improbable day, he and Jamie would mentor the kid, and Chaddy would keep the secret for as long as he could. They'd take it one day at a time.

One day turned into many, and though Chaddy never was sure how Mickey managed to spend so much time at the farm without anyone noticing, the kid showed up on time every day. From the little he overheard up at the house, Chaddy knew Mickey's father was caught up in a whole heap of trouble and spent most of his days either begging his father-in-law for money or barricaded in his study, drowning his troubles in drink. Apparently, there was no one else to care what happened to his kid, but Mickey was happy in the barns, and that was enough for the old trainer.

Weeks went by and seasons changed. Before a year had passed, Mickey had seamlessly become one of them—the people who had given their lives over to their love of horses.

Chapter Nine

"Come in. The door's open." Hannah knew she needed no invitation, but her arms were laden with snacks, as were Sylvia's. "Our arms are full, Lacy," she called back.

The kitchen door swung open a moment later. "Oh, goodness, let me take something from you. Welcome, Sylvia. I'm so glad you decided to join us. Hannah, when did you have the time to do all this?" Lacy exclaimed as she set a box of food on the counter.

"I was restless after we got back. I couldn't stop thinking of the nameplate we saw." They'd told Sylvia, who had dug out some brass polish from the cleaning supplies and cleared away the dirt and tarnish. There was no full name, but the initials *K.A.* had been clearly engraved. Could it be that the missing horse had once been there, or was Hannah jumping to conclusions?

"You know me—I cook when I'm nervous or excited. I started out puzzling over the horse mystery and thinking what else we could do, but once I got caught up in my recipes, I almost forgot we had a mystery."

Lacy gave a mock gasp.

Hannah grinned. "I said 'almost.' Besides, it felt good to cook for my friends."

"So, what did you bring us?"

"Well, since it got wet and cold, I decided to go for comfort food. I made apple pumpkin lentil soup, and I have some crunchy crouton bites to go with it. There are also some finger sandwiches for anyone who is not in a soup mood, and I have fondue."

"Oh my goodness," Lacy exclaimed. "I haven't had fondue in forever. I didn't think anyone even made it anymore."

Hannah gave a sheepish grin. "I was looking through a Best of the Sixties website for racing information, and there was so much fondue that I found myself craving it. I figured we could use the long forks to avoid sticky fingers while we're doing the puzzles."

"That sounds amazing. I have hot cider to go with it. Allison is bringing harvest doughnuts for dessert. But tell me—did all your research and thinking time come up with any answers about Kentucky's Angel?"

Hannah's shoulders sagged. "No, just a whole lot more questions."

"Any response from your boss, Sylvia?"

The woman shook her head. "He's been strangely secretive. I'll try to push for more answers once I'm back in the office. I'll be in touch."

"You'd better be," Lacy told her. "You're our friend now. Don't push so hard you get yourself in trouble though. We'll keep investigating from here. Maybe one of the ladies from our church group will remember something," she suggested. "They've lived here their whole lives."

Hannah smiled. "We can ask, but Miriam and Evangeline didn't mention anything when I told them about finding the box."

"Can't hurt to ask again, and I have the perfect lead-in."

Before Hannah could ask what it was, the front door opened, and Lorelai poked her head in. "Lacy? Can we come in?"

Lacy rushed forward to welcome the rest of their friends, who were shaking off rain on the wide front porch. Lacy took their wet coats and looped them over the racks that she pulled out whenever she had visitors.

Evangeline rubbed her hands together. "It's gotten nasty. I hope there will still be leaves left on the trees when this storm is over. I always love it when the trees still look pretty for our Thanksgiving Gratitude Feast."

"Oh, we should talk about the feast," Connie chimed in. "We need to schedule a meeting before everyone gets caught up in their own family Thanksgiving preparations."

Lacy led them all into her large kitchen. "Come in and warm up. Hannah's been cooking. Wait until you see what she brought."

"Oh, Hannah. It smells glorious in here." Vera Bowman rubbed her hands together as she peeked at the food. "Did you make fondue? It was all the rage when I was younger, but I haven't had it in ages."

Hannah repeated what had led to the fondue while the other ladies deposited their own snack offerings. Soon the wind and rain were nothing but a memory as the women eagerly filled plates and settled around the big farm table. Their happy chatter filled the room as everyone caught up on their busy weeks and family plans for their upcoming Thanksgiving dinners.

"Hannah, has Jacob thought about catering Thanksgiving dinners?" Miriam wondered.

"He mentioned it, but I told him I thought it might be nice to prepare a dinner for the fire department instead, since at least some of the guys will be scheduled to work."

The answering smiles and knowing looks made her blush.

"What?" she demanded. "I always find it sad that our emergency response people have to miss dinner with their families. We'll take some to the sheriff's office too."

"And if Jacob is busy in the kitchen, who could possibly bring that feast to the firefighters? Oh, Hannah, maybe you should, since it's your restaurant that is feeding them. I'm sure seeing you would improve Thanksgiving for the poor overworked dears." Allison's teasing words were met with laughter around the table.

Hannah couldn't help but laugh along. It was apparently common knowledge in Blackberry Valley that she and Liam enjoyed spending time together, but they were both so busy at work that so far nothing more had come of it. She kept telling herself that maybe someday, when her restaurant was stable, things would be different.

Hannah smiled to herself. She could hear her father's response to that line of thought as if he were sitting right next to her. Dad, too, was a big fan of her finding time for Liam. To be honest, lately she found herself wondering if she really wanted to wait so long to find out if Liam felt the same.

"Earth to Hannah."

Hannah blushed again. "Sorry."

"Somebody was daydreaming," Connie teased.

"Don't we have some puzzles to work on?" Hannah begged.

Lacy jumped up. "We do, and I have a surprise for tonight." She dashed to her puzzle closet and pulled the top two boxes down from a shelf. "I ordered the Thanksgiving one in advance, but then I found a special one at the store yesterday and knew it was perfect for tonight, Hannah."

She set the box down on the table, and Hannah burst out laughing. The thousand-piece puzzle showed eight horses breaking from the gate at Churchill Downs. Colorful silks, majestic horses, fanciful hats, and the excitement on the faces in the crowd captured all the splendor of Derby Day.

"Oh, this will be fun, Lacy. Look at all those colorful silks."

"Why horses, Lacy?" Lorelai asked.

"Oh, Lorelai, you must have missed meeting Sylvia at church yesterday. Some of you probably heard Hannah talking about it, but now we have more to add to our story about how we met her. And there's a mystery."

"Of course there is," Evangeline joked.

"Let's get the puzzles set up," Hannah suggested. "Then we'll tell you all about the mystery. We're hoping you can help us again, Evangeline. I guess this puzzle choice was meant to inspire." She gave her friend a hug. "Thanks, Lacy. This is perfect."

Outside, the storm picked up in intensity with rain and wind lashing the windows, but the friends were cozy in Lacy's warm kitchen as they unboxed the puzzle pieces. Sometimes puzzle night became a friendly rivalry to see who could get their puzzle completed first, and sometimes there was more chatting and snacking than puzzling, but tonight everyone's attention was focused on Hannah and Lacy as they recounted their visit to the estate sale.

"So," Hannah finished, "when we finally got a chance to see what was in the box, we found a mystery about a horse and jockey who disappeared on the eve of the Derby."

Over soft exclamations and murmured voices, one question stood out. "What year was this, Hannah?" Miriam asked.

"The programs and trophies covered a couple of years from the mid-1960s, but the newspaper said they went missing in 1963, so the question is who of us might have been old enough to remember hearing about it?"

All eyes turned to Miriam, who sat up straight in her chair. "Well, yes, of course I was old enough, but I paid no attention to the horses. My full attention was on a fine young man, hoping he would fall for me."

"I remember." Evangeline spoke up. "Not when it happened, as I was only a toddler then, but I went through my own *Black Stallion* phase as a child and devoured every book about horses. One of my teachers saw me reading and mentioned that we had a local horse mystery, but I never heard that it was solved."

"Well, if anyone can solve it, Hannah can," Miriam said. "She and Lacy can solve any mystery, as well I know."

Hannah said, "Thank you, Miriam. We'll try our best. But right now, we have puzzles to solve, so let's get to them."

Happy voices floated on the air as the women divided themselves between the two puzzles and set to work. As always, there was a hint of competition, but everyone had a role, whether it was sorting pieces by color or figuring out how the shapes connected.

Hannah was studying a particularly complex section of the famous Churchill Downs twin spires when a thought occurred to her. Her father had talked about the records at Keeneland, but what about Churchill Downs? Did they keep historical records of the races won there?

Kentucky's Angel had never actually raced in the Derby, but what about some of the races for younger horses? Had she raced in those? Maybe someone at the track would remember or know how to check. Hannah could also go through the programs in the box again to see if there were any for Churchill Downs.

A flash of brilliant light was followed immediately by a crashing boom of thunder, startling Hannah from her thoughts. The friends barely had time to make eye contact across the puzzle table before another flash of lightning sizzled and an answering boom shook the house.

Lacy jumped up from the table. "I need to check on the animals."

"Lacy. Wait. You won't do the animals any good if you get blown away," Vera warned.

"Dorothy was in Kansas, not Kentucky," Lacy joked. "I know you're right, but the girls are scared of storms, especially Hennifer and Eggatha. Rocky will take cover, but I don't like the sound of this wind."

"I'll go with you." Allison stood up from the table and grabbed her coat from the rack.

While Lacy and Allison ran out to check on the chickens, the other friends began clearing the food and dishes, trying to distract themselves from the fierce wind and rain outside. Fortunately, the line of storms passed through quickly, and by the time they were done cleaning, the wind had died down and the rain had eased. They were all breathing sighs of relief when Lorelai's phone rang.

She smiled at the screen. "It's my husband. Bob is probably worried about me being out in this." Answering the call, she said, "Hello, dear, I'm safe here with the women." She listened to his reply and then said, "Oh, my. Are you okay?" She listened some more, and Hannah noted her shoulders ease as she responded, "Praise the Lord. Yes, we'll be careful. No, you don't need to come. I can get a ride. I'll see you soon."

Everyone watched with concern as Lorelai ended the call.

"Bob said a tree fell through the wall of the community center," Lorelai told them. "Thank goodness no one was hurt."

The door flew open, and Allison stamped her boots on the landing before entering. "Chickens and horses are all accounted for, but they're in a state, so Lacy wants to stay with them. She apologized for the abrupt end to the night, but I assured her we all wanted to get home and check on our loved ones anyway."

The other women agreed, and Lorelai filled Allison in on what had happened at the church. "Bob said there are branches down everywhere. Parts of town lost power," she added.

"Oh, that's terrible," Allison replied. "I could see some branches down when we were walking to the coop. Fortunately, Lacy saw no damage to the farm buildings."

Fear gripped Hannah's heart at Allison's words. The Hot Spot wasn't far from the church. Had her restaurant been damaged? The old firehouse had certainly withstood its share of storms over the years, but so had the church. All it would take would be one devastating gust of wind knocking over a tree, and everything she had worked for could be gone in a flash.

Hannah's anxiety was mirrored on the faces of all the other women.

Lorelai must have noticed. She took the hands of the women on either side of her, and soon they all stood in a circle, hands clasped. "We trust in the Lord," Lorelai said. "All physical damage can be repaired. Lord, we pray for the safety of our Blackberry Valley families. Please give us strength."

When Lorelai finished praying Hannah said to her, "I heard you tell Pastor Bob that you would get a ride back. Would you like to come with me?"

"Thank you, Hannah. Bob dropped me off because he needed the car to visit an ill parishioner. He was going to come get me when we were done."

"I'm sure he'll be busy seeing to the damage. I'm dropping Sylvia at the inn. I can easily take you home too."

Allison spoke up. "If there's so much damage, it will be safer if we leave at the same time. We can form a caravan. But let's wait for Lacy to come back."

The other women agreed, and it wasn't long before Lacy appeared in the doorway, phone pressed to her ear. She held up a finger for them to wait as she said goodbye and ended her call. Her voice shook as she addressed them. "I'm glad you all haven't left yet. That was Neil. He said he tried to come back as soon as the storm started because he knew the animals would be anxious and I would need help." She paused and took a deep breath before continuing. "A large branch barely missed his car. He said there are branches down all around."

Lorelai reached to hug Lacy, then related what had happened at the church. "Bob said it's bad all over. We'll wait with you until Neil gets here."

"Oh, Lorelai, no," Lacy protested. "You don't need to do that." "I'll be fine. You all need to get safely home."

"And we will, but first we will wait with you."

Hannah could hear the tremor in the woman's voice and knew she was eager to get back to her husband, but Lorelai led by example, putting others' needs before her own.

It wasn't long before Neil's car pulled up to the farmhouse, and amid plenty of warnings about driving slowly, the women headed back to town in their convoy. Hannah took the lead, followed by Evangeline driving Miriam and Vera, and Allison brought up the rear with Connie as her passenger.

As she avoided one downed branch after another, Hannah couldn't help thinking that in the mysteries she loved to read, storms like this often revealed some hidden box caught within the roots of a toppled tree. But she already had her mystery box, and nothing about this storm was likely to reveal the whereabouts of the missing horse or jockey.

Chapter Ten

Hannah wasn't sure what to expect as she headed toward Grace Community Church. The road in from Lacy's farm was littered with tree branches, and more than once she'd had to stop the car to clear the road enough to get through. At least the rain had stopped and the skies had cleared.

"Hannah, why don't you drive by the Hot Spot first?" Lorelai suggested as they entered town. "I know you must be worried."

Hannah smiled her appreciation. "Damage in town doesn't seem as bad as on the road, so let me get you to the church first."

"I insist, dear."

Knowing when to concede, Hannah acquiesced and made a slight detour. She breathed a pent-up sigh of relief when she saw the old brick building standing tall.

Knowing that all was well, Hannah didn't bother to stop, but went on to drop Sylvia at the inn. After extracting a promise to stay in touch, Hannah continued down Main Street with Lorelai until they could see the church. The façade, front porch, and steps were intact, but as they pulled around behind by the fellowship hall, both women gasped. Even though they'd been told a tree had come down, they couldn't have imagined the sight they beheld.

A huge old oak had been uprooted and taken a wall of the fellowship hall down with it. Hannah could only imagine the devastation that lay beneath the wet autumn leaves.

Already the buzz of saws filled the air, and Hannah realized that the Blackberry Valley Fire Department truck was blocking most of the lot. Spotlights from the church and from the nearby fire engine lit the entire scene, and she spotted Liam hard at work. Gratitude filled her heart, and if the little kick it gave at seeing Liam was something more than gratitude—well, so be it.

Hannah let Lorelai out and then parked in a corner of the lot. She climbed out and hurried over to where a small crowd had gathered, hoping there was something she could do to help. The fire department and a group of local men had the tree situation under control with chain saws and rakes.

When Archer took a break to speak with his girlfriend, Bryn Reynolds, Hannah joined them to ask the firefighter, "Is there anything I can do to help?"

"Thanks, Hannah. Not really. This is a job for the pros. We have a long night ahead of us with storm debris all over town, but this tree took priority because it pulled down some power lines that were throwing off sparks. Don't want to risk an electrical fire. When we're done here, the county crews need us to help with cleanup elsewhere." He kissed Bryn's temple and hustled away, but he left Hannah with an idea.

She spotted her server, Raquel, among the spectators and went to speak to her. "The firemen will be working all night here and around town. I'm sure they'll be starving from all the exertion, so I figured I'd run down to the restaurant and pack up some food for them. Want to help?"

Raquel nodded enthusiastically. "Why don't I ask Marshall to come too? He was helping with the heavy work, but Liam just roped off the area and asked us to back up. It was getting to a critical point, and Liam didn't want anyone hurt."

"Sure. The more hands, the faster the work." Hannah still couldn't believe how Marshall had turned from Hot Spot Enemy Number One with his scathing review, into Raquel's boyfriend and the Hot Spot's most frequent customer. Her mother had always said that God works in mysterious ways, and this was a prime example. "As soon as I figure out how to get my car out of the lot, I'll meet you out front."

Raquel glanced back at the parking lot. "There are so many cars and trucks blocking you in now that it would be faster to walk, but that would limit how much food we could bring. Marshall is parked on the street. Why don't we let him drive?"

"That would be great. Let's go."

Hannah had intended to make a quick trip to the restaurant and gather what could be easily eaten, but when she saw the selection of leftovers, she decided the workers deserved better. "I don't know how much time we have, but I know the guys all love the wings. What else do you suggest, Marshall?"

"Archer told me they'll be there for hours still. Liam promised Pastor Bob that once they got the tree removed, they'd cover the opening to prevent further damage. I vote you make slider versions of the Breakfast Burger, if that's not too complicated. And fries of course."

Hannah agreed and got right to work. As she'd told Lacy earlier, it felt good to be cooking for others.

"I can put together some of the Pull Box sandwiches," Raquel offered. "I've certainly watched Jacob make them often enough while waiting on an order."

"That would be great. Maybe when you're done you can gather up some desserts."

"What can I do?" Marshall asked.

"There are some boxes in the storage room. We'll need them lined with foil to transport the food. There should be some plastic tablecloths and battery-operated candles left over from Halloween in there too. If you bring them, we could set up the cars like a tailgate party."

"What a great idea," Raquel enthused. "I'm going to call a friend and have her bring some chips and soft drinks to be sure we have enough food."

"Where will she get them at this time of night?" Hannah asked.

Raquel laughed. "She has three teenagers. Her house is always stocked. And we can always send someone to the convenience store."

Hannah smiled at her friend. "I think I'll double up on what I was planning to bring. I'm sure once people smell the food, everyone will be hungry."

The trio worked efficiently, and before long they were back on the road in a car packed full of food.

"I may sleep in this car tonight," Marshall joked. "It smells heavenly."

Hannah laughed. "That may be the strangest review my cooking has ever received."

When Marshall pulled up in front of the church, Hannah suggested that he and Raquel wait in the car. "I want to check with Liam about where to set up, so we don't interfere with their cleanup."

She hopped out of the car and hurried around to the side where she was pleased to see how much progress had been made in the short time they'd been gone. The pile of brush had grown high, due in part to the number of people who had arrived to help now that the storm was over. Good thing they'd brought extra food. This community spirit was just one of the things she loved about Blackberry Valley.

Hannah headed back toward the yellow tape the firemen had used to create a safety zone. It didn't take long at all for her to zero in on the dedicated firefighter working alongside his men. Hannah pressed up against the yellow tape and called his name.

He didn't notice, but that was hardly surprising. She could hardly hear herself over the whine of saws. One of the other firefighters tapped Liam's arm and directed his attention her way. Hannah didn't even try to fight the thrill she felt as his face lit up at the sight of her.

He picked up the huge branch he'd just finished cutting and dumped it atop the rapidly growing pile on his way to her. When he reached her, he removed his helmet and shook out his black hair. "What can I do for you, Hannah?"

She smiled at him. "It's more what I was hoping to do for you and your men. Raquel, Marshall, and I thought you all might be hungry, so we brought some food from the Hot Spot. If it's okay with you, we'll set it up tailgate style, and your men can come get something to boost their energy whenever they need a break. You all must be starving."

The smile that burst across Liam's tired features warmed Hannah's heart. "That's so generous of you, Hannah. I don't even know what to say. 'Thank you' doesn't seem enough. I guarantee the guys will appreciate this as much as I do."

Hannah ducked her head, overwhelmed by his gratitude. "Feeding you seemed the least we could do after all this exhausting work you're doing for the town. I hope you'll enjoy what we brought."

He cocked his head. "Did you bring wings?"

"You bet."

"Then you know Archer will be happy. We're close to wrapping up here, since we've done about as much as we can until morning. We just need to hang a tarp over the opening. If you want to set up in the parking lot, I'm sure all the people who've been helping out would be happy to eat—if you think you've got enough."

"I made sure to bring plenty. This is the kind of work that builds an appetite."

"You've got that right. Let me know when you're ready, and I'll make an announcement."

"Great. I'm just going to explain to Lorelai, and then we'll get set up."

Liam headed back to tree-cutting, and Hannah went to find the pastor and his wife. As she approached the couple, she could see that Lorelai looked a little overwhelmed. Pastor Bob was keeping a brave face, but she knew he must be equally concerned.

"Hello, Lorelai, Pastor Bob." She gave them each a hug. "I'm sorry this happened, but I come bearing good news—well, at least good food." She quickly filled them in on her plan.

"Oh, Hannah, we don't want to cause you any trouble," Lorelai objected.

"You're not causing me trouble. I love to feed people." She took Lorelai's hands. "I wanted to help."

"Thank you, dear." She turned to her husband. "Isn't this a silver lining, Bob?"

The pastor beamed at Hannah, his eyes glassy with unshed tears. "Let's get you set up, and then I will offer a blessing, if you like."

"I wouldn't have it any other way."

With Marshall organizing the cars to use as makeshift tables and the church group arranging the food, it wasn't long before Hannah could signal to Liam that they were ready.

Liam reached into the driver's side of the fire truck and honked the horn.

The saws cut off, and heads swiveled toward the truck.

"Thank you all for coming out to help," Liam called out. "The spirit of Blackberry Valley is strong tonight."

A chorus of cheers arose from the group.

Liam's deep voice rose over the noise. "Now, for those of you doing the dirty work, a surprise!" He moved the spotlight from the truck to illuminate the cars parked in a semicircle of open hatchbacks, trunks, and truck beds. "The Hot Spot has been kind enough to provide a meal for us. Thank you to Hannah Prentiss for her incredible generosity in cooking for us after hours. Pastor Bob, would you lead us in a blessing before we dig in?"

The pastor stepped up beside Liam. "Thank you, Liam. Thank you, Hannah. Disasters such as this tree falling through the wall of the fellowship hall are often referred to as acts of God. But when I think of an act of God, I prefer to think of the heart of this blessed community, always stepping up to help a neighbor in need. Lorelai and I are so grateful to all of you for coming out tonight to help us clear away the debris."

Hannah smiled. She'd been thinking exactly the same thing.

"Tomorrow, we'll take a look at how extensive the damage is and plan how to rebuild, but for tonight, I am grateful to all of you for your hearts of service and your spirit of generosity. And to Hannah, who embodies both so well, thank you also for the food."

After another round of applause, Pastor Bob spoke again. "Please bow your heads as we ask for God's blessing over our food and the good people who share it." When the crowd obeyed, he went on. "Dear Lord, You are with us always, in times of plenty and in times of loss. We thank You tonight for this generous bounty, and we ask Your blessing over our food and those who share it with us."

He lifted his head, and the people answered, "Amen."

He scanned the crowd. "Hannah, is there anything you would like to say?"

Smiling, Hannah said, "I'd like to thank Raquel and Marshall for jumping in to help me prepare all of this." She raised her hands to applaud her hostess and friend, and the community followed suit. "Now, let's eat!"

Excited chatter spilled through the crowd as people made their way to the various cars, checking out what was available. Hannah leaned against her Subaru and took it all in. Her heart was full watching her friends and neighbors talk and enjoy the food she'd brought.

Liam came up beside her with an overflowing plate. "This is amazing, Hannah. I don't know how you managed it all so quickly, but thank you."

"My pleasure," she replied, and she meant it.

Pastor Bob and Lorelai joined them. Pastor Bob raised his plate in a salute. "Hannah, I didn't even realize I was hungry until I sampled this slider, but it's fabulous. I hope it's going on the regular menu."

While Liam and the pastor worked out a plan for the morning, Hannah laid a hand on Lorelai's arm. "Are you okay?"

Lorelai glanced up, and Hannah could see worry etched on her face. "It just hit me, with all this talk of being thankful. What are we going to do about our Thanksgiving Gratitude Feast?"

Her husband and Liam heard the question and fell quiet. Lorelai turned pleading eyes on Liam. "Please tell me it's possible to repair this damage in time."

Hannah watched Liam shift uneasily, and she knew the answer before he even spoke.

"I'm not the construction expert. We'll need a better look in daylight." He shook his head. "But from what I can see, I'm afraid that isn't very likely."

Hannah's heart sank. The annual Gratitude Feast had been held in the fellowship hall for as long as she could remember. It had been a highlight of her childhood, and she knew everyone in town looked forward to it each year.

Pastor Bob wrapped an arm around his wife and whispered something to her—encouragement, no doubt. They would trust in God to provide, and in time the wall would be rebuilt.

But the church wasn't the only group to suffer the effects of this loss. Hannah glanced over at Evangeline, whose expression was nearly as stricken as Lorelai's. She must have overheard the conversation. The kindly head librarian would never draw attention to herself, but Hannah knew that this year's feast had been earmarked to raise funds for a critical upgrade for the library. What would Evangeline do to make up the shortfall?

Pastor Bob raised a hand. Everyone fell silent and turned expectant faces his way. "I know you'll all be disappointed to hear this, but it seems unlikely we'll be able to host our annual Gratitude Feast this year. We'll just have to improvise so the library doesn't lose funds. Maybe we can do a raffle or..."

His voice trailed off as he saw the dejection on their faces. A raffle was fine for fundraising, but the Thanksgiving Gratitude Feast was much more than just a fundraiser. It was a celebration of Blackberry Valley and who they were as a community.

And then Hannah realized she had the perfect solution.

Liam bent his head toward Hannah and murmured, "Are you thinking what I think you're thinking?"

"I think so." She winced. "Am I crazy?"

He smiled. "Well, you did an amazing job pulling this off tonight, and they only need a venue. The actual meal is a potluck. I'll help with whatever you need, so don't let that hold you back."

"I mean, I don't even know if that's what they want," Hannah hedged.

"We can still have the feast if we find another location, right?" Liam called out.

Pastor Bob nodded. "Yes, but I don't know where we—"

"We can hold it at the Hot Spot," Hannah announced.

She gulped when cheers rose around her. *No backing out now.*

Chapter Eleven

Hannah was still in shock the next morning as she slowly sipped her coffee and tried to wrap her mind around the notion that not only had Liam encouraged her to host the Gratitude Feast, but she had actually volunteered, and then the community members who had been there enthusiastically adopted the idea.

She was honored of course, but also completely overwhelmed. How in the world was she supposed to pull this off? And how could she have suggested it without talking it over with her staff first? Not that they had to do all the work—Lorelai and Evangeline assured her that there were committees to handle most of it—but still.

When her phone chimed, she glanced down to see a message pop up from Jacob. What's this about a feast I hear we're hosting?

Hannah sighed. She should have realized that the Blackberry Valley gossip network would have spread the news before she could alert him.

No details yet. If you heard that, you probably know the fellowship hall was damaged and can't host. Fill you in later. Have to run errands.

He responded quickly. Was visiting friends in Cave City and missed everything. No worries. I'll be thinking of recipes.

Her head chef was a blessing. His talent in the kitchen and his signature dishes were a huge part of what made the Hot Spot such a success, regardless of his occasional thinking too far outside the box. She should make sure the box was clear to him for this event.

She typed a message back. THINK TURKEY.

He sent back a smiling face emoji next to a turkey and pie slice.

Hannah laughed out loud. Jacob was sending her emojis? What was this world coming to?

It wasn't hard to figure out that she was on edge because she felt overwhelmed. The best way she knew to fix that was to spend some time in prayer.

First she refilled her coffee, because it would take more than one cup to feel fully alert this morning after all the unexpected excitement last night. Once she had doctored it to her liking, Hannah brought her mug to settle in her favorite armchair by the window that let her look out over the town.

The weather this morning was sunny and brisk, a sharp contrast to last night's storms. The view was a constant reminder that God had been so good to her, leading her back home, helping her find the strength to open her restaurant and persevere through the difficulties. She was grateful, which was all the more reason to host the community Gratitude Feast.

The problem was that she was already so busy with the restaurant and plans for Christmas in another month, plus her quest to find out what happened to Kentucky's Angel and her jockey. She took a breath and tried to calm her racing mind. If God wanted her to solve this mystery, He would lead the way. She had to remember to honor Him and keep Him first in her heart.

Hannah sat back and flipped through her Bible to the Gospel of Luke, since Pastor Bob's preaching from that had impacted her so on Sunday. The pages fell open to chapter three, and she began reading. When her gaze fell on verse five, she paused and began to read carefully. *Every valley shall be filled, and every mountain and hill shall be brought low; and the crooked shall be made straight, and the rough ways shall be made smooth.*

Hannah took another sip of coffee as she pondered the verse. What better reminder could there be that God was in control, and that all would be made right in His perfect timing?

She took a deep breath and let her shoulders relax and the stress fade away. She didn't have to handle everything alone, as long as she remembered to place her trust in the Lord.

Once she'd finished her coffee and meditation, Hannah grabbed a pen and paper to plan out her morning so she could be sure to make it back to the Hot Spot in plenty of time to open. The library would be her first stop. She hoped to enlist Evangeline's help in discovering who had owned the property that Sylvia's company managed. With any luck, that information would solve at least part of the mystery and point her in the right direction.

If that didn't take too long, maybe she would treat herself to a pastry and cup of coffee at Jump Start, where she would try to wrap her head around this feast she was suddenly hosting.

Her phone rang, and Hannah groaned at the interruption. It had been ringing off and on all morning, but so far she'd avoided answering. This time it was Lacy, and Hannah breathed a sigh of relief. Lacy would be a voice of reason.

"Good morning, Hannah. I hear you and our fire chief were quite chummy last night."

Chummy? "Who told you that?"

"A little bird."

Hannah shook her head. "Did the bird also tell you I'm now hosting the Thanksgiving Gratitude Feast?"

"Yes, and that Liam promised to help." Lacy paused. "When are you going to admit there is something special there? You like him, Hannah, and I'm pretty sure it's mutual."

Hannah closed her eyes as she tried to think how to answer.

"Hannah?"

"Sorry, Lacy. It was a long night, and I'm still tired."

"You're trying to avoid answering."

Was she? "Look, I do like him, and maybe someday it will be more, but right now my focus has to be the Hot Spot."

"All work and no play makes Hannah a dull girl."

"Well, there are mysteries to solve, and they aren't dull."

Before her friend could respond, another incoming call lit her screen. Liam. Despite her protestations to Lacy, Hannah's heart did a little dance. "I've got another call coming in, Lacy. Talk to you later."

She disconnected and switched the call over. "Liam?"

"Good morning, Hannah. I hope I'm not interrupting anything."

"Not at all." *Unless you count my best friend's interrogation.*

"I wanted to call and apologize for last night. I hope I didn't pressure you into taking on a mammoth task like the Gratitude Feast if you didn't really want to."

Hannah laughed nervously. "I thought you said it was 'only a venue' they needed." She could imagine Liam squirming, as he fumbled for words.

"It is, but it's a big deal in the community, and I felt guilty about it all night."

"All night while you and your team were out clearing debris?" It was time to let him off the hook. "I'll admit I was a little shocked at first, but I'm okay now. I may live to regret saying this, but I'm actually looking forward to it."

She could hear the relief in his voice as he responded. "You'll do a terrific job with it—I know that for sure. But don't forget you don't have to do it alone."

"I know. There's an entire team that runs this every year. My mother headed the committee once when I was young. It's always been one of my favorite traditions here in Blackberry Valley. I'm honored you believe I can do it, and I'll do my best to live up to expectations."

"I'll be your number one cheerleader and lend a hand for whatever you need."

With an uneasy laugh, Hannah said, "You might have to fight my dad for the honor, but thanks. I'll hold you to that."

Hannah approached Blackberry Valley Library with hope in her heart and a sense of anticipation. This library held so many cherished memories from her childhood, but as an adult she had developed an entirely new appreciation for the services they provided beyond checking out books—though she certainly made good use of that.

"Good morning, Hannah."

Startled, Hannah said, "Evangeline. You caught me daydreaming."

The librarian, who had become a friend since Hannah's return, smiled. "You were always daydreaming with your head stuck in a book—horses and mysteries. I always made sure to set aside the new ones when they came in that I knew you would like."

"I always appreciated that."

"Then you'll be thrilled. I did just that this morning. I know you're here about the estate ownership, but since you have horses on your mind, I thought you might enjoy a trip down memory lane." Evangeline reached under the counter and pulled out an old copy of *The Black Stallion*.

Hannah's face lit up. "Alec and the Black. Oh, Evangeline! I have no idea how many times I checked that book out. You probably had to order a new copy because I wore out the pages. My mother eventually bought me my own."

Evangeline chuckled. "I should have saved the old card as a memento for you. Anyway, I came in early to check the records before the library officially opens."

"You didn't have to do that. I could have waited." Hannah laughed. "Impatiently, but I would have waited. You must have been exhausted after last night."

Evangeline smiled. "Actually, it had the opposite effect. I was invigorated by the warmth, the sense of community. It was nice to see the young people helping, and you turning the disaster into a community tailgate party was truly inspired."

Hannah released a satisfied sigh. "It *was* a lovely evening. Things like that are daily confirmations that Blackberry Valley is where I'm meant to be."

"And who would solve all our mysteries if you weren't here?" Grinning, Evangeline picked up a notebook from her desk. "So this is the name of the property owner, but I doubt it will do you much good. He passed away several years ago. I guess his family is finally getting around to clearing things out."

"But who was he?" Hannah couldn't let go of the hope that the name would reveal some sort of connection to the mystery horse and rider.

"His name was John Randolph Chandler. Does that mean anything to you?"

Hannah shook her head.

"Me neither, so I looked him up. I couldn't find anything local, but a California newspaper from the mid-seventies had a small article about a leading businessman who'd been severely injured in a skiing accident. At the time the article was written, they didn't know if he would survive. If that's the right man, it would seem he owned this property before the accident, but didn't live there at the time."

"That doesn't exactly sound like someone who would have a connection to a missing racehorse, does it?"

"No, it doesn't, so I researched the owner before that. His family was from up north and was only there briefly while he was guest-lecturing at the university. That was in the early sixties, so it was the right time frame, but again, no connection to racing. He was a botany professor. Before that, the same family had farmed the land there for decades. I could give you their name to see if they had any connection to racing, but that seems unlikely, given that they sold the property before Kentucky's Angel was even born."

Hannah agreed. "If the Chandler family owned the farm for so many years, I imagine one of them would have cleared out anything left behind from previous owners. When did the lecturer's family live there?"

Evangeline consulted her notes. "From 1960 to 1962."

Shaking her head, Hannah said, "It couldn't have been them anyway. The 1963 trophy for Kentucky's Angel was in the box. I guess that also rules out the farm family. It must be someone who lived here after that."

"I didn't know if you'd had a chance to speak with Elaine about this, but I was curious, so I called her," Evangeline said. "What's interesting is that her family didn't know the people who lived there. They've been around this area forever, and farm families generally have a bond. But she knew nothing about the Chandler family. Didn't even remember hearing the name."

Hannah drummed her fingers on the table as she puzzled over the anomaly. "Maybe they were reclusive due to his injuries?"

"Could be."

"Or maybe they owned a racehorse that had disappeared with its jockey, and they didn't want anyone to know," Hannah suggested.

Evangeline shook her head. "I don't think so. The article made it sound like he was a prominent businessman and a competitive skier. Doesn't sound like someone who would want to be caught up in a scandal over a missing horse."

"True," Hannah acknowledged. "But I think I will do some more research into his life and see if I can find a connection anyway."

"Good idea. I'll do the same if I have some free time between story hours and youth book club. What's your next step?"

"I am going to drop in and see Jack to ask if he thinks there might be anything in the *Chronicle*'s archives. Dad also suggested visiting the museum at Keeneland."

As she was speaking, Hannah picked up the copy of *The Black Stallion* from the counter and absently fanned through it.

"You know," Evangeline said softly, "most of the other girls wanted to check out *Black Beauty*. But you always wanted Walter Farley's books."

Hannah smiled at the memory. "It was the wildness of the stallion that called to me. How much he loved to run."

She still had a smile on her face as she headed out the door, thinking of her girlhood fascination with horses. Was that why she was so keen to solve this mystery?

Chapter Twelve

Hannah knew it was silly to have her hopes dashed just because the lead about who owned the farm hadn't panned out. That was the way of sleuthing. Not every clue led to a solution.

She certainly had no intention of giving up, but first she desperately needed coffee.

As she opened the door to Jump Start Coffee and inhaled the aroma of cinnamon and freshly ground beans, Hannah's spirits immediately lifted.

Zane Forrest, Jacob's brother who owned the shop, stood behind the counter as she approached. She greeted him and then stood breathing in the aromatic air. "I wonder how much caffeine there is in just the aroma of coffee."

Zane laughed. "Drinking it is better. What are you having this morning? Cinnamon Danish and a coffee?"

"I'm thinking of shaking it up. What tastes good?"

"Everything, of course. But I have cranberry walnut muffins if you want something seasonal."

"That sounds perfect. I'll take one of those with my regular coffee."

"Sure thing. You have your pick of seats. The morning rush just cleared out. I'll bring it over as soon as it's ready."

The café bell jingled, and Hannah turned to see Liam stepping through the door. His face lit up when he saw her, and she wondered if her own delight was as obvious.

"Run out of coffee at the Hot Spot?" he teased.

She laughed and parried. "Run out of coffee at the firehouse?"

Liam shrugged. "Colt may be a whiz kid at bacon, but his coffee-making skills can't match Zane's fresh grind."

"I have it on good authority that the cranberry walnut muffins are scrumptious, if you want something with your coffee."

"So cranberry muffins and coffee for two?" Zane asked, watching them with an amused smile.

"Oh, I'm sure Liam's is to go," Hannah said. "But I'll be at the corner table."

Liam walked beside her. "I'm actually on my way back from checking in with Pastor Bob and Lorelai about the state of things, so I'm in no rush. Unless you don't want company."

Hannah hesitated, but then she had a sudden memory of Raquel choosing to be brave about asking Marshall out. She wouldn't go that far, but there was no reason not to admit she wanted Liam to stay. Smiling warmly, she said, "I'd love your company."

Based on Liam's answering grin, that had been the right answer.

She returned her focus to the first part of what he'd said. "How are Pastor Bob and Lorelai? I was going to drop by and see them when I finish here. Well, after I visit Jack over at the paper. I'm working up some questions for him about the missing horse."

Concern etched Liam's face. "There's a horse missing? No one called us in to search."

Hannah laughed. "Not now. Well, sort of, but there's no search."

Liam's concern morphed into confusion.

"You must be the only person in town who has missed hearing me talk about my new mystery."

Liam grinned in understanding and said over his shoulder to Zane, "Definitely staying, so make that coffee a double, please." He followed Hannah back to her table and pulled out her chair for her. He raised a questioning eyebrow at the copy of *The Black Stallion*. "Is this connected to the missing horse?"

Hannah smiled again. She seemed to do that a lot around Liam. "Evangeline checked it out for me. Maybe she thought a trip down memory lane would give me some clues."

"About the missing horse? I didn't know you were into riding."

"I went through a horse phase when I was a girl. My mom fed my love of reading with horse books, and my dad used to take me to visit a friend of his who was a trainer at Keeneland."

"Is that where the horse went missing from?"

"No. Short version is that Lacy and I went to an estate sale on Saturday morning and ended up with a mystery." She went on to tell him about Sylvia and the box of trophies and programs. "So now my brain is obsessed with finding out what happened to the missing horse and rider." She gestured to the book. "Blame it on Alec and Black Stallion."

Hannah paused while Zane delivered their coffee and muffins. She pinched off a bite of hers and tasted it. "This deserves every bit of the hype."

"I'm glad you like it," Zane said. "I want to hear more about the horse."

He was just starting to pull over a chair to join them when the bell at the front rang again and Jack Delaney walked in.

"Just the person I was coming to see," Hannah greeted him. "I was planning to bring you coffee."

Jack walked over to the table. "Am I late to a party?"

"No, I was just filling Liam and Zane in on a missing horse mystery. I was going to visit you about it after I finished my coffee."

"Oh, Pippa mentioned that you'd probably be in," Jack said, nodding. Pippa Nelson was a young reporter who worked for the paper. "Something to do with a box of horse memorabilia, right? Good thing I ran into you here. I was actually heading over to talk to Pastor Bob, so I would have missed you. But if you can wait for me to grab a coffee, I've got some time to listen now."

"Pull up a chair," Zane suggested. "I'll get the coffee." He disappeared behind the counter and returned a few minutes later with a steaming carafe and a basket of warm muffins. "Now, let's hear it from the beginning so Jack gets all the details."

Hannah took a sip of her coffee and began. "It all really started when a dog ran out into the road in front of my car."

The three men leaned forward in their seats, and Hannah continued, telling them about rescuing Sylvia, helping her for the day, and then getting to examine the box.

"Let me get this straight," Jack said as Hannah paused to sip her drink. "You just want to find out what happened, right? You don't expect to find the horse and return it?"

Hannah made a rueful face. "I'll admit that the ten-year-old girl in me wishes I could find her, but I know that's not possible. Kentucky's Angel was racing almost thirty years before I was even born. But maybe in packing up for the estate sale, someone missed this box. It holds precious memories, possibly family history. I'd like to return the box to its rightful owners."

Jack scratched his head. "I haven't been here long enough to know if the *Chronicle* ran any stories, but I'll see what I can find. Maybe you should check the library at Keeneland."

"That's what my dad suggested," Hannah said.

Liam had been resting his chin in his hand, thinking as he listened. "I could ask my gramps. I think one of his buddies was a huge racing fan."

The mention of Patrick Berthold filled Hannah's heart with warmth. Ever since she'd gotten to know him when she found his wife's brooch, she'd enjoyed his company. "I would love any excuse to visit with Patrick. You should bring him and his friend by for dinner at the Hot Spot some night."

"He will love that idea," Liam said. "He was just asking about you the other day."

From the flush on his face, Hannah wondered if Patrick's questions had looked like the teasing she regularly got about Liam.

Liam changed the subject. "Couldn't Sylvia's company contact the person who hired them to run the sale and find out?"

Hannah crossed her arms and mock-glared at him. "I don't get to research horses that way. Where's the fun in that?"

Jack laughed. "He's got a point. It would be a whole lot easier that way."

"Well, Mr. Let's-Be-Sensible, Sylvia is going to ask for me, though she said her boss is being secretive about it. So, in the meantime…"

"In the meantime, you have a Gratitude Feast to organize," Zane reminded her.

She grinned in amusement. "And people to assign duties to, which begs the question, do you want to help?"

Their discussion turned to the feast. Jack promised to run some ads, and Zane offered to supply the beverages. "Have you talked to Jacob about it yet?"

Hannah chuckled. "I don't think he's grasped the potluck part. He texted me about recipe ideas at seven a.m."

"That's my brother."

"And I'm assigning the firehouse to the setup and teardown." She winked at Liam.

Before he could respond, his phone issued a loud alert.

"Oh no, is there a fire?"

Liam's shoulders shook with suppressed laughter as he put the phone back in his pocket. "No, Mrs. Henderson's Maine Coon is stuck in a tree. Again. Archer offered to take the truck over, but she wants me."

"You have to wonder if she chases that cat up the tree just to be able to call you over," Zane teased.

Pink rose into Liam's cheeks. "She's lonely. I don't think she has many friends left. My mom used to visit her until she and Dad moved to Florida. Now it's become kind of a thing. I rescue her cat, and then I stay for tea and whatever she baked that morning."

Hannah was impressed by the fire chief's tender heart. "That is so kind of you."

Liam's flush deepened. "Only one of her daughters still lives around here, and it's a lot for her on her own. The daughters all want their mom to go live at Clarkston Commons, but she's not ready to leave her home. I get it. Gramps had a tough time moving too, but he loves his life there now."

That got Hannah thinking. "Maybe I could invite her to dinner at the Hot Spot the night you bring Patrick."

"Matchmaker Hannah," Jack teased.

"No, of course not. Patrick was a one-woman man, and he still loves Bridget. But I think maybe hearing how happy he is there could interest Mrs. Henderson a bit."

"That's an excellent idea, Hannah," Liam said. "Maybe I could suggest Mrs. Henderson's daughter bring her. I'll arrange a night with Gramps and clear it with you." He pushed back his chair and stood. "But for now, I should get going. Cat duty calls."

"Jack, are you going to the church now?" Hannah asked as the newspaper editor also stood. "I could walk with you and check with Lorelai about my new feast responsibilities."

"That's a fine idea," Jack said.

"I'll stay here serving coffee to the lovely folk of Blackberry Valley," Zane added. "And start thinking of some holiday beverages to rival whatever my brother cooks up for the feast."

"I love the competitive streak, but maybe you could ring up some coffee and muffins for us to bring to the pastor and his wife before you tap into your creativity," Hannah suggested.

"Gladly. But they're on the house."

"What are you thinking, Hannah?" Jack asked as they headed down the street.

She gave a quick laugh. "Is it that obvious? I'm wondering if I'm wasting time and energy on this mystery that could be better put to running my restaurant and hosting the best Gratitude Feast ever. Maybe Liam is right, and I should just wait to hear from Sylvia. I'm probably turning this into way more than it warrants when there are other pressing responsibilities."

Jack matched his stride to hers. "That does not sound like the Hannah I know. How badly do you want to know about this horse?"

Hannah gave him a sheepish glance. "Really badly."

"Then keep digging. Sylvia's company may not give you an answer. In fact, I'd be shocked if they did, with confidentiality agreements and all that."

"But if it was a mistake and the person wants the box of memorabilia returned to them? They'd tell me then, right?"

"That they want it back, yes. But they still wouldn't have to tell you what the connection to the missing horse was—unless you make it a condition of parting with the box. You did say you bought it, and they were hired to sell the contents of the estate, so the sale is legal."

"I could never keep the box if they wanted it. These are someone's precious mementos."

"If that person is even still alive," Jack countered gently. "Years of reporting the news has made me a realist. Not every story has a happy ending. I know you know that, but I also know you're hoping for one."

"Who wouldn't?"

"I'm not trying to dissuade you, Hannah. I think if you want to solve the mystery, you should try. And I'll do what I can to help."

As they rounded the corner and were met with the destruction of the church property in the full light of day, all thoughts of mysteries and horses were driven from Hannah's mind. What a loss for their community. It must have been hard for Pastor Bob and Lorelai to face the devastation. Hannah was especially glad for the coffee and muffins Zane had sent.

The pastor and his wife were speaking with a local contractor, so Hannah and Jack waited at a respectful distance.

"Whatever happened to the dog at the farm?" Jack asked.

Consternation filled Hannah. "We don't know. He disappeared that afternoon. Lacy and Sylvia and I went back out there yesterday, but he was nowhere to be seen. I was thinking of driving back once I'm done here."

"I can run a piece in the paper if you think that would help."

"Oh, Jack, that would be terrific. So many people read the *Chronicle* to know what's going on in Blackberry Valley. What do you need to know about him?"

"You don't have a photo, do you?"

"No. I can only describe him as a hound, brown and white. Probably about seventy pounds. Really friendly. He had a collar, but we couldn't see a tag."

"That should do it. I'll run it in the next print issue and put it up on our digital page."

"Thank you. My heart will rest easier knowing we're doing what we can to locate him and possibly reunite him with his owner. Elaine thinks he's probably a farm dog who wanders. But I'd like to know."

"A horse and a dog. Are you sure you didn't mean to be a veterinarian instead of a restauranteur?"

"Veterinarian was my goal when I was six. It fell in between teacher and lawyer. Pastor Bob is waving us over."

Pastor Bob gratefully accepted the hot coffee Hannah offered, and then he and Jack set off to examine the damage and talk about plans for rebuilding.

Hannah joined Lorelai, who seemed calmer this morning. After letting Hannah have a quick glimpse of the mess, Lorelai invited her inside to share coffee and muffins while they talked over plans for the feast.

"You know, Hannah, you are the reason I'm so calm today despite the mess outside."

"Me? Do you have me mixed up with someone else?" Hannah laughed. "Like some big fireman wielding a chain saw?"

Lorelai rested a hand on Hannah's arm. "You helped me more than you can ever understand. First you brought food and turned what felt like a disaster into a true show of community spirit. And then you volunteered the Hot Spot for the feast. I was reminded that no matter how dark it may seem, God provides. And last night He provided through you."

Hannah was humbled at the kind words. "Lorelai, I don't even know what to say. I just did what anyone would."

The pastor's wife shook her head. "The fact that you believe your kindness is instinctive shows what a special person you are."

Uncomfortable with the praise, Hannah decided to change the topic. "Are you very busy? I mean, that must seem like a silly question given the mess, but is there anything you have to do right now, or would you like to come for a drive to get away for a bit? I have a dog to look for."

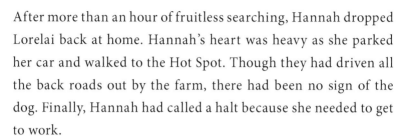

After more than an hour of fruitless searching, Hannah dropped Lorelai back at home. Hannah's heart was heavy as she parked her car and walked to the Hot Spot. Though they had driven all the back roads out by the farm, there had been no sign of the dog. Finally, Hannah had called a halt because she needed to get to work.

Her heart lightened a bit, as it always did when she unlocked the door and stepped inside her restaurant. Before she could even switch on any lights, her phone rang. Hannah dug it out of her coat pocket. "Hello, Lacy. I hope this isn't another call to play matchmaker."

Lacy's voice was bubbly as she replied, "Not unless you know a lonely female pup."

"What?" Hannah shrugged out of her coat.

"After you had to get off the phone this morning, I was worrying about the farm dog in the storm last night, so I drove out there."

Hannah started to laugh. "Brilliant minds think alike. Lorelai and I just got back from doing the same."

"Bet you didn't find him."

Hannah's shoulders drooped. "No, but how did you know?"

"Because I did. He's bedded down in my barn right now."

Now Hannah understood why Lacy's voice sounded practically jubilant. "That's the best news I've heard all day. How did you manage to capture him?'

"I lured him with treats. He was only too happy to jump into the truck to get them."

"Smart move. Can you snap a photo and send it to Jack Delaney? He promised to run a missing dog notice, but it would be better if he had a photo. Now, he'll have to change it to trying to find the owners."

"Sure thing. I also wanted to volunteer to help out with whatever you need for the Gratitude Feast."

"Thanks, Lacy. I'll let you know once I wrap my brain around it. But now I have to prep for dinner service tonight. Thanks for letting me know about our dog friend."

Once Hannah disconnected the call, she got right to work with pep in her step. One by one, the members of her staff arrived, and she greeted each with a cheery smile. She really was grateful to have such a terrific crew and such a wonderful life.

"Someone's mighty cheerful for having just taken on a huge responsibility," Elaine commented.

Hannah beamed. "That's because I live in the best community to be grateful for and have the best staff to help me pull off the feast. And Lacy found the missing dog."

They launched right into prep, which smoothly gave way to the dinner rush. Before Hannah knew it, closing time had arrived. So many people had dropped by for dinner, eager to talk about the storm and volunteer for the Gratitude Feast. Hannah's heart was full as she climbed the stairs to her apartment.

Once inside, her gaze settled on the box sitting on her table. They might have found the dog, but she was no further along in her search for the horse and jockey. Since she was too wired from the busy evening to sleep yet, Hannah chose to make a cup of herbal tea and spend more time going through the box while there was nothing to distract her.

She decided to be orderly about her search, so she pulled out all the programs and lined them up one by one. As she did, something struck her. Mickey was the only jockey ever listed with Kentucky's Angel. And Kentucky's Angel was the only horse ever listed for Mickey. The other horses had frequent changes, but Mickey and the filly were consistently paired. Why?

Realizing that she had never finished researching the pair, Hannah turned to her laptop and put both names into the search engine. There was surprisingly little information about Mickey and it was always in the context of Kentucky's Angel's victories. She saw no mention of him ever riding any other horse. That was almost as puzzling as his disappearance, given how frequently other jockeys switched mounts. Grabbing her pen and pad, Hannah added that question to her notes.

She found several references to the horse having been born and raised on Camden Farms. Suddenly, the random letters she'd picked up from the trophy—*C*, *M*, and *N*—made sense. She'd just been missing some of the letters from *Camden*.

Excited by the possible lead, Hannah searched that out next. She lifted her mug and sipped as she waited for the images to load. When they did, a happy sigh escaped her lips. Dozens of glorious thoroughbred horses in a verdant pasture filled her screen. Kentucky bluegrass waved in the fields, and frame after frame showed frolicking horses.

Mesmerized, Hannah read through the website, learning the history of the family and the legacy of champion horses. Kentucky's Angel was mentioned in passing for her victories, but there was no mention of her disappearance.

Hannah sat back in her chair and mulled over the new information. She supposed it made sense that they wouldn't want to highlight the disappearance of a horse, but Kentucky's Angel wasn't just any horse. She'd been a favorite to win the Run for the Roses. How could a farm history fail to mention a detail such as that? Surely they would have wanted to publicize it in case anyone could help them track down the missing thoroughbred.

Unless they wanted to cover it up.

The unpleasant thought pricked at Hannah's brain. She was no naive girl. Even though she loved the horses, she knew horse racing could be an unsavory business. Was there an insidious reason that the investigation had been unsuccessful?

Smothering a yawn, Hannah clicked on a tab that brought her to the tours page. She bolted upright as she scanned the page. The farm offered guided tours of the grounds on Mondays and Wednesdays, including visits with the horses.

She glanced at the clock. It was too late to call Lacy, but she was sure her friend would be up for the trip if they coordinated schedules.

Unfortunately, given the distance, the timing of the tours and her responsibilities at the Hot Spot, they wouldn't be able to go until the following Monday. Hannah knew her curiosity would be running wild by then, but the mystery of the missing horse and rider had gone unsolved for sixty years. Surely it could wait another week.

In the meantime, she needed sleep. She picked up the copy of *The Black Stallion* and headed to bed. Maybe she'd just read a few pages to lull herself to sleep.

She woke the next morning to a voicemail from Liam. She'd stayed up much too late reading and must have slept through her ringing phone.

"Hey, Hannah," the recording said. "I called my grandfather last night. He remembered the story about the horse. Apparently one of his buddies was obsessed with it and full of conspiracy theories—everything from insurance fraud to the trainer throwing the race. Unfortunately, his friend is no longer alive, and Gramps never heard any definitive answers. I guess that gives you more to think about though. Hope it helps. See you soon."

Hannah stretched and headed to the kitchen. Liam's message certainly gave her something to think about as she made her morning coffee.

She discounted the idea of insurance fraud right away. There must have been an investigation before any insurance payout was made.

But the idea of the trainer being involved was new and disturbing. She hated to think it might be something so unsavory. Her research on the farm's website indicated that Jamie Chadwick had been Kentucky's Angel's trainer, assisting his grandfather who was head trainer. He had been at the farm his entire life, growing up as an apprentice to his grandfather, James Chadwick Sr. In the photos, both men appeared attentive to the horses. How could anyone with their history and apparent devotion to the horses in their care have done anything so unscrupulous?

The latest information showed that Jamie Chadwick was still alive and actively involved in horse training even though he was in his eighties now. That made up her mind. She and Lacy would be taking a tour of that farm, and they would make a point of talking to him.

In the meantime, she had a lot to keep her busy over the next few days.

Chapter Thirteen

Lexington, Kentucky
May 1960

"Can't we do something?" Mickey looked from the horse's heaving flanks to the old trainer. "Can't we pull the legs or something?"

The unflappable trainer patted the kid's shoulder. No longer a kid, but the name had stuck. "If you go near the mare now, it will only stress her."

"But she knows me."

He shook his head. "She's in the middle of foaling. The only thing she should be focusing on is her baby."

"But she kept getting up and down. She's in distress."

"Nope. That's normal. She was doing that to help reposition her baby in the birth canal. Now that the legs are free, her baby will be coming along soon. You'll see."

"But wouldn't it help her if we pulled the baby out?"

Chaddy almost laughed. "Mickey, one of the things that has always made you so good with the horses is your patience. Things happen in their own time. The baby will be born when it's good and ready. Sometimes the mare needs to rest. Foaling is a tiring business, but it's a natural one."

Mickey stared up at him through pain-filled eyes.

Chaddy rested an arm around the kid's shoulders and squeezed. "Mama is doing just fine. She's doing everything right. You can trust me."

The kid nodded, but Chaddy knew the only thing that would help would be the foal's safe delivery.

Chaddy's grandson, Jamie, sat on the straw and beckoned Mickey to sit with him. Chaddy could hear their low voices as Jamie related his first experience watching a foal come into the world. "I kept covering my eyes," he admitted with a laugh.

Jamie kept talking, and Mickey slowly relaxed. But when the filly finally burst free, Mickey hurried forward.

Jamie caught Mickey's arm. "Let her be. You'll be glad you did."

Mickey sat back down and watched in awe as the mother and baby got to know each other. The mare curved her neck, leaning toward the filly, and the baby struggled to reach her mama. Little by little, their noses came closer as the foal shifted her newborn body until they could touch. The mare nuzzled her baby and began to lick her clean. Soon the filly found her legs and struggled to stand on wobbly knees.

Mickey let out a soft gasp as the foal faced her. "Look at that mark on her forehead. It's shaped like a halo. She's an angel horse, born here in this stable in Kentucky." Mickey stared solemnly at Chaddy and Jamie. "That should be her name. Kentucky's Angel."

Hours later, when Chaddy came back to check on the mare and foal, he stopped short at the sight of Mickey sitting cross-legged in the straw, cuddling the foal and gently stroking her head while the mare nuzzled from above.

He shook his head in amazement and slowly backed out, all the while praying that nothing would destroy this newborn bond.

Chapter Fourteen

The week had flown by between managing her restaurant and planning for the feast, but Hannah was beside herself with excitement to finally be heading out to Camden Farms. She drove to Bluegrass Hollow Farm to pick up Lacy, and the two friends were soon on their way.

Lacy held her hands up to the heater. "This feels very much like our drive out to the estate sale, except it's gotten much colder."

"Speaking of that, how's our pup doing?" Hannah had been out to Lacy's farm several times to visit him and had fallen head over heels for the sweet boy.

Lacy's face creased in a frown. "He doesn't like being constrained. The first night I locked him in the barn, he dug his way out. Now I leave the door ajar so he can come and go at will. He always shows up again the next day. It's as if he has a family somewhere but loves to roam, so I don't want to prevent him from going home."

"That's so strange. Jack says no one has responded to his notices in the paper. I sent your photo to the vet, but no one recognized him there either." Talk of the dog had Hannah paying extra close attention to the road. She didn't want a repeat of a creature running out in front of them and her not being ready.

"So long as he keeps coming back, I'll know he's safe," Lacy added. "But it's a mystery for sure. Now, why don't you bring me up to speed on everything you've learned about our other mystery—the horse and the jockey."

"Sure. Talking it through might stir something loose in my brain too."

Hannah quickly filled her friend in on the conversations she'd had, the research she'd done, and the questions rattling around in her head. "I haven't had much time to do any more digging over the past few days. I've hit a dead end online, and this visit to the trainer feels like the only lead that can help. I did read one interesting article last night. You know how I mentioned that Mickey seemed to only ride Kentucky's Angel?"

Lacy turned in her seat to face Hannah. "Yes, and that's strange, because most jockeys ride plenty of horses over the course of a career."

"It gets even stranger. Apparently, Mickey only applied for a jockey license so he could ride Angel. The track reporters say that he could get her to run like no one else. He never rode anyone else, and they never ran a race together that they didn't win."

Lacy tapped her fingers on her leg as she thought about the new information. "That opens a whole pool of suspects, doesn't it? I'm not accusing anyone, but all the other owners, trainers, and jockeys must have been beyond frustrated. What would it have taken to make one of them snap and do something extreme for a chance to win?"

"Good point. To complicate it even more, why was there never much of an investigation? I don't know what would be normal for missing livestock. Do they put out a missing horse bulletin like they would for a person? And what about the jockey? Did he have no family demanding answers about what happened to him?"

"That does seem unusual. Have you checked with Sheriff Steele?" Lacy asked. "He might have a way of checking records we don't have access to."

"I considered it," Hannah admitted. "But a few people have been asking me why I care so much about an unsolved mystery from sixty years ago, so it seemed kind of frivolous to bother the sheriff."

"Do they know you? Who cares how long ago it was? Presenting you with an unsolved mystery is like offering candy to a child, even if you didn't love horses so much."

"Well, yes, but should I really be doing this or am I being totally ridiculous? I mean, why do I really need this mystery solved?"

"Who are you, and what did you do with my best friend?" Lacy teased.

Hannah laughed. "Maybe I needed a reality check. I know I get carried away, but more than anything I want to return the items from the box to the person they belong to."

"And you want to know what happened to the horse."

"There's nothing wrong with that, is there? I mean, people open cold cases all the time."

Lacy chewed on her lip and stared out the front window.

When she didn't respond, Hannah prompted. "Tell me what you're thinking."

"I'm just wondering." Lacy took a deep breath and turned to her friend again. "I asked about this the other day, but you didn't really answer. What if the reason the box was on a shelf in the tack room was because someone was trying to hide it? Maybe because they didn't want the secret to get out. They didn't want to be found."

Hannah glanced over at her friend. "Are you saying we shouldn't be looking into this?"

"Not necessarily." Lacy was thoughtful. "I'm just saying we should proceed with caution. There's no harm in going to this horse farm today. They do public tours, and that's what we're going for. If we have a chance to talk with Jamie Chadwick, then we seize it and ask him if he has any idea who the box could belong to. If he doesn't, no harm, no foul. But if he does, then we decide from there how to handle it. After we talk to Jamie, if we don't have an answer, you have my full support to involve Sheriff Steele."

Hannah nodded. "That makes perfect sense, Lacy. Thank you. You really are the best friend ever."

They continued driving, and the conversation turned to planning for the Thanksgiving feast and the reconstruction of the destroyed fellowship hall.

"Can I admit something?" Hannah asked sheepishly. "I'm nervous about hosting the Gratitude Feast."

"But you run the restaurant every day."

"That's different. It's business," Hannah said. "This almost feels like I'm auditioning for a part in the community."

"Now you *are* being silly, Hannah. You don't need any audition. You were born here, so that makes you one of us. And even if that weren't the case, you've already won everyone over with your open heart and generous spirit. Everyone loves you."

"But what if I mess up? What if it's a disaster?"

"You won't, and it won't be. Remember, you have a whole committee to help." Lacy eyed her sharply until Hannah gave her a small smile. Then she said, "Now, let's talk about what really matters."

"And that is?" Hannah couldn't think of anything more important than the mystery and the Gratitude Feast.

"You and Liam."

Hannah groaned. "Not that again. I'm not even sure what there is to say about it."

Lacy was undeterred. "You like him. He obviously likes you. What's holding things up?"

Hannah hesitated, trying to figure out the best way to explain the situation without digging herself in deeper. "I can't speak for him, but I'm not sure I'm ready to be anything more than friends. I have a business to build."

"So what? Neil built his bookstore business, but he still had time to marry me."

Hannah tightened her grip on the wheel. "Whoa, we were just talking dating, and you fast-forwarded to marriage."

"Has he asked you out?"

"You know I would have told you if he had."

Lacy crossed her arms. "I'm not so sure of that. If you turned him down, you probably wouldn't admit it to me."

Hannah sighed in resignation. "I promise if Liam asks me out, you will be the first person I tell. And I won't turn him down."

"You will call me immediately?"

Hannah rolled her eyes. "If the time is appropriate."

"Any time is appropriate. I don't care if it's the middle of the night."

"Neil might care."

"So send a text."

Hannah snorted. "You do realize how ridiculous this sounds, don't you? We're not teenagers."

"Love is never ridiculous."

Hannah struggled to keep her eyes on the road rather than gape at her friend. "How did we get from a date to love?"

"Because it's obvious. Half of Blackberry Valley has already decided that you two are perfect for each other."

Hannah gulped, not daring to ask what the other half thought. "Oh look, there's the turnoff just ahead. Time to focus on horses."

As they drove up a tree-lined lane to the horse farm, Hannah considered Kentucky's Angel being trained in this very place. The trees were sixty years older, and the people and horses were different, but the overwhelming sense that she was driving into thoroughbred history was so exciting. "Look at this, Lacy. It's incredible."

As far as her eyes could see were fields of bluegrass, starting to brown now as the temperatures dropped. And everywhere there were horses. Some grazed, some played together, but some raced across the field with a wild abandon that called to Hannah's heart.

The white-rail fence that surrounded the fields added to the magic. Hannah had the strongest urge to pull over and climb up on a rail in hope that one of the majestic horses would visit, but she stopped herself. That would probably not be the way to make a good first impression on the owners.

Her pulse pounding with excitement, Hannah followed the signs to park for the tour, and she and Lacy started toward the gathering spot. Hannah had brought the box of memorabilia along, but she left it locked in the car until later. So much would depend on whether they could find Jamie and what his reaction might be. In her dreams, he would be overjoyed to meet them, would answer all their questions, and would know who the box belonged to and where to find them. But there was no guarantee of that.

There was still time before the tour was scheduled to begin, so Hannah wandered over to one of the paddocks to admire the horses. Captivated by their beauty, speed, and grace, she said to Lacy, "I might look like my thirtysomething self on the outside, but inside, right here, right now, I am ten and totally freaking out over these horses."

There was a part of her that wished she had thought to bring her dad along, but even though he'd been the one to take her to Keeneland, he'd mainly wanted to visit his friend. It was her mother who had shared her love of horses.

A sharp stab of grief came with the thought. It constantly surprised her the way a thought would pop up without warning and remind her of her loss. Her mother would have loved the idea of this tour, though, and would want her to enjoy it.

A young female guide came out to greet them along with a small group that had gathered. She started by introducing them to the horses currently in the paddock. "These are yearlings, which means they're about a year old. They still need to mature a little more before we start to train them to wear a saddle or even consider training them to race."

The tour was fascinating from the start, and Hannah almost forgot their real reason for being there. As they strolled across the grounds, they heard the history of the farm and some of its famous horses, and they paused at headstones for some who had passed on. Hannah's thoughts immediately strayed, wondering where Kentucky's Angel had been buried.

The next stop on the tour gave them a chance to see a few of the assistant trainers working with the horses. "Now if we can find Jamie Chadwick, maybe we can get some answers," Hannah murmured.

Lacy took the lead and asked the tour guide, "Does Jamie Chadwick still work here?

The young woman smiled. "They will have to carry him out of here in a box. He isn't the lead trainer anymore, but he still lives here, and he still dishes out advice. Why, do you know him?"

"No," Lacy replied. "I just heard some stories about him recently."

The guide's face fell, and her friendliness vanished. "If you're talking about those old stories about him throwing the race, I can tell you they are all lies. I have never met a more honest man in my life, and Uncle Jamie would never do that to his horses."

Hannah felt their chances to speak with Jamie slipping away, even as she realized that must have been the rumor Liam's grandfather mentioned. Not wanting to blow their opportunity to meet the legendary trainer, she jumped in to explain. "No, she didn't mean that at all. I'm sorry for the misunderstanding. It's my fault. I came across a story about Kentucky's Angel and Mr. Chadwick's success in training her. My friend and I were hoping to meet him."

The tension in the woman's face eased a bit. "I'm sorry. I shouldn't have come on so strong. I wasn't alive then, but he's my uncle, and I know it was a hard time in his life."

"I understand that, but I don't want to accuse him or bring up painful memories," Hannah insisted. "I have something that might interest him."

The woman's expression tightened again, and she didn't respond for a moment. She finally agreed that they could complete the tour and then she would check with her uncle to let him decide if he wanted to speak with Hannah and Lacy.

With that concession, Hannah focused on enjoying the rest of the tour and soaking up every last bit of information the guide gave about thoroughbreds. When the group finally returned to the starting point and the other tour members departed, the guide turned back to Hannah and Lacy. "This time of day, Uncle Jamie is probably supervising the assistant trainers. We'll check the stallion barn. You can wait outside while I see if he's up to talking with you."

As they walked toward the barn, Hannah tried to ease the tension by chatting with the young woman. "If Jamie Chadwick is your uncle, do you ride, or just lead the tours?"

The guide's expression grew wistful as she answered. "I used to be a training rider. I wanted to be a jockey. Unfortunately, I inherited the family gene for height, so I'm too tall. But I still get to exercise the horses and ride for fun. Do you ride?"

"I took lessons as a child, but I haven't been on a horse in years. I was living in California. I just moved back home and opened a restaurant. If you're ever in Blackberry Valley, stop by the Hot Spot and see us."

"I'll do that. The Hot Spot is an interesting name for a restaurant."

"It used to be a firehouse, but Hannah converted it to the best restaurant in Kentucky," Lacy said with pride.

"That sounds fun. I'll definitely put it on my bucket list. Here we are. I'll go in first and check with Uncle Jamie. What is it I should tell him about why you want to see him?"

Hannah debated what to say. "Tell him we found some racing memorabilia for Kentucky's Angel."

The guide's eyes widened. "Oh no. This is not a good idea."

"Wait," Hannah said. "Please hear me out. Or let Mr. Chadwick have the chance to tell me no himself."

"Erin? Is everything okay?" The white-haired, elderly man who walked toward them had the bowed legs of a horseman and wore an expression that showed concern for his niece. Hannah recognized his face from her internet search. It was Jamie Chadwick.

When he reached them, he wrapped an arm around Erin's shoulders. "Who are your friends?"

Erin's features were stony. "Not my friends, Uncle Jamie. These ladies are from the tour, and they were just leaving."

"Mr. Chadwick," Hannah interrupted. "We mean no harm. We just wanted to talk to you for a minute."

"I'm so sorry, Uncle Jamie. I told them they couldn't visit with you."

"Why not?"

Erin hung her head and scuffed her boot against the gravel, clearly not wanting to explain. Hannah suddenly empathized. The young girl was trying to protect her uncle from hurt the same way Hannah herself would try to protect Uncle Gordon.

Hannah spoke up. "She's worried that we'll upset you because we want to talk to you about Kentucky's Angel. But I can assure you that we're not here to cause trouble. I have something I want to share with you."

She couldn't read his expression at the mention of the lost horse.

Hannah rushed on without giving him a chance to turn them away. "Honestly, I'd never even heard of you or Kentucky's Angel until a week or so ago. I was at an estate sale where I bought a box that turned out to be full of racing programs, news clippings, and two of Kentucky's Angel's trophies."

Mr. Chadwick didn't say anything, but she could see she had at least piqued his interest.

"I have the box in the car."

He studied Hannah long enough to make her squirm. "Why would discovering a box of memorabilia bring you here?"

His voice had a kind tone, but there was a bite beneath it as hard as any horseshoe.

Hannah pondered how best to answer. She wanted him to understand that it was not idle curiosity or some desire to reawaken scandal. "It seemed like whoever saved those items cared deeply about the horse. I'm trying to find out who the box belonged to so I can return it."

"If it was an estate sale, wouldn't that mean the person wanted to get rid of it?" Old pain was evident in his voice.

"Not necessarily. The box was stored up on a shelf in the tack room. The person running the sale in the barn happened to notice it. She tried to look into it, but the trophy made the box heavy and it fell on her, knocking her off the ladder."

"How did you get it?"

"It's a long story about a dog that led us to find her. We helped her, and I was intrigued by the trophies, so I bought the box. It was only later that I saw all the programs for Kentucky's Angel's races. The flowers she won were pressed in an album. Someone obviously took great care to preserve those memories. I can't believe that anyone who cared that deeply and put that much effort into saving those items meant to discard them. It must have been a mistake."

As Hannah finished, she noticed tears in the man's eyes. Her heart leaped. He must know who the box belonged to.

And then he dashed her hopes. "I'm sorry, young lady. I can't help you."

Hannah couldn't give up so easily, not after coming all this way. "Don't you want to look at what I have? Maybe it will spark a memory."

He smiled gently. "You're a persistent one, aren't you? You remind me of someone I knew long ago. She had the same tenacity. I'll look at your box, but don't hold out any great hopes." He turned to his niece. "Do you have time to escort them back to my office?"

"Are you sure you want to do this?" Erin asked him softly.

He hesitated only a moment before answering. "Yes."

Once they had retrieved the box, Erin led Hannah and Lacy to where Mr. Chadwick was waiting in a small office in the barn. He had cleared a section of his desk, and Hannah set the box down. Lacy was carrying the heavy trophies and placed them beside it.

Mr. Chadwick picked up the smaller trophy and smiled as he showed it to them. "This was from Kentucky's Angel's first race. It wasn't official. She was a yearling, and we don't race yearlings or even ride them, but Angel never stopped running. The moment she was in the pasture, she was free as the wind, racing across the fields. None of our other yearlings could hold a candle to her. Later, when Mickey rode her…" A dreamy smile wreathed his face. "They would take your breath away. It was as if they were one. At the end of the season, I had a special trophy made for Angel as the Yearling Champion and wove a garland of wildflowers to drape around her neck. Mickey insisted on braiding ribbons into her mane, and they paraded around the paddock as if they'd just won the Triple Crown."

That explained why she had never been able to match the trophy to a race. Excited, Hannah reached into the box and pulled out the album. She flipped it open to a page with a circle of pressed wildflowers.

Mr. Chadwick was speechless as he ran his work-roughened finger over the flowers that had been sealed inside the page. Their colors had faded, but Hannah could tell he was seeing them in all their fresh-picked glory. He flipped through the pages, studying the flowers. "I never realized Mickey saved them all."

"Are you okay, Uncle Jamie?" Erin asked.

He gave her a sad smile. "You never know what the Lord plans for your days. I surely never would have predicted this, but it's an unexpected blessing. Thank you, ladies. This was a very special time in my life that I tried to forget about because of what happened later."

"If it's not too much to ask, I would love to hear your side of that story," Hannah told him.

Mr. Chadwick leaned back in his chair, clearly gathering his thoughts. "My grandfather was the lead trainer back then. I was a young kid who thought he would rule the racing circuit one day. Pipe dreams. But when Angel was born, I just knew. She was the one. She was so special. We joked that her birth was like she was breaking from the starting gate. That horse was born to run."

"You trained her?"

"In name, yes. But really, there was only one person she responded to."

Goose bumps rose along Hannah's arms, and she drew her jacket closer even though the sensation had nothing to do with cold air. "Mickey Dawes."

"Yes, how did you know?"

Hannah dug back into the box and pulled out the pile of programs and booklets. "I saw his name listed with Kentucky's Angel in the official programs. Some of this is confusing to me, but the name of the jockey is clearly listed."

Mr. Chadwick took the program in his gnarled hands and again seemed to be lost in memories. "This was Angel's two-year-old finale. She and Mickey won every race they ran that year. No need for invented awards. They swept them all. They were unstoppable together."

"What is this?" Hannah asked, holding out a different set of booklets. She had organized them by type.

"Those are condition books. The track puts them out with all the information about the race, the horse, the handicaps, the bloodlines, track conditions. Everything you need to know for the race is in there."

"Some of these names are funny," Lacy said with a laugh. "Mr. Tink. Succabone. I'd go for a horse named Fightin' Scot."

"Not if you didn't want to lose your shirt," Mr. Chadwick replied. "It got so no one wanted to back any other horse. Angel left them all in the dust. There were some that said she was ruining the fun of the season, but she was just a horse who loved to run. If someone was chasing her, she only ran faster."

Hannah's ears perked up. Could that have had anything to do with Angel's disappearance? Could Lacy be right that aggrieved owners or trainers had done something to give their horses a chance at victory?

Hannah opened her mouth to ask, but Mr. Chadwick was deep in thought, holding the other trophy.

"This cup was from the last race she ran. We didn't think anything of it at the time. It was just a Derby prep race, and she won it running away from the pack." His hand lovingly stroked the cup. "We had no idea it would be her last time in the winner's circle." He cleared his throat and suddenly asked, "Why did you really come to see me today? Surely not just to bring this box."

Hannah and Lacy exchanged a glance, and Lacy nodded that Hannah should speak.

"We had two reasons for coming, Mr. Chadwick, though if we'd known how much seeing these would mean to you, we would have come anyway. After holding this trophy, seeing all these programs, and doing my research…" Hannah hesitated as emotion clogged her throat. "I really wanted to see where she was born, where she learned to run, where she lived and was obviously adored by Mickey."

"That filly didn't *learn* how to run here. As I said, she was born with running in her heart." Mr. Chadwick's voice was husky as he spoke. "Mickey had some difficult moments during the foaling, but the horses were fine. The minute those wobbly legs hit the ground, she was ready to move."

"Why was it difficult for Mickey?" Hannah prompted.

"Mickey's mother died in childbirth, so watching the foaling was rough, but once Angel was born, they took to each other right away. They connected instantly in a way you see sometimes, but I've never seen a bond like they shared. We all loved Angel, but the love between the two of them was something special. Unique. Lovely. It actually hurt sometimes to watch them because they were so perfect together. It was the innocent love of a horse and rider." He cleared his throat. "What was your other question?"

"I wanted to know if you knew where I could find Mickey. I wanted to return this box."

Mr. Chadwick hung his head a moment, and when he lifted it, his face was clouded with grief. "If I knew the answer to that, it would have saved me many a sleepless night. Mickey and Angel well and truly vanished that night, and I have no idea where they went."

Shortly after that conversation, Hannah and Lacy left. Mr. Chadwick clearly had no answers, and Hannah was sorry to have revived his grief. The friends were quiet as they walked to the car. Hannah's gaze still roved the field, and she reveled in the sight of the horses racing across the pasture. She pictured Kentucky's Angel racing across the green grass, wind in her mane and her tail streaming behind her. And astride the horse, bent low over her neck, whispering encouragement, was the mysterious jockey, Mickey.

Hannah wished she could have asked Mr. Chadwick more about Mickey, but the old man had seemed so sad when telling the story. He didn't know where the rider had gone, so what was the point of forcing him to wallow?

"Lacy, wait here a moment, please." Hannah grabbed the smaller trophy and dashed back.

Mr. Chadwick sat at his desk, his eyes closed, and for a moment she thought he was asleep, but as she entered, he opened his eyes. "Did you forget something?" A tear stood in the corner of his eye.

She recalled Lacy's remark earlier about why they were doing this. Answers to her questions suddenly didn't matter if they meant bringing sorrow to a kind, old man.

Hannah held out the trophy to him. "I thought you might like to have this."

He blinked, then shut his eyes, and Hannah sensed he was trying to hold back overwhelming emotion. When he nodded, she stepped forward and placed the trophy in his hands. "It belongs with someone who loved her."

His eyes flashed open so quickly that Hannah thought maybe she had said something wrong.

"You clearly loved Kentucky's Angel," she clarified, "and since I have no way of tracing who owned this box, I feel like the trophy should stay with you."

He swallowed hard. "Thank you."

Hannah slipped out of the office, but glanced back over her shoulder. The old man ran his hand over the golden horse, much as he must have once run it along the filly's withers and down her back. Tears built in her eyes, and she swiped a hand over them as she joined Lacy and explained what she'd done.

"I probably should have asked your advice first," she concluded.

"No," Lacy said firmly. "You did the right thing. That trophy belongs with him. But I still wish we could find Mickey."

"You and me both," Hannah said. "If for no other reason than to bring Mr. Chadwick some peace."

Chapter Fifteen

Lexington, Kentucky
March 1961

Early evening shadows lanced through the high barn window and fell across Chaddy's desk. He leaned against the wall of his office, arms behind his head, feet resting on a stool, and soaking in the calm after a busy day. The barn was quiet except for the occasional snort or shuffle of a horse. This was his favorite time of the day, alone with the horses. Soon Jamie would arrive so they could review training plans for the next day, but for now he soaked in the peace of a place that had been home for most of his life.

Chaddy knew his days as lead trainer were winding down. He'd been training his grandson to take his place. Jamie would make a fine lead trainer. He had it in his blood the same way Mickey did.

Run for the Roses

He closed his eyes, envisioning a farm with Jamie at the helm, another generation of Chadwicks working side by side with the Donahues to produce the finest thoroughbreds in all of Kentucky. Jamie and Mickey would make quite a team.

A soft knock at the door jolted him from his daydreams. "Come in, Jamie. I'm just resting my eyes." But when he opened his eyes, it wasn't Jamie standing there.

"I'm sorry to bother you." Mickey kicked a booted foot at the floor and didn't look up at the trainer. "There's something I wanted to ask."

Chaddy had never known Mickey to be shy, so this tentative tone surprised him. "You know you can ask anything."

"I want to ride."

The quickly uttered words hung in the air between them as Chaddy chewed on a piece of hay and mulled over the request. "You already ride any time you want. You don't have to ask to ride one of our horses."

"Maybe I should have said I want to race."

Chaddy whistled low against the hay. "Now that's a horse of a different color."

"I don't want to ride just any horse. I want to ride Angel."

Jamie came into the room in time to hear this declaration and stopped short, his eyes wide.

Chaddy breathed a sigh of relief. "You know she isn't ready to be ridden yet. You're still getting her used to a saddle and bridle."

"I know it's too early, but there are times I think she sees the other horses racing and wants us to do it too. I don't mean now. I mean in the spring, when she's ready, I want to be the one to ride her."

"But you can't ride," Jamie objected. "You're—"

Chaddy silenced him with a raised hand that cut off the words. "Why do you want to ride, Mickey?"

"Because riding is everything. And riding Angel is all I want in life."

Chaddy stood and walked across the room to where he could see the horses. "Your granddaddy brought your mama out to this barn to meet his horses on the very day she was born."

Mickey's eyes widened. "Really?"

"Yes. Your grandmama was not at all happy about it, but he said a girl needed to meet her horses as soon as she breathed air."

Mickey's expression grew wistful. "I wish he'd done that with me instead of sending us away."

Chaddy smiled as he peered back in time. "Your own mama brought you here to visit before you were born. She snuck out here when she knew her father was away. She said it was a mistake to keep you away and wanted to introduce you to the horses while she had a chance." Chaddy shook his head at the memory.

"Apparently you gave quite a kick when the horse neighed."

Tears welled in Mickey's eyes. "You never told me that."

"I'm telling you now. Because this is my answer. Riding is in your blood, child, and I cannot deny it. We'll start with letting you ride training runs on some of the other horses this year. But racing..." He heaved a sigh. "I will have to speak with your grandfather about that. Let's have you start with exercising the horses so we can show you off when the time comes."

The smile that grew across Mickey's face near broke Chaddy's heart. He wished he was as confident in the old man's decision as he was in Mickey's ability to ride.

Chapter Sixteen

"You're unusually quiet," Lacy commented as they drove back along the highway.

"I'm thinking." Hannah groaned. "My brain is tired. Thankfully, traffic is light."

"I know it's not traffic making your brain hurt," Lacy teased. "What are you thinking?"

"So many things. I'm so sad for Mr. Chadwick. He clearly loved Kentucky's Angel like she was his own. I feel awful that we reminded him of such a horrible time in his life."

"Yes, but we also brought up many happy memories for him," Lacy pointed out. "After he warmed up, he seemed to enjoy sharing them."

"That's true, and his stories made me desperately wish we could have seen Angel run. Imagine how it must have felt to see her racing across the pasture with such abandon, or to watch her in a race leaving all the other horses behind. My father showed me a video of Secretariat doing the same thing. All those years later, and through a computer screen I could still feel the thrill of the beautiful horse racing for sheer joy. Imagine what it must have felt like for Mickey to ride her when she was running like that."

"I think I'd have been a mix of elated and terrified," Lacy said. "I never go much faster than a canter across the field with mine." She owned a few horses herself.

"Which brings me to the topic of Mickey. Kentucky's Angel didn't disappear by herself. She disappeared with Mickey. Do you think the reason Mr. Chadwick doesn't want to talk about it is because he suspects Mickey betrayed him and stole the horse?"

Lacy was quiet. "If he did, there had to be a good reason. The way Mr. Chadwick described it, he and Mickey got on very well. I know I'm basing my opinion on what others have said, but I just can't believe Mickey would betray the man he worked for."

"Unless he was forced to."

"What do you mean?"

Hannah tapped the wheel. "Remember what Mr. Chadwick said about how everyone was tired of Angel winning every race or demolishing the competition? Maybe it really was as simple as some other owner or jockey being tired of losing every race. Eliminating the favorite gives the others a chance at the winner's purse."

"I don't like thinking about that," Lacy said softly.

"No one does, but if we're going to figure out what happened to Kentucky's Angel, we have to be willing to consider all possibilities."

"I thought we were just trying to return a box of memorabilia to its rightful owner."

"We were," Hannah replied. "And we will, but Mr. Chadwick's comment sent my mind in a different direction, and now I need to know."

"Hannah, I should know better than to try to talk you out of a mystery no matter how old, but don't you think whoever investigated at the time would have followed up all these leads?"

Hannah squared her jaw. "Not if someone was being paid to look the other way."

Lacy gulped. "Wouldn't that make it really dangerous for you to dig into it now?"

With a shrug, Hannah said, "I'll be careful. Most of the people involved are probably dead by now anyway."

"But the reputations of their farms rest on their memories. I'm worried about you getting in over your head."

Hannah tossed her friend a smile. "It's probably just my overactive imagination anyway. I'm sure there was a much less criminal explanation."

"I don't know how there could be. An expensive racehorse went missing on the eve of a race where she would have won a handsome purse—not to mention all the breeding fees that would have come with a victory. Imagine if she had gone on to win the Triple Crown."

Hannah swallowed hard. "I know this was many years ago, but it makes me angry on Mr. Chadwick's behalf."

"I understand," Lacy replied. "But everyone lives through sad times. Like Erin said, that was a terrible time for her uncle Jamie, but look at what a long, successful life he has led. Mr. Chadwick has been blessed with a lifetime of living on a beautiful farm and working with his beloved horses."

"You're right," Hannah said. And Hannah had been blessed with such a wise friend.

"I may be right about this, but I forgot to ask Neil about horse books. Maybe you can satisfy your horse mania with a reread of *The Black Stallion*. Or *Seabiscuit*. Did you read that? I know Neil ordered a copy recently."

"Evangeline loaned me a copy of *The Black Stallion* the other day. She remembered how often I used to check it out as a child. I haven't had much time for reading lately, and I miss it. If you remember to ask Neil, tell him I'd love to read anything he recommends."

When they arrived at Bluegrass Hollow Farm, Hannah got out to give her friend a hug. "Thanks for coming with me today."

"It was such fun," Lacy replied. "Maybe we didn't make much progress in finding the owner of the box, but it was good to meet Mr. Chadwick and see the horses."

After dropping Lacy off, Hannah decided to stop by to see her dad. She could use some time with him to get her mind off the missing horse for tonight, so maybe she would make dinner for him and Uncle Gordon.

But that didn't mean she was abandoning her mystery. Despite Lacy's warnings, Hannah couldn't forget about the horse and rider who had disappeared. She promised herself she would do her best to avoid trouble, but dangerous or not, she intended to pursue this investigation. Her ten-year-old, horse-loving self would allow for nothing less.

Chapter Seventeen

The next morning, Hannah was up early. Dinner with her dad and uncle always centered her, so she felt refreshed and ready to take on the world—or at least her part of it. A full day at the Hot Spot lay ahead, including a meeting with Jacob about the Gratitude Feast.

Hannah had the sense that her chef had been hard at work creating festive dishes. Hopefully he hadn't gone over the top, forgetting that this was usually a potluck feast, but if the samples coming out as specials in the last week were any indication, Blackberry Valley was due for a Gratitude Feast that would have people begging for recipes.

That put an idea in her head. Maybe she should speak to him about putting out a cookbook of recipes to help with fundraising efforts. *Hot Meals from the Hot Spot.*

Would that sabotage her business? If people could make their own favorites at home, would they still come to her restaurant? She didn't really think it would be a problem. People came out to share a meal with friends and family—one they didn't have to cook. That was the kind of environment she was trying to create. She wanted the Hot Spot to become much more than merely a place to eat. Volunteering to host the Gratitude Feast had been a step in the right direction. She needed to start thinking of some festive ways to draw the town in for Christmas.

As the coffee brewed, she turned her mind to creative ideas. The Christmas season would be a great time to hold festive gatherings. Maybe she could host a Christmas movie dinner night or a caroling session after dinner. That reminded her of the packages Sabrina wanted to coordinate between the Blackberry Inn and the Hot Spot. So much to look forward to.

But first, Thanksgiving.

Her phone rang as Hannah was filling her mug, and she was surprised to see Lorelai's name on her screen. She answered at once. "Hi, Lorelai, how are things going at the church?"

"The contractors are making good progress. There's nothing much I can do here without being underfoot, which is why I called. I know it's early, and I don't mean to be a worrywart, but I've managed this feast for so long that it feels like I'm being irresponsible if I don't have any work to do. Are you sure there isn't anything you need help with?"

Hannah heard the undercurrent in her friend's voice and was ashamed of herself for not picking up on it earlier. The pastor's wife felt left out of her own event. "I have a meeting with Jacob this morning to go over some ideas. Would you have time to join us and give your experienced opinion?" Now that she'd suggested it, Hannah didn't know why she hadn't thought of it before. She hadn't been to the feast since she was a teenager, but Lorelai had been running it for years. Of course she should be offering guidance.

"That sounds wonderful. What time should I come?"

"Let me check with Jacob, and I'll text you."

"Perfect. I'll be there."

Once Hannah had agreed on a time with Jacob and sent a message to Lorelai, she refilled her coffee and settled in with her devotional. With all that was going on, some quiet contemplation would make a good start for her day.

Half an hour later, feeling refreshed, Hannah glanced at her clock and saw that she had a little more time before she had to head downstairs. She decided to dive back into the box from the estate sale. She was eager to go back through the programs and condition books now that Jamie had explained what they were.

But poring over the charts and trying to decipher bloodlines and weights and jockey names and purse amounts only confused her and gave her no clues as to the fate of the missing rider and horse. By the time she needed to go downstairs, she was no further than she'd been before.

As she packed everything back in the box, Hannah's gaze fell on the album. Jamie Chadwick had been particularly interested in that and had lingered over the pages, especially the one featuring the wildflowers he'd picked so many years before.

Hannah stared at the page. There was something about this album that nagged at her, but she couldn't quite place what it was. She decided to leave it on her coffee table to look at before bed. Maybe when she was winding down from the day, she would figure out what it was about the album that called out to her.

Hannah finished her coffee and set her mug in the sink then changed into the slacks and shirt she would wear for the evening. She trotted down the steps to work.

Lorelai hadn't arrived yet, which gave Hannah time to duck into the kitchen and let Jacob know the pastor's wife would be joining them. Mouthwatering aromas greeted her as she pushed through the swinging doors. "Jacob, it smells so enticing in here. What are you cooking?"

She was rewarded by his broad smile. Even confident chefs liked to hear praise for their work. Despite his tendency to add questionable flair to his dishes, Jacob was an accomplished chef, and she counted herself extremely lucky to have him on her staff.

Before he could answer, Hannah's phone dinged. "Lorelai's here. She was feeling a bit left out, so I invited her to join us and give feedback. I hope that's all right."

"Sure thing," Jacob replied. "That will help us maintain a consistent feel with previous years' feasts."

"I'm glad you feel that way. I'll go let her in and we can get started."

Hannah hurried through the dining room, reveling in the sense of accomplishment it always gave her to see the fulfillment of her dreams.

A chilly breeze blew in as she opened the door to welcome Lorelai. "Come on in. Jacob is waiting for us in the kitchen, where it's warm and everything smells divine."

Lorelai paused in the entryway to the dining room. "It's so odd to see the room without a crowd. Usually there are dozens of laughing, chatting people enjoying Jacob's creations. You have something really special here, Hannah."

Hannah beamed at her. "I was just myself thinking how special this place is. It's brought my dreams to life." She led Lorelai through the room and into the kitchen. "This is where the culinary magic happens."

Jacob was balancing a full tray, but he called out a greeting. "Hi, Mrs. Dawson. Welcome to my home away from home."

"Lorelai, please, or I'll have to call you Chef Forrest."

"That wouldn't be so bad," he said with a grin. "But Jacob is fine."

Jacob reached for the coffeepot and gestured to stools he'd set around his gleaming worktable. "I thought we could discuss first. Then I'll share some samples I've been trying out."

"That sounds delightful," Lorelai said.

Jacob filled their cups while Hannah and Lorelai settled on their stools. "So, Lorelai," he said. "You've run this Gratitude Feast for as long as I can remember, and it's always been run flawlessly, so tell me your secrets. How do you get it all to appear so effortless?"

Hannah could have kissed her chef for his kindness. One quick glance at Lorelai's face told Hannah exactly how much Jacob's words meant.

"You are too kind, Jacob. It's teamwork, pure and simple. The church ladies' group organizes everything, and we have the advantage of having run it for years. It's a lot of work, but we're not exactly reinventing the wheel." She was a humble soul, so her response didn't surprise Hannah.

"Then we won't reinvent the wheel this time either, but we might have to make some adjustments. The Hot Spot is a very different environment compared to the community hall. We have less flexibility in seating for example. Do you have any suggestions on how we should handle that?"

Lorelai seemed to consider the question. "I'd suggest we do it buffet-style for the dining, but if it's okay with Hannah, I'd really love to have a meeting with the committee here to brainstorm plans on-site."

Hannah nodded, then sat back and watched as the two continued in serious conversation.

"Let's talk about the menu," Jacob finally suggested. "I know exactly how the potluck version goes, since I've eaten at it for years, but I had something different in mind."

The moment of truth. Hannah didn't think Lorelai would object, but she held her breath until the pastor's wife encouraged Jacob to share his thinking.

"I don't want to speak for Hannah, and I probably should have cleared this with her first." He gave Hannah a grin. She couldn't blame him for speaking out since she was the one who'd sprung Lorelai on him.

"Go ahead, Chef," she teased so he'd feel comfortable.

Jacob cleared his throat. "All of us here at the Hot Spot are supremely grateful for how Blackberry Valley has embraced this restaurant. You've really exceeded our dreams, right, Hannah?"

She beamed at him. "You're absolutely right, Jacob."

"I was thinking," he continued, "that we could make the main entrees as our gift back to the community. Our way of saying thank you for welcoming and supporting us."

Hannah was amazed. Why hadn't she thought of that?

"I also don't want people to feel neglected, so I'd like to offer to cater the main part of the meal, but then anyone who wants to bring their favorite side or dessert would be welcome to do that as well. We could set up the tables in the center of the room and then the booths would be available for seating, as would any leftover tables. If the weather cooperates, we could even spill out onto the sidewalk and street—maybe with small fire pits, though we'll have speak to Sheriff Steele and the fire department about that part."

Lorelai clapped her hands in delight. "That sounds absolutely perfect, Jacob—except for one thing. Hannah has already taken on the expense of opening the restaurant to us, and this would be adding to that. The church does have a small budget allocated for the feast, and I'm sure the committee will vote to offer it to you to offset the costs. What do you think?"

"I'd appreciate that," Hannah replied. "Jacob captured every feeling that has been overflowing my heart these past few months. This feast is a wonderful opportunity to share our gratitude with Blackberry Valley, and Jacob dreamed up the perfect way to express it."

"I'm glad you feel that way," Jacob said. "I do have another idea. Since we're showcasing so many local products, we may be able to get some donations of them as well. Now, if that's settled, are you ready to sample some of what I had in mind for a menu?"

Hannah was enjoying how much her chef had gotten into planning the feast. It was wonderful to see this side of him.

He started toward the stove. "In keeping with our farm-to-table model, I designed a number of dishes around the produce and poultry we source from local farms." He took a tray from the warming oven. "I didn't cook a turkey today. I think we all know what to expect from that, though I will give it my own flair." He winked at Hannah. "I wanted to show you some other recipes I've come up with. Most are a bit of a twist on the traditional. I didn't include anything from our regular menu, like our wings and burgers, but I can if you want."

"That's okay. I think this is different," Hannah agreed. "Maybe we can find one five-alarm recipe, but let's see what you have."

Lorelai laughed. "Bring it on, Jacob. All this talk of food has me ravenous."

Jacob set the tray on the table. "I made some sample appetizers. Our guests will likely bring cheese and crackers and the traditional Thanksgiving crudités, but I also made these sweet potato puffs. There's a surprise in the center."

"Oh, what fun." Lorelai popped one in her mouth and smiled. "Cranberry sauce. It's delicious."

"That makes me think of a hot recipe you could use, Jacob," Hannah chimed in. "What if you made jalapeno poppers with sweet potatoes?"

"I could do that. We could call them Hot Potato Poppers or Sweet Tater Hots."

"They'd better come with a warning," Lorelai joked. "And keep them away from the children's table."

"Oh, that's right. I'd forgotten there is usually a children's table. I'll have to get to work on some creative ideas to entertain them."

"What else do we have as appetizers?" Hannah asked.

"Stuffing is probably everyone's favorite part of Thanksgiving dinner, so why only have it for the main course? I made these stuffing toasts with dollops of cranberry-fig jelly, and then I have celery filled with a squash puree and sprinkled with chopped pumpkin seeds. These baby wild mushroom quiches are flavored with thyme and rosemary and topped with maple bacon that Colt will make en masse for us."

Hannah's mouth watered with every additional item Jacob listed.

Lorelai was speechless. "I want to taste everything."

Jacob set out plates and used tongs to place a variety of items on each one. "Save some room for the main course."

"There's more?" Lorelai's eyes were wide

"Well, the turkey, but I also have been trying out a ground turkey shepherd's pie on the menu lately. We're calling it Fireman's Pie, and it's been well-received."

"Don't be humble, Jacob," Hannah said. "It's the first thing people ask about when they make their reservations. 'Is the Fireman's Pie on the menu tonight?'"

Jacob grinned wryly. "It'll be challenging to come up with a Christmas menu to top this. But I do have some ideas. Have you tried the Fireman's Pie, Lorelai?"

She nodded. "I did. Raquel recommended it when I was in for dinner last week. It was delicious. I raved so much to Bob that now he wants to come try it."

Jacob smiled his gratitude. "I'm working on a vegetarian version with lentils and whipped parsnips as well."

"Yum. I love lentils and parsnips together, but I haven't had them in ages," Hannah enthused.

As the discussion continued, Jacob pointed out the squash, sweet potatoes, brussels sprouts, and corn he'd mentioned coming from local farms. He had an arrangement with a Blackberry Valley poultry farm for their organic free-range turkeys, and the herbs were grown in a local nursery.

Lorelai made a delicate face at the idea of brussels sprouts, but Hannah advised her, "Don't bet against Jacob. He can make a believer out of you."

Jacob was in his element. "There are two varieties of brussels sprouts—the first are roasted in apple cider vinegar, and the second are candied in bourbon maple syrup from a Kentucky farm to give it a local flair. The alcohol cooks out," he added.

Lorelai still looked doubtful, but she gamely gave the dish a try. Her eyes widened in amazement as she took a second bite. "Can I order this for our own Thanksgiving feast?"

Hannah was pleased to see how the compliment touched her chef's heart.

"We don't do catering," he replied. "But I'll whip up a special batch as a thank-you for being a taste tester."

Lorelai's eyes sparkled with joy. "Thank you. Bob is going to love this."

"So, do we have everything settled?" Hannah asked.

Jacob nodded, but Lorelai shook her head. "Jacob, I already admitted to tasting your shepherd's pie, but what I didn't say is that I've been thinking about it ever since, and I had an idea. What if you made a crust with cornmeal? I know traditional shepherd's pie doesn't use a crust, but I was thinking of the juices from the turkey soaking into it instead of being lost. What do you think?"

"That's an intriguing idea. Tell me more." And just like that, the two of them were off debating the merits of different crusts.

"Personally, I like the idea of a stuffing crust," Hannah interjected.

"No, no, no." Jacob waved a hand. "Lorelai is onto something with this cornmeal idea."

Lorelai beamed. "I'd be honored for you to try it." She stood and pushed back her stool. "Now we're done, but please let me help you clean up."

Jacob declined and shooed them out. As Hannah led the way back into the dining room, Lorelai glanced at her watch. "I should head to the church. Bob and I are meeting about the property repairs in half an hour. Knowing his busy morning, he may not have had a minute to stop and make his lunch. Any possibility of leftovers?"

"I heard that," Jacob called out. "Box lunch coming right up."

Once Lorelai left, Hannah settled down to do some paperwork until the rest of her staff arrived to start setting up for dinner. That was always a favorite part of her day, when they all gathered together to make sure everything was ready to ensure a smooth evening and wonderful experience for their patrons. As she watched Elaine, Raquel, and Dylan fall into their comfortable routine, she was again overcome with gratitude for her treasured staff.

The restaurant started to fill shortly after opening, and Hannah delightedly spent the evening chatting with her diners and filling in as needed. Sometimes she had to pinch herself that this was her life—especially when Liam and his friend Archer strode in an hour before closing. They wore fresh clothes, but they carried enough of a whiff of smoke that Hannah was concerned.

"Busy night?" She tried to cover her worry with a cheerful smile.

"A lucky one," Archer replied. "There was a small brushfire outside of town, but thankfully someone spotted it right away and we were able to extinguish it quickly."

Hannah glanced at Liam. He didn't seem as cavalier about the result as his friend, and she hoped everything was all right.

She led them to a table and announced as they sat, "Dinner is on the house for two brave firefighters. Choose whatever appeals to you. My treat in thanks for your quick work."

"Thanks, Hannah, but you're already giving enough. We'll pay for our food." Liam smiled at her, and she didn't miss the fatigue in his eyes.

"Don't you worry about him, Hannah," Archer chimed in. "He's only tired because he stayed up too late last night reading the book Neil gave him."

"Oh, what book, Liam?"

"*Seabiscuit*," Archer teased. "Because it's about horses."

Archer gave a sudden yelp, and Hannah suspected he'd just been kicked under the table. She fought back a laugh and ignored Archer's teasing as she addressed Liam. "Please tell me you didn't take the last copy. Lacy suggested I read it."

"I'll be happy to loan it to you when I'm done," Liam said at once.

"Thanks. Now let me get you some menus so you can go home and get some rest."

"No need for a menu. We know it by heart," Liam said. "I'll have the Glowing Embers Wings, and Archer will have the Inferno."

Hannah laughed, thinking back to the first time Liam had gotten revenge on Archer with Jacob's hottest chicken wings. She winked at the younger firefighter. "*Two* servings of Inferno coming right up."

She walked away, humming a happy tune. It warmed Hannah's heart to think Liam might have chosen the book because of her love of horses. Yes, she had a lot for which to be grateful.

Chapter Eighteen

Hannah was in the middle of dinner prep on Wednesday when she saw that Jack Delaney had left a voice message on her phone.

"Hi, Hannah, I might have some information for you. Any chance you could stop by the *Chronicle* office this afternoon?"

Hannah was torn. She didn't want to leave before dinner, but her curiosity would eat her alive if she had to wait until morning. "Elaine, can you take over for a bit? I have to run out."

"Of course. Take your time. We have everything under control."

Hannah grabbed her coat and hurried down to Jump Start. The least she could do was bring the newspaper editor a coffee. "Hello, Zane. Isn't it a fabulous evening?"

Zane looked from Hannah to the window that was being battered by a misty wind. "Sure, Hannah. If you like this kind of weather."

"I do. It's better if you can curl up inside with a cup of coffee and a good book, but I'm here to pick up an order to go. I need whatever Jack usually orders. You wouldn't happen to know how Pippa and Marshall take their brew, would you?"

"Do you know Liam's favorite order at the Hot Spot?"

"Why does everyone keep asking me that?"

Zane winked. "Because we know you're so good at keeping track of your customers' favorites, just like I am. Which is why I know exactly what to give you for Pippa and Marshall at this time of day."

Hannah rolled her eyes, but she happily paid for the drinks and headed over to the *Chronicle*.

She had never visited the office before and was curious what she'd find as she approached the brick storefront. The door was unlocked, so she let herself into the small reception area. No one was at the front desk, but she could see past it to the newsroom, where Marshall hunched over his computer, chewing on a pencil. Filing cabinets lined one wall. Several desks held computers or piles of newspapers, while a few others sat empty. Beyond the newsroom, she saw the door to Jack Delaney's office, but she didn't feel comfortable walking in unannounced, so she called to Marshall.

"Hey, Hannah. What brings you here?"

"I have a meeting with Jack. Okay to go on back?"

He nodded. "If he's expecting you."

Marshall lowered his head to focus on his work again, so Hannah walked over and set the coffee beside him. "Maybe this will taste better than graphite and save some poor unsuspecting restaurant a scathing review."

When he saw the coffee, his expression lightened, but then shifted to suspicion. "Thank you, Hannah. To what do I owe this?"

"Nothing special. Is Pippa around? I was hoping to finally meet her, so I asked Zane what I should bring for her."

The food critic's face eased into a smile. "I appreciate the coffee. Thanks. Pippa was here a minute ago, but then she got a call. If you want to leave it, I'll explain when she gets back."

"Thanks. Bye, Marshall."

"Bye, Hannah. Say hi to Raquel for me."

"Okay, but I'm sure she'd rather hear it from you directly." Hannah grinned as she walked away, loving the besotted expression on his face.

The door to Jack's office stood ajar, but Hannah knocked lightly on the frosted glass panel anyway.

Jack looked up and waved her in. "Hannah, hello. Thanks for coming. I'm sorry I couldn't meet you at the Hot Spot, but deadline is looming."

"I can come back at a better time, if you like," Hannah offered, even though her heart sank at the idea of waiting for his reply.

"No, no. Have a seat. This is fine. I'm waiting for Marshall to finish his review, and Pippa just raced out to chase down a lead on a story she's been following."

Hannah settled in the chair across from his desk and glanced around the office as Jack took a grateful sip of his coffee. It was the exact opposite of the stereotypical newsroom. Everything was in place, the desk was clear, and one would never guess he was trying to send an issue to print. "Is it okay if I rest my cup on your desk?"

"Sure. Everything okay?"

"I guess I was expecting chaos in here," she confessed. "You know, the way it is on television news shows."

Jack laughed heartily. "I think better when my desk is neat. Clear desk, clear mind."

Hannah took a sip of her coffee. "So, you have something for me?"

"A couple of things actually."

Her ears perked up. "Yes?"

"After I left the church and was walking back, I was thinking about our conversation. I may not have been around back then, but

I realized that I know some other newspeople who were, so I made some calls."

Sitting up straight, Hannah asked, "Did they remember anything?"

"Yes and no. One friend had only a vague recollection, but he promised to think on it. Then I thought of Frank. He was my mentor when I was first starting out. He knows everything there is to know about Kentucky history. He remembered the story immediately. Said it was quite the scandal at the time."

Hannah was beginning to think Jack enjoyed playing with her. "Okay, Jack. What did he say? I'm dying to know."

"Well, sorry to say he didn't have any real answers. Just a lot of gossip from the time and a few people who were considered suspects."

"What do you mean?"

"Well, the racing prize wasn't as large back then as it is now, but it was still a considerable haul for the winning stable, and the acclaim for a champion horse meant additional money in breeding fees. When the favored horse vanished on the eve of the big race, the first suspicion was foul play."

Hannah sat back hard against the chair. She had hoped for another explanation, but Jack's explanation made sense. "Whom did they suspect?"

"A range of people were questioned. They started with the owner and the trainer."

"Liam's grandfather heard rumors of the race being thrown."

Jack nodded. "Yes, that was one of the ideas that was tossed around, but it didn't make sense. Traditionally, if a race is thrown, the horse actually competes and loses. And they try to make it look normal. The horse simply disappearing and not showing up for the post wouldn't have worked for that."

"True." Hannah didn't know much about betting, but this theory sounded reasonable.

Jack continued. "When they couldn't come up with a plausible reason to blame the owner or trainer, suspicion turned on the competition. It goes back to the big prize money. If one horse had dominated all the races leading up to the big one, it stands to reason someone might have wanted to eliminate the winner."

"Would someone really do that?" She had come up with the same idea on her own, but didn't want to believe that anyone would harm a horse. She could tell from Jack's expression that it was a naive belief. Still, she couldn't wrap her head around kidnapping—or worse—a magnificent horse over money.

"Horse racing is not just about the love of the animals, Hannah. It's big business."

"I know. It just seems so heartless."

"It's a controversial sport for sure, and a lot of the controversy centers around the treatment of the animals as assets rather than living creatures."

"So did anything come of that investigation?"

"No. And that's where it got interesting." Jack picked up his coffee and took a long sip before continuing. "My friend remembers being puzzled that the investigation never amounted to anything. It seemed like the police ran into a few dead ends and then the entire matter was apparently dropped."

"You're telling me a champion racehorse vanished into thin air, and the police dropped the ball on the investigation?" Jack's information was backing up what she had deduced from her own research, but it was still wild to think.

"Frank said the general consensus was that the owner wasn't interested in further pursuing the investigation. But that's not the end of it. A few years later, a new horse emerged on the racing circuit. A champion from the first race he ran."

"A colt?"

"Yes. Kentucky's Dawn. Had the same unusual halo markings as Kentucky's Angel, and with the similarity in name, of course there was talk."

Hannah sat in silence mulling over this new information. After a few minutes she had a question. "Was it the same owner?"

"No. This one was owned and raced by Kentucky's Angel's trainer, Jamie Chadwick. Said he received him as an anonymous gift complete with papers certifying his bloodline. And yes, the colt was descended from Kentucky's Angel."

Hannah was lost in thought as she headed back to the Hot Spot. Everything Jack had told her tumbled around her brain, but it was his bombshell revelation that blew her away.

Jamie had held out on them. Kentucky's Angel had a colt. She had looked him up on her phone and found a long list of races the thoroughbred won. Kentucky's Dawn had been the horse that cemented Jamie's name on the racing circuit, and he had never even mentioned the colt.

Which made her wonder what else he hadn't told her and Lacy.

Questions spun through Hannah's mind as she walked. Where had Kentucky's Angel gone that she was able to foal with no one knowing or pursuing the investigation into her disappearance? Had anyone raised questions about the veracity of the colt's bloodlines? Or did someone know where the filly had been all along? Hannah had to admit that all the horse knowledge she thought she had gleaned from the Black Stallion books left a lot to be desired.

"Earth to Hannah."

She looked up in time to just barely avoid walking into Liam's chest. "Oh!" She shook herself. "Sorry, I was woolgathering."

"Must have been some pretty tangled wool. You looked a million miles away."

She laughed. "Only as far as Lexington."

Liam studied her with a humorous glint in his eyes. "Thinking about the horses again?"

"No, this time I'm thinking about the trainer who held out on us when Lacy and I talked to him."

"Sounds intriguing."

Hannah made a face. "More like annoying. But I know I'm being ridiculous. He had no obligation to tell us everything about his life."

"Whoa there." Liam held up a hand. "Want to start at the beginning?"

She glanced at the time on her phone before answering. "I've got to get back to the restaurant. I left Elaine in charge because Jack wanted to talk to me about his findings, but I've been gone too long."

"You can tell me as I walk you back."

Hannah took a moment to appreciate what a good friend Liam was. "Thanks. Maybe you can help me make sense of all of this."

As they started to walk along the street, she told him first about her visit to Camden Farms and Jamie Chadwick, and then what she'd just learned from Jack. She quickly filled Liam in on the details of the suspects, the incomplete investigation, and the biggest news of all—Kentucky's Dawn.

Her mind ran back over all the questions she had been considering earlier, so she tried them out on Liam. "If Jamie didn't tell us about Kentucky's Dawn, was he hiding something, or did he just think it was information he wasn't required to share with two nosy women who had no skin in the game?"

"Either is possible, but you explained to him about the box you found, right?"

"Not only did we explain it, we brought it to show him. And I gave him one of the trophies." Hannah wanted to kick herself. "I feel so foolish now. I got the feeling it meant something to him, but he must have hundreds of trophies like that, and if he raced Kentucky's Dawn, then he must still have some connection to the colt's dam."

"Could he know more about the disappearance than he let on?"

"That's what I'm wondering," Hannah replied. "I've been mulling it over, and it's the only thing that makes sense. Which means he moves to the top of my suspect list."

"But he didn't know who the box belonged to?"

"No." Hannah's voice deflated. "Unless he pretended not to because he didn't want to let on. Liam, do you think they could have been kidnapped? Maybe something happened to the filly and they didn't want to admit it and have her value decrease, so they kidnapped her and her jockey."

Liam chuckled. "I think you might be letting your imagination run away with you, Hannah."

She laughed. "I guess I got a little carried away. I just want to find out who this box belongs to so I can return it to them."

"And that's all?"

She peered up at him. "I need to know what happened. I have a gut feeling that Jamie knows more than he let on."

"So go back and talk to Jamie again. I'll go with you if you want."

Her eyebrows rose. "You will?"

"Sure. We can drive up on my next day off. Maybe he'll open up when we confront him about Kentucky's Dawn together."

"Maybe."

They'd arrived at the Hot Spot. Liam opened the door, and Hannah's heart filled with joy. Happy people chattering and eating, delicious aromas of something spicy wafting on the air, her excellent staff keeping everything running smoothly—these were the good things she had to focus on right now. And Liam. "Thanks for being such good company and for listening to all my wild ideas."

He glanced down at her with a look that made Hannah catch her breath. "Any time. And I'm serious about going with you. Just let me know when is good."

"Will do." Hannah wished him a good night, but as she watched him walk away, she suddenly wished he would stay. Did she also wish he could be more than a friend? She had a growing suspicion, fostered by half the town's speculation, that maybe she did.

Shaking off the question, Hannah turned and headed into the Hot Spot, but she couldn't help one last glance at him. When he turned and waved, she knew she was well and truly caught—in more ways than one.

Chapter Nineteen

Hannah forced herself to focus on her business. Elaine was about to seat a new group of diners, but as she gathered menus, she pointed to a bag at the hostess station. "Neil dropped that off for you. Said you'd know what it is."

Hannah hoped it was the book Lacy had suggested. Maybe Liam hadn't snagged the last copy. Maybe if she read it, they could have coffee and—

"Yoo-hoo, Hannah."

Turning, Hannah saw Connie waving to her from her favorite table. This time she was with her husband, Hal, and her grandson, Trevor, instead of their friends from the church group. Hannah cast a longing glance at the bag, but she knew it would have to wait. As she made her way through the restaurant toward the church secretary's table, her gaze fell on the occupants of a different table. Sheriff Steele and his wife, Geraldine.

Hannah had been hoping to ask him if there were records regarding a past investigation into Kentucky's Angel or Mickey's disappearance, and now the opportunity had landed in her lap. She resisted the urge to go over. The sheriff had earned the right to eat in peace with his wife, so she wouldn't interrupt his dinner. But she would keep an eye out to catch him before he left.

Connie was still waiting for her, so Hannah continued on to her table. "Hi, Connie, Hal." She turned her attention to Trevor. She'd met him a few months before at the local outdoor outfitters. "It's good to see you again. How's work at the store? I've been meaning to stop by and look for some new hiking boots."

"Come by anytime and I'll be happy to outfit you."

Connie's eyes had a mischievous glint as she studied Hannah. "Planning to do some hiking with someone, Hannah?"

It was all Hannah could do not to laugh at the not-so-subtle question. "I loved to hike in the mountains on my rare day off in LA. It's so beautiful around here that I thought I might get back to it. In my free time, that is." She playfully rolled her eyes.

"How's the mystery coming along?"

"Not as well as I'd like. Everything I learn just leads to more questions."

"You'll solve it," Connie assured her. "We all believe in you." She gave a delicate cough, and Hannah realized she was about to hear the real reason Connie had called her over.

"We believe that you'll do a fabulous job hosting the Gratitude Feast too, but some of the committee members were wondering if we could get together for a meeting. Lorelai mentioned that Jacob has been planning the menu."

"I'm so sorry, Connie. I should have asked you all to a meeting sooner. Why don't we plan to meet here later this week?"

"That would be lovely, Hannah. I'll pass the word to the other ladies, and you can let us know the date and time."

Out of the corner of her eye, Hannah noticed Dylan clearing Sheriff Steele's table and Geraldine, phone to her ear, headed toward the front door. This was her chance. "I'll check with Jacob when we close and then call you in the morning. Enjoy the rest of your dinner now. I have to speak with Sheriff Steele before he leaves."

"Far be it from me to stand between you and answers," Connie said with a laugh.

Hannah strolled back across the room. "Good evening, Sheriff Steele. I hope you enjoyed your dinner."

"Please call me Colin, Hannah. I'm off duty."

And that was that, Hannah told herself. She couldn't pester him with questions while he was enjoying dinner on his private time. "May I offer you coffee and dessert? Jacob has been working on some cranberry treats for the Thanksgiving feast, and we'd be happy to have you sample them."

"That would be nice, Hannah. Thanks."

"I'll have Raquel bring some right over."

The sheriff leaned back in his chair. "Why don't you have her bring coffee and dessert for you too, and then you can ask me the questions that are rattling around your brain."

Hannah was horrified. "No, it wasn't meant as a bribe for your time. You're having dinner with your wife. I—"

Colin cut her off with a laugh. "I saw your face when you noticed me here. It was like a light bulb went off."

Hannah chuckled. "I guess that's why you're such a great sheriff—all that deductive reasoning."

"You're not a bad sleuth yourself, from what I hear."

Hannah ducked her head. "I guess I've developed a bit of a reputation, but mysteries seem to keep falling in my lap. Although in this case, it literally fell on someone else."

"Well, now you have me intrigued. Please get me up to speed."

Hannah cast a glance around the restaurant. Everything was under control, and this was the opportunity she'd been waiting for.

After placing an order for the treats and a cup of decaf for herself, she settled in across from the sheriff. "My brain is already spinning so hard that I don't dare have caffeine now or I will never sleep tonight."

"Will talking to me help?"

"I hope so." Hannah said. "I have some general questions that you might be able to answer."

"Try me."

"Why would there not be any real investigation into a missing thoroughbred?"

Colin's congenial manner evaporated. "You know something about a missing horse?"

Hannah sighed, remembering a similar conversation with Liam. "I should remember to give a warning when posing hypothetical questions. This is about a horse that went missing in the 1960s."

"Kentucky's Angel?"

"You know of her?" Hannah could barely keep the excitement from her voice.

"Liam mentioned that you were trying to solve a mystery about her. May I ask why?"

Hannah made a face. "I guess if you're talking to a law enforcement officer about a possible crime, there's no such a thing as hypothetical—especially if it involves a real cold case."

"Maybe you should start at the beginning."

"I probably should," she agreed. "Lacy and I were at an estate sale, and a mystery sort of fell into our laps." She continued the spiel she had perfected to fill people in on the salient details. "I was talking to Jack Delaney this afternoon, and he told me he talked to a friend of his who remembered it. Apparently it was quite the news sensation."

"I imagine it was," Colin agreed. "We take our horses seriously here in Kentucky."

"Jack's friend told him that initially the county sheriff launched an investigation, but apparently it sort of fizzled out. No leads were ever presented. No theories given. The horse was never found, nor was the rider."

"That sounds both suspicious and complicated. Was the rider an adult?"

Hannah had to think about that. "That's a good question. I don't know. How old do you have to be to become a jockey?"

Colin shrugged, and Hannah added *jockey age* to her mental list of things to research.

"For the sake of our discussion, let's presume the jockey was a legal adult," Colin suggested. "If no one filed a missing persons case, it may have been presumed the jockey left voluntarily with the horse."

Hannah gasped, but as she noticed heads turning at nearby tables, she quickly lowered her voice to speak. "You mean the jockey might have *stolen* the horse?"

"It seems a logical line of investigation if they disappeared at the same time."

Tapping her index finger on the table, Hannah said, "But then why didn't the owner pursue an investigation?"

"Now that is an interesting question." Colin took a sip of his coffee and had another bite of cranberry apple compote with cinnamon whipped cream. "Be sure to tell Jacob this has my vote."

Hannah smiled through her impatience. "It has mine too, but I want him to turn it into a crisp with toasted oats and nuts."

"That's brilliant." Colin sipped his coffee then sampled a bite of caramel brownie. His brow was visibly furrowed, so either Jacob's second dessert option wasn't living up to the compote or he was thinking. "This is terrific too, but the cranberry apple wins." He cleared his throat and set the fork down. "I guess I should save some for Geraldine."

"I hope she isn't staying away because of me."

"No, she had to take a phone call from her mother. Those tend to last a while. So, back to your investigation question. One reason the investigation might not have been pursued is if there were no leads. Remember, there weren't cameras everywhere like there are today, and no one would have thought it odd for a jockey to be walking his horse. The investigation probably went nowhere, and if the owner wasn't pushing, it would have gone cold. Especially if there were other, more active cases."

Hannah felt like sputtering at that idea, but she waited because Colin wasn't done.

"However, the most likely scenario is that the owner figured out what happened and didn't want it to be made public, so he called a halt to the investigation. He probably had some influential friends who could see to it."

She sat forward with her chin in her hands. "That's the part I don't understand. Why would the owner not want it pursued? Racehorses are valuable."

"Yes, and from what Liam told me, this one had a greater value than most because there was a lore developing around her."

"So, how do you explain it?"

He shrugged. "The only person who could tell you the truth about that is the owner. Is he still alive?"

"I don't know." Something else to add to the list. "The trainer is. I visited him, but I didn't ask him about that. Maybe he could tell me." *Unless he's to blame.* Hannah chalked that up as another reason for her to go back and see Jamie.

"Will he talk to you?"

"I think so." She hoped he would.

Colin pointed at his empty plate. "Maybe take him some of Jacob's dessert, and you'll be able to persuade him."

Hannah's brain was still spinning with the ideas Colin had planted when she finally grabbed the bag Neil had left for her. She locked the restaurant doors, switched out the lights, and headed upstairs hoping that some reading time would quiet her mind enough to sleep.

She set the bag on the table while she prepared for bed. When she finally pulled out the book, she was surprised to find it wasn't the one she'd expected. Neil had taped a note to the front.

Sorry, Hannah, Liam had already taken my copy of Seabiscuit, *but I thought you might enjoy this book about one of the first female jockeys instead. It's a lively story. Let me know what you think.*

Reluctantly setting aside her ideas of a book discussion with Liam, Hannah turned her attention to the pages. Within minutes, she was hooked. For all her professed love of horses and her dreams of riding, she'd had no idea of the hurdles women faced to be licensed as jockeys.

Before long, Hannah was fighting back yawns as the day caught up with her, but she didn't want to stop reading. A memory flashed of Archer ribbing Liam about staying up reading. If *Seabiscuit* was half as interesting as this book, she totally understood. She'd read just one more chapter.

Hannah woke after a restless night of dreams about riderless horses streaming across a pasture, with angry men running in pursuit waving fistfuls of hundred-dollar bills. That was what she got for continuing to read long past the next chapter. Stories of jockeys boycotting races rather than allowing a woman to compete had twisted in her mind with the disappearance of Kentucky's Angel.

She pushed back her blankets, though the clock on her nightstand said that it was only six a.m. Normally she would sleep later after a long night at the restaurant, but the dream had left her unsettled. The kind that made her wish she could call her mom. Since that wasn't possible, she would start her morning routine.

Still yawning, Hannah wrapped herself in her warm robe and made her way to the kitchen to start the coffee maker. The dream had left her strangely hungry and craving bacon. Since there was none in her refrigerator, she settled for toast instead. It popped up as the coffee finished brewing. After slathering it with butter and her favorite harvest jam, Hannah gripped the mug, balanced the plate on her arm, and headed for her chair. She could see frost on the trees as she set the mug on an end table with the toast beside it. Wrapping the robe a little closer, she curled up on the chair and opened her devotional.

Prayer time calmed her, but questions started stockpiling in her brain as soon as she closed her book. The morning reading had been from Matthew today. Hannah knew *seek and you shall find* had not referred to the missing racehorse, but the mystery was never far from her thoughts. Colin had done such a professional job of outlining the possibilities that Hannah wished she could talk to one of the deputies who had actually participated in the short-lived investigation. Were any of them still alive?

With that question in mind, Hannah refilled her coffee and headed to her laptop. One advantage of the Hot Spot not opening until dinner was that she had the whole morning to devote to her investigation.

As she sipped her coffee, she read article after article about the missing racehorse and jotted down all the names she came across. Next, she started searching those names. One detective, Nick Jones, appeared more frequently than the others, and when Hannah dug a little deeper into his history, she found that he was now in his late eighties and residing in a local nursing home. Maybe he would like a visitor.

A quick call to the nursing home to confirm that they allowed visitors, and Hannah was on her way shortly afterward.

When she arrived at his room, the elderly retired detective was sitting in a chair by the window, working on a crossword puzzle. He raised his head at her knock. "What's a four-letter word for a Spanish dessert?"

"Flan?"

He penciled in the word. "Right you are. Thank you. That one was stumping me."

Hannah smiled warmly. "I own a restaurant. I know desserts."

He studied her closely. His eyes were clear, and apparently his mind was sharp. "Since you probably didn't come merely to help me with my crossword, what can I do to return the favor?"

She entered the room and sat in a chair across from him. "Detective Jones, my name is Hannah Prentiss. I was hoping to talk to you about a cold case." She quickly explained her mission.

"I'm not a detective anymore, just Nick." But as he set the crossword book and pencil aside, Hannah noted that he sat up straighter in his chair. "Ah, the missing filly." He shook his head, and Hannah could see him slipping deep into his past.

"I was hoping you could tell me about the investigation."

He snorted. "What investigation? I was as stumped as anyone about what happened. We were still interviewing people when word came down from above that the case was closed."

Whatever Hannah had imagined he would say, it wasn't that.

Nick met Hannah's gaze. "If you ask me, that 'investigation' was all for show. Once the initial uproar over the horse's disappearance died down, so did the investigation."

"Did you have any suspicions about what was really going on?"

"It felt like an inside job to me. That's the only reason I can come up with that Charles Donahue wasn't squawking and demanding justice. He would have earned a pretty penny on that horse."

Hannah's ears perked up. "Insurance, maybe? And who is Charles Donahue?"

He shook his head. "No claim was ever filed. That was another mystery. Donahue owned Kentucky's Angel. If your promising champion racehorse was stolen, wouldn't you have filed a claim? I still wonder about that horse every May. The Derby rolls around, and others are pulling out mint julep cups and fancy hats, but I pull up memories. If you saw that filly run, you never forgot her."

"That's one of the things I don't understand," Hannah said. "People apparently did forget."

He shrugged. "Maybe someone wanted them to. That's horse racing. There are the greats that everyone remembers, but there's a new crop of horses every year. You know that saying, 'time and tide wait for no man?' Well, neither does the racetrack." He peered at Hannah. "Why are you so interested? That filly must have died before you were even born."

Hannah told him about the box, and that perked him up. "Probably belonged to the missing jockey. That was another odd thing. No family turned up looking for him. No missing person's report filed. It was almost as if he hadn't existed."

Hannah braced herself to ask the question she dreaded. "Did anyone suspect the jockey of stealing her?"

"As I said, we barely got around to interviewing people, but I never heard any suspicion of the jockey. Strange that was, since he went missing too, but people were more concerned about him than suspicious. Said he would have done anything for that horse. They were a bonded pair."

But would "anything" have meant stealing Angel, if Mickey felt it was for the horse's protection? The question nagged at Hannah as she wrapped up the interview.

"I almost forgot. Did you know about the horse, Kentucky's Dawn?"

"Yes, the colt showed up about seven years after Kentucky's Angel disappeared. Of course, there were questions when he appeared out of thin air, but the horse's papers were determined to be legitimate and no one pushed to reopen the investigation. Kind of confirmed my original theory, but since there was no proof of a crime, no insurance claim—so no fraud—and no evidence of foul play, there was nothing for us to do."

"No one questioned the bloodlines? I mean, couldn't anyone have produced false papers?"

"I tried to check into it, but the owners closed rank."

Hannah was frustrated. She reluctantly admitted to herself that the retired detective didn't know much more than she did about what had happened all those years ago.

But at least one piece of information had come out of this meeting. She knew that Charles Donahue had owned Kentucky's Angel.

She said her goodbyes and promised to let him know if she discovered anything. She'd enjoyed the time she spent with him, and she thought it had put a bit of light into his life to reminisce with her.

The trip hadn't been a waste, she decided. Although Detective Jones hadn't had much information, he had given her a lot to think about. One of his comments in particular echoed through her mind.

It was almost as if he hadn't existed.

Chapter Twenty

Hannah was back in her car when her phone dinged with a text message from Connie. Sorry for the short notice, but would it be possible for the committee to meet at the Hot Spot this afternoon?

Guilt surged as she realized she'd forgotten to call Connie once she had fixated on the detective this morning. She'd been off on a wild-goose chase over a horse that vanished six decades ago while her chef spent all his free time testing recipes and the committee was waiting for her to meet about the event that was happening sooner than she would have believed possible. She immediately texted back that she would be happy to host them.

Then, with fingers crossed, she sent another text to Jacob to ask if by any chance he had any samples for them.

His reply was immediate. Do I ever!

Hannah chuckled at her chef's enthusiasm. She was grateful one of them was on top of this. More importantly, she had to make sure Jacob got credit for all his efforts.

With the meeting scheduled, Hannah glanced at the clock. She had enough time to get home, have a bite to eat, and do a little more research into jockeys of the sixties. She couldn't escape the lingering feeling that this was all somehow tied to Mickey Dawes.

Once she reached her apartment, Hannah reheated some soup and made a grilled cheese sandwich. Even chefs sometimes wanted an old standard to warm and nourish themselves. Then she settled at her computer.

She tried *Mickey Dawes* in the search engine again, but once more it brought up only stories related to Kentucky's Angel. She was inclined to revise the detective's comment. It was almost as if Mickey hadn't existed—except in relation to the filly. Was that a clue? Hannah revisited her hunch that finding the jockey was the key to all of this. But how was she supposed to find someone who seemed not to exist apart from a horse that was no longer alive?

The book that had intrigued her so much last night beckoned, but Hannah knew that opening it carried the risk of reading right through meeting time. Maybe she'd research the women jockeys she'd been reading about instead.

She opened a new search window and typed in, *woman jockeys 1960s*. There were pages and pages of results, but one summary jumped out at her. The first time a woman had been licensed as a jockey was in 1968. Hannah clicked the link and began to read. Kathryn Kusner had applied in the early 1960s but been denied because she was a woman. She had to sue the racing commission to be allowed to race. This confirmed what Hannah had read in Neil's book last night.

Hannah hurried to read the rest of the article before her meeting. There was so much fascinating information, beginning with a story about the first woman to own a champion thoroughbred. She had received the horse as a wedding gift from her husband, and it had won the 1904 Kentucky Derby. But it wasn't until 1970 that a woman, Diane Crump, was allowed to ride in the Derby. People had argued the fear that chivalry would make male jockeys defer to female jockeys, giving them an unfair advantage.

As Hannah read about people boycotting races and hurling insults, she was amazed that anyone had persisted. Apparently, the love of horses was stronger than threats, warnings, or opinions about female fragility and belonging in the kitchen.

Wondering how many women had raced in the decades since those pioneering jockeys, Hannah did another search and was surprised yet again. Only six women had ever raced in the Kentucky Derby. She didn't have to wonder why this time, not after everything she'd read.

The tour guide's childhood dreams of being a jockey came back to her. Little girls with that fantasy likely weren't aware of the difficulties they would face. Which made her wonder—why had some succeeded where others hadn't? Maybe by the time they grew up, the love of riding was too fierce to surrender.

A few names popped up repeatedly as Hannah continued to read. Julie Krone, the only woman to ever win the Belmont Stakes. Rosie Napravnik had won the Kentucky Oaks, the premiere race for fillies held on the day before the Derby each year. That story made Hannah wonder why Kentucky's Angel's owner had planned to race her in the Derby instead of the traditional Oaks. Was she just that good?

Curious now, Hannah decided to watch some of the female jockeys and see for herself if their gender made a difference, so she turned to videos. Viewing the horses race sent thrills along her spine. She would have sat there all day, glued to the screen, if not for her meeting. Which was starting soon.

Hours later, after a productive committee meeting and a smooth, profitable dinner service, Hannah was exhausted. When she locked up for the night after the busy day, she went straight to bed without daring to glance at either the book or her computer.

She was still sound asleep the following morning when her phone rang. Stifling a yawn, she reached to see who was calling. Liam. His voice was warm and friendly when Hannah answered, and she was instantly alert.

"I hope I'm not calling too early, but I have the day off and was wondering if you wanted to make an early trip up to Lexington. If we leave in the next hour, we should be back in plenty of time for your dinner rush."

Hannah didn't even need to think about it. "That would be terrific. After I left you the other night, I had a conversation with Sheriff Steele. Then yesterday I met with one of the original detectives, so I have even more questions for Jamie."

"I want to hear all about it when I pick you up. Forty-five minutes okay?"

She agreed and then spent half that time figuring out what to wear. Since they were headed to a horse farm, she finally settled on jeans with a sweater and slipped on a pair of ankle boots. Liam texted that he was downstairs just as she finished packing up some snacks for the road.

Hannah was heading toward the door to meet Liam when her phone rang again. Seeing that it was Sylvia, she was tempted to answer, but she and Liam had limited time for their trip, and she didn't want to keep him waiting. She would call Sylvia back later.

Liam waited beside his vehicle with two cups of steaming coffee when Hannah emerged from the Hot Spot. He handed her one and then opened the Jeep door. Her phone stuck out of her pocket, and he tugged it out and shut the door before she could stop him. He paused to fiddle with her screen. When he climbed in the driver's side, he handed it back.

She immediately opened it, curious to see how he'd designated himself this time—it was their little joke—but the first thing she noticed was a voicemail from Sylvia. After making a mental note to listen to it, she switched to her contacts list and chuckled when she saw *Liam "Champion Chauffeur" Berthold*.

"Shall I move to the back seat, sir?"

Liam's face fell. "I hadn't thought of that. Let's have you stay up front to rate my driving skills."

Hannah took a sip of the perfectly brewed coffee. "Maybe you should change it to 'Coffee Connoisseur.' This is excellent."

Liam winked at her. "I'm a man of many talents."

"And humble too," Hannah teased, though privately she agreed with his assessment.

"Where are we headed?" he asked as he backed out of the parking spot. "Do I need to put the address into the GPS?"

She tossed her head in mock pride. "No need. You have me as navigator extraordinaire." She grinned and took another sip of her coffee.

"Also humble. We're well matched."

Hannah was momentarily speechless. How was she supposed to respond to a comment like that? It was probably the most overt statement of interest Liam had yet made.

Instead of replying directly, she took a conversational detour. "Would you mind if I listen to Sylvia's message? She was going to try to find out some information for me, and I'd like to know if she did before we meet with Mr. Chadwick."

"Be my guest. I'm almost as curious as you are."

Hannah opened her voicemail and set it to speaker so Liam could hear.

"Hi, Hannah. Sorry I missed you. I have to go back to the farm tomorrow. I didn't get to finish everything before I had to leave last time, and I have another client meeting in Lexington. I figured I'd knock out both in one day, and I was wondering if you or Lacy would like to visit. Let me know when you get a chance."

Hannah made a mental note to check in with Lacy later, then turned her attention back to Liam as he asked, "So, what did Colin have for you?"

She swiveled in her seat to face him, and her heart gave a little flip as she took in his classic profile. It would be easy to be attracted to him for his looks alone, but now that she had gotten to know him, she knew the fire chief was so much more than just his appearance. He had a heart for others and was always available to help anyone in need, the way he was helping her today.

"Hannah?" he prompted.

She ducked her head, embarrassed at having been caught staring. "Don't repeat this, but I sort of bribed Colin with desserts."

Liam chuckled. "When did you have time to make desserts with all the investigating you're doing?"

"I didn't. Jacob is doing them as part of his planning for the Gratitude Feast. He wanted a themed menu. I'm going to have to find a way to thank him properly because he has thrown himself heart and soul into this feast."

"Jacob's a good man," Liam agreed. "And his cooking could bribe even the most stalwart officer. Did Colin have anything useful to say?"

"He did. He gave me lots of ideas about why the investigation may have stalled. That's why I followed up with a detective who originally worked the case. He was the one who explained that it hadn't stalled. It was shut down." She continued, recounting her internet search and subsequent visit to the elderly detective. She shared everything he had told her, including his comment about Mickey. "It all comes down to the jockey one way or another. I'm sure of it."

The drive passed quickly as they tossed ideas back and forth.

As Hannah was giving final directions to the horse farm, she thanked Liam for indulging her. "You'd make a great detective if you ever need a second job," she teased.

"Firefighting often does require investigating, as you well know."

Hannah thought back to the very first case they'd worked on together, trying to determine whether a fire in Miriam's house had been accidental or arson. "We're a good pair."

Liam pulled into the parking lot at the farm, stopped the car, and faced her. "Yes, we are." The gleam in his eyes gave Hannah the distinct impression he was talking about more than detective work.

As she caught a glimpse of an exercise rider racing around the farm's track, Hannah imagined the nerves fluttering through her must be similar to the ones jockeys felt at the beginning of a race. So much uncertainty lay ahead, but the promise of victory beckoned. Was she ready for whatever came next?

Recovering herself, Hannah climbed from the Jeep and led Liam over to the fence that surrounded the training track. They stood side by side, watching the powerful horses pound the turf.

"Hello, Hannah. Who's your friend?"

Hannah had been so absorbed in watching the horses that she hadn't heard Mr. Chadwick's approach. She turned to greet him and was suddenly overcome with a mass of conflicting emotions. She liked the elderly trainer and was genuinely happy to see him again, but her mind was filled with concerns about the details he'd neglected to tell her and the suspicions that had been raised about his possible involvement.

She forced a light tone. "Hello, Mr. Chadwick. This is Liam Berthold. He's the fire chief in Blackberry Valley."

"Welcome to Camden Farms, Chief Berthold. I hope this is not a formal visit. I'm certain we are up to code on everything. The lives of our horses depend on it."

As Liam assured Jamie that he was here as a guest, Hannah's heart lifted. If there was one thing she could be sure of, it was that Kentucky's Angel had come to no harm at the hands of a man who loved horses as Jamie Chadwick did.

Mr. Chadwick and Liam started chatting, so Hannah stepped up onto the first rail of the fence to watch the training runs. Her research kicked in, and she realized they were doing timed sprints.

She leaned forward, eager to watch because she recalled Jamie's niece saying she sometimes did the runs. Was she racing today?

As she studied the riders, Hannah realized she had an answer to one question—even without their racing silks, she could not distinguish between male and female riders as they flew around the track.

Suddenly, the pieces tumbled together in her mind. Goose bumps rose along her arms as she gripped the rail and stared into the distance, into the past. Her heart raced as she stepped down and faced Jamie Chadwick. "Mr. Chadwick, when did you realize Mickey Dawes was a girl?"

Mr. Chadwick looked startled as he turned away from Liam. He didn't meet her gaze. His voice was husky when he finally spoke. "What are you talking about?"

In that moment, Hannah knew without a doubt that she was right. "Is that why they disappeared? Did someone threaten to expose that your champion filly had a female jockey?"

Chapter Twenty-One

Lexington, Kentucky
April 1962

Three men stood trackside, watching Mickey do a practice run with Kentucky's Angel.

At two years old, the filly was already showing a natural affinity for racing. Chaddy had invited Mickey's grandfather to observe the morning workout. The time had come to reveal that the exercise rider was Charles Donahue's granddaughter and see if he would let her ride. So far, his reaction to the suggestion of allowing a woman jockey to ride his prized filly was far less promising than Angel's performance on the track.

As the filly rounded the homestretch and raced toward the imaginary finish line, Mr. Donahue voiced his thoughts. "I agree she's good, better than good even. But why risk putting a woman up on the horse when you know it's not done? The jockeys won't take it well, and we don't need a scandal."

Chaddy knew that was an understatement, but he also knew Mickey and Angel. "The filly won't run like this for anyone else. They were born to ride together."

Mr. Donahue was just pointing out how ridiculous that sounded when the jockey dismounted. As she began to walk the horse toward them, she lifted a hand to remove her riding cap.

Chaddy felt, rather than saw, the old man freeze. He stared at her with dawning recognition, and the ice thawed, but then heated to rage. When Mickey walked a horse, she was the spitting image of her mother at seventeen. Chaddy had hoped the resemblance would work in their favor, but it had the opposite effect, and as the old man's face grew red, Chaddy feared he might have apoplexy.

"What does Dawes think he's doing? Trying to pull one over on me? If that derelict who stole my daughter thinks he can winnow his way into an inheritance by putting his daughter on my horses—"

Chaddy interrupted the rant with quiet words. "He's not involved."

"Then why is she here?"

Chaddy answered in a measured tone. "There was a day, years ago, when Dawes came asking for money. There was a lot of arguing."

Donahue harumphed. "Not just one day. He came begging whenever one of his schemes failed. What about it?"

"Mickey was with him that particular day. When the two of you started fighting, she came to watch the horses." Chaddy noticed a slight softening of the old man's expression, so he pushed his luck. "I remember someone else who always went to the horses when she was upset."

"Don't you dare bring my daughter into this to change my mind. She has nothing to do with—"

"Forgive my saying so, sir, but she has everything to do with it. I think you know that. Mickey is her mother's daughter to the bone. She's kind, she's gentle, everyone loves her—and she has the same touch with the horses that her mother had." The old trainer looked the owner, his boss, straight in the eye. "But I don't have to tell you that, because you've seen it for yourself."

Mr. Donahue's jaw twitched, but he didn't reply.

Chaddy let the words sink in before he continued. "After that day, she came back by herself day after day and just sat and watched the horses from a distance—until I invited her in." He crossed his arms and spoke defiantly. "If you want to blame someone, blame me. Her father doesn't know she's ever been here, let alone that she arrives by sunup every morning. Mickey has been working here since she was ten. She mucks stables with the best of them, intuits when a horse is in trouble, and has the hand of a champion rider. I'm telling you the girl is magic with horses. Especially Kentucky's Angel."

"I should fire you for this." Donahue's face was still red, but the anger had left his voice.

Chaddy shrugged. "That's your choice, of course, but it would double your loss." He waited a beat to let the words sink in. "Give the girl a chance. She's the best rider this farm has ever seen. And she and this horse share a bond like I've never seen. Unlike your daughter, this girl will never give up her horses for a man. I know that like I know my own name. Horses are her one true love."

The owner grumped and muttered, but Chaddy sensed that in the end, he wouldn't deny what his own eyes could see. The girl and the filly were a thing of beauty together.

A long silence pulsed with tension, but when he finally spoke, Donahue's voice was rough with emotion. "Let her get a jockey's license as Mickey. Then we'll see."

A cheer rose in Chaddy's throat, but he swallowed it and nodded solemnly instead. "I'll keep you apprised of her progress."

"No need. I'll be watching her myself." Donahue turned on his heel and stalked toward the house.

Chaddy smiled to himself. Of that he had no doubt. His only question was whether, through her riding, Mickey could find a way into her grandfather's heart as deftly as she crossed a finish line.

Chapter Twenty-Two

Jamie Chadwick glanced over his shoulder to make sure there was no one within hearing distance. When he turned back to Hannah, his face bore an expression of resignation, and she realized he wasn't going to try to argue with her. He seemed to have accepted what she knew.

When he finally answered, she heard decades of pain in his voice. "Did someone threaten to expose that Kentucky's Angel had a female jockey? Maybe. I really don't know, because as I told you last time, I don't know what happened the night they disappeared."

Hannah waited, hoping he'd provide more information.

He shrugged tiredly. "We tried to keep her true identity a secret, but I've always wondered if it was connected to the disappearance, if someone had found out. But I don't know what that even would mean." He caught Hannah's eye. "If you think you need answers to this mystery, trust me—I know how you feel. I've been waiting more than half a century for them. No one needs to know what happened that night more than I do."

Her heart went out to him. "I've done some research. I understand how unacceptable it was at the time. I imagine it's been a hard secret for you to keep, but this all happened years ago. Why have you never told anyone before?"

Mr. Chadwick's eyes were sad. "It wasn't my story to tell."

"Who was she?"

"That is still not my story to tell."

Hannah had to admire the man's loyalty, but as she studied him, she realized it was more than that. "You loved her."

"How could I not?" His face creased in the widest smile Hannah had ever seen. "Everyone loved Mickey. She just had this way about her. She was magic with the horses, but people loved her too."

"Did they know she was female?"

Mr. Chadwick shook his head. "To my knowledge, only three of us knew—my grandfather, the owner, and me. Others may have suspected, but she was part of our barn family. No one would have given her away."

Hannah felt a story coming on. "Tell me about her."

Mr. Chadwick started to walk away, and Hannah wondered if she had pushed too hard, but he beckoned them to follow. She was glad for her boots as he led them across the drive to a paddock.

"The first time I saw her was right here, talking to my granddad. I didn't realize who she was. She was such a tiny little girl then, always small for her age. She climbed up on the paddock fence like she owned it. The horses naturally gravitated to her. There wasn't an ounce of fear in her, even when the horses came flying across the field to meet her. When my granddad, who was never without a pocketful of peppermints, gave her one, she held it out in her hand and a colt snatched it. She didn't even flinch. I was too young to fall in love then, of course, but I was old enough to understand that she was special."

Jamie uttered a long, pained sigh before he continued. "Her father had been fighting with her grandfather. He was in a rage, which only increased when he saw her with the horses. He ordered her into the car."

"Were they from around here?" Hannah asked.

Jamie laughed. "Nice try, but I've been around the track one too many times to be fooled so easily. I'm not going to give you anything to help figure out who she is, but I'll tell you what I remember."

Hannah wanted to argue that she was less likely to find Mickey without knowing her identity, but Jamie went on.

"She came back about a week later—without her father that time. I knew right away that it was her. My grandfather pointed her out. She'd ridden her bike and would sit there under the trees, day after day all that week, watching the horses. When she came back the next week, he invited her in and asked me to train her to work in the barns. She was dressed in old jeans and a baggy shirt. I guess everyone assumed she was a boy. No one ever questioned it when he gave her a job mucking out stalls."

Mr. Chadwick's jaw tightened. "My grandfather, Chaddy, never set out to deceive people. He just didn't want her grandfather to find her and kick her out. That's why he called her Mickey, and it's why she continued to dress like that. Granddad had a soft spot for her. He'd known her mother, and he could tell the farm was the only place Mickey ever found peace and people who cared for her. And she loved the horses. Oh, how she loved them. And they loved her right back."

Hannah tucked away the knowledge Mr. Chadwick had inadvertently given her. If Mickey had ridden a bike, she must have lived somewhere nearby. "The horse from that first day—you called him a colt, so it wasn't Kentucky's Angel?"

"Oh, no. This was years before Angel was born."

Mr. Chadwick kept talking while Hannah and Liam soaked in every word. It was as if, after having to hold in the story for over sixty years, a dam had burst.

"I'm confused about one thing," Hannah said when he finally paused. "Why didn't Mickey ride as a jockey for other horses? If she loved to ride so much, why hadn't she raced before?"

Mr. Chadwick laughed as he replied. "Before Angel, Mickey was content to train the yearlings and prep the two-year-olds for their first races. She had a gentle but firm hand, and they all responded to her. But there was never any talk of her riding them in races. As you learned, it wasn't done at the time.

"Angel was different. In some ways, they grew up together. Mickey was about sixteen when Angel was born. Mickey had cared for the broodmare all through her gestation, and she gave birth in the middle of the night. Mickey and Angel bonded from the very first moment. From then on they were inseparable. It was as beautiful as it was baffling. When it came time to train Angel, Mickey begged to be the one to ride her. She could coax speed from her like no one else. But that was the problem. Angel would only run like that when Mickey was astride her. I overheard my granddad talking with the owner one day. They had decided to let Mickey register as a jockey. No one would question her name, but it would be our secret to keep, because many of the jockeys were boycotting races if there was any hint of a woman jockey."

Hannah knew that from her research. She also remembered one of the women registering with her initials so as not to give away that she was female.

"They raced together, and Angel started racking up wins. They were the talk of the racing world, but our secret held. There were no problems I was aware of…until the night they disappeared."

Hannah believed him but there was one more thing to question. "What about Kentucky's Dawn?"

Jamie rubbed his forehead. "You don't miss anything, do you?"

Liam, who had been quietly taking everything in, spoke up. "Nothing gets by her. She's building a reputation for it." Pride rang in his voice.

"Then we needed her sixty years ago, because no one could figure out what happened."

"The detective told me the case was closed on an order from higher up," Hannah told him.

Jamie's eyes widened with shock. "But why?"

"I was hoping you knew." Hannah hesitated, wondering if she was about to overstep some invisible line. She decided to risk it. The worst Mr. Chadwick could do was refuse to answer. "You told Lacy and me that you don't know what happened the night before the race when Mickey and Angel disappeared, but is there anything about that night that stands out to you? Anything that might be a clue that would explain either where they went or why the investigation was closed?"

He hunched over, leaning heavily against the fence. "I've replayed that night in my mind so many times. Sometimes before a race, Mickey would sneak into the stables and sleep in the stall with Angel. That night I knew Mickey was nervous because she was about to ride in the biggest race of her career thus far, so I figured I would find her in the barn. When I got there, though, the stall was empty. I assumed she had taken Angel out for a walk to work out some nerves. But they never came back."

Liam whistled low.

"I waited for a while, and then I went looking for them. When I didn't find them, I called my grandfather. He had no idea where they could be, so he called Mr. Donahue. He had no answer either, so I kept looking. I walked all over Churchill Downs, searched every inch of the grounds. I called for Mickey until my voice was hoarse. Someone notified track security, and eventually the sheriff. It's all kind of a blur after that. The next day, the race went on as scheduled—without the favored filly. I never saw Mickey or the horse again."

Mr. Chadwick was suddenly showing his age. He walked over to an ancient-looking tree that shaded the paddock and sagged against the rough bark. "You asked about where Kentucky's Dawn came from. Would you believe me if I said I don't know? It's the truth. Years after Angel went missing, Charles Donahue, who owned this farm then, called me into his office. He told me my grandfather had decided to retire and he was appointing me head trainer. Granddad would stay on to help, but I was in charge, and to show his faith in me, he had a special gift. We walked outside and there was a horse tied to the fence."

Closing his eyes, Mr. Chadwick spoke as if he was seeing the horse in his mind. "The minute I saw his markings, I knew. He had that halo I had only ever seen on Angel. When Angel was born, Mickey took one look at that white marking on her head and said she was an angel."

Hannah could see how hard this was on him, but she needed to know everything he knew if she had any chance of solving this mystery—for his sake as well as her own. "Where had the colt come from?"

He shrugged. "I don't know. The owner said he was a gift, and I didn't question it." He wiped his hands over his face. "That was probably cowardly of me, but I didn't want to know. Mickey broke my heart when she disappeared. To this day, I don't know if she took Angel, or if she left because the horse was gone. All I know is that my grandfather told me she and the horse were gone, and he didn't think they were coming back. No matter who I asked or how many times I questioned it, there was never an answer. For a long time, I struggled to care about anything. I did my job, but my heart wasn't in it. I don't know how to explain it, but when Kentucky's Dawn showed up, something in me came to life again. I didn't ask any more questions because I think I was afraid of the answers."

Tears glinted in his eyes, but he swiped them aside and forced a laugh. "You know the expression, don't look a gift horse in the mouth? That was me. I accepted him without question because it felt good to care again."

Hannah wiped away her own tears. "It worked out well for you."

"Professionally? Yes. Dawn made my career. And now there's a new colt, Kentucky's Future, from his line. You saw my niece riding him when you got here. Angel's blood is still running through the thoroughbreds on this farm."

Hannah was quiet in the car on the way home.

Liam left her to her thoughts for the first ten minutes before he asked, "How did you know?"

She dragged herself from her odd mood. "About Mickey?"

"Yes. I'm pretty sure when we got out of the car you weren't thinking that she was a girl."

"You're right, mostly. Some things had been nagging at me because they felt off."

"Like?"

"The preserved flowers in the scrapbook for one. That didn't seem like something a man would do."

Liam glanced over with a teasing smile. "You mean I shouldn't have a scrapbook of all the news articles about fires we put out?"

"You do?"

He swallowed his laugh. "No. But my mother kept all those articles about my father."

"But that's my point. It was your mother. I know some men keep scrapbooks, but do you know any who keep scrapbooks of flowers? I guess maybe gardeners would, and it's fine if you want to. I did wonder if there was a woman in Mickey's life who might have done it, but there was no mention of one. Now I know why."

Hannah shifted in her seat to face him. "I was also thinking of the tour guide. After she told me about being too tall to be a jockey, I went home and watched videos of women racing. I was struck how, in their silks astride their horses, they were indistinguishable from the male jockeys. It stuck in the back of my mind, but when I was watching her ride today, I realized I wasn't sure if it was her or one of the male jockeys. That's when it really clicked."

"I don't think that would have occurred to me," Liam admitted.

"There was one other thing that I didn't think anything of at the time, but now I'm rethinking it. When I gave Mr. Chadwick the trophy, I said it belonged with someone who loved her. He reacted in a way that made me wonder if I had said something wrong, so I quickly explained that I meant Kentucky's Angel. But his reaction makes sense if he thought the 'she' I referred to was Mickey."

"This is all very interesting, Hannah, and you showed great instincts, but you know we didn't really solve anything, right?"

"Aren't you the spoilsport?" She frowned at him. "Maybe not directly, but I have more to go on, and I've ruled Jamie out as a suspect. Sylvia's message earlier said she was going back out to the farm tomorrow, and I could come if I wanted to." She grinned. "I definitely want to."

They'd barely arrived back in Blackberry Valley when Liam's phone chimed. He pulled over to take the call, and his expression became grave. After hanging up, he turned to Hannah. "Sounds like a big one. They're calling in all surrounding teams. My apologies, but I need to drop you at the door and run."

"No need to apologize. And you can drop me right here. The rest of the walk will allow me to clear my head." She paused with her hand on the door handle. "Come back when it's over, and I'll cook you a late dinner as a thank-you."

Liam's expression flashed from tense to tender. "I may take you up on that if it's not too late. I'll call."

Hannah walked back to the Hot Spot and tried to immerse herself in serving her guests, but as the dinner hour rolled on, fear crowded in. Was this what it had been like for Bridget, Liam's grandmother, every time Patrick was out at a fire?

When her phone finally rang right before closing, she heaved a sigh of relief to see Liam's name. "Hello there."

"Hi, Hannah." He sounded exhausted.

"Are you starving?"

"I can't ask you to cook for me this late. I'm sure your kitchen is closed by now."

"The restaurant's kitchen is, but I have one in my apartment, and that is never closed to a friend who's been fighting a fire. Come on over and let me feed you."

She heard his weary exhale. "Thank you."

When Liam arrived twenty minutes later, Hannah met him at the restaurant door and led the way to her apartment upstairs. He was fresh from a shower, but Hannah could still smell lingering smoke. "Come in." She welcomed him into her home. "Have a seat. Dinner is ready."

Liam sniffed the air appreciatively. "It smells amazing in here. What did you make?"

She lifted the pan to show him. "A ratatouille omelet." She expertly slid it onto a plate as she talked. "The filling is tomatoes, zucchini, olives, eggplant, cheese, and locally grown herbs. The eggs, of course, are courtesy of Hennifer and Eggatha." Hannah added some toasted bread to his plate and placed it in front of him. "Dig in."

Liam waited while Hannah made a plate for herself. When she joined him, he said a blessing and then began to devour his omelet. He'd eaten half of it before he paused. "Where did you learn to cook like this?"

The awe in his voice warmed Hannah's heart. "My mom taught me the basics, but this recipe comes from one of the restaurants I worked in. It was owned by a husband and wife. She was French, and he was from Spain. The menu was an eclectic mix of both cultures, but every night when service was done, he would cook for the staff, and we would sit at one long community table and laugh and eat and generally unwind from our day."

Liam nodded. "I get that. We sometimes do something similar after fighting a tough fire. But no one cooks like this."

"His ratatouille omelet was my favorite. He'd pair it with crusty French bread. It's been years, but I still remember how much I loved it."

"If you ever decide to take over from Jacob, this should go on the menu."

She grinned at him. "I'd have to think of a sauce to add."

As Liam continued to eat, Hannah sat back and simply enjoyed his company. It felt good to be here in her kitchen with a man who made her heart flutter. A man who was good and kind and entirely too handsome for her peace of mind.

Thinking of relationships made her consider the one between Jamie Chadwick and Mickey. Had she felt about Jamie the way he clearly had about her? If so, why would she have left without telling him?

She suddenly noticed a questioning look in Liam's eyes. "You caught me woolgathering again."

"What about this time? More recipes?"

She laughed. "You wish. I was wondering about Jamie and Mickey."

"Do you think she wanted him to follow her?"

That was a different angle. "You mean to bring her back?" Hannah pondered the notion a moment longer, then shook her head. "No, I don't think she left so he would follow. I think if she did leave with the horse, it must have been for a very good reason. The eve of the Derby isn't a time for silly games. And if she was doing it for an important reason, she'd have found a way to make sure he knew to come after her." Unable to explain why she was so sure of that, Hannah rose and started clearing the dishes away.

"Hannah?"

She glanced over her shoulder. "Another hypothetical question?"

"No, this one requires a yes or no answer."

"Go ahead."

"Will you go out with me?"

"Outside? Okay, but it's cold, so let me get my coat." As the words left her mouth, Hannah realized that was not what he meant.

But now they had to go outside.

They went back down the stairs and through the restaurant toward the Hot Spot entrance. Embarrassed, Hannah struggled to fill the suddenly awkward silence. "You know, I don't ever walk through this room without thinking of your grandfather fighting fires from here. I'm so grateful to both of you for sharing his memorabilia with me."

"And we appreciate the care your father and uncle put into making the display case to honor them."

They stopped in front of the diary entry she had framed. Liam touched it, and Hannah sensed he was feeling the connection to his grandmother. "I imagine you miss her as much as I miss my mom."

Liam nodded. "With my parents in Florida, my grandfather is my only local relative. I miss having family nearby." He ran his finger along the edge of the frame. "Shall we go for that walk?"

He held the door, and Hannah stepped out onto the familiar street.

As she and Liam strolled beneath the old gas lamps, he posed a question. "Do you ever regret giving up the excitement of Los Angeles for small-town Kentucky?"

After his response about family, Hannah sensed that her answer was important. "Never."

"Why did you leave Blackberry Valley?"

"I wonder that myself sometimes. I thought it was to learn from the best professional chefs. From the time I first started cooking with my grandmother and mother, I knew I wanted to run my own restaurant. A place where I could make people feel at home, where they'd want to come."

He stopped under a streetlight and drew her around to face him. "Back there, I wasn't asking if you wanted to go outside."

Hannah dipped her head a minute before looking up at him with a grin. "I kind of figured that out a bit too late."

Liam shook his head slowly and chuckled. "So, we went for a walk."

"It's a nice night for one, even if it is cold."

"Are you going to answer the question I was really asking? Will you go out on a date with me?"

"We're both very busy people."

"Not too busy to take a walk together or spend a day exploring caves."

Hannah hesitated a fraction too long.

He released her. "It's okay. If you have to think that hard about it—"

"It's not that, Liam." She laid a hand on the sleeve of his coat. "I like you a lot, and I really value your friendship. I'm afraid of losing that." She took a deep breath. "But I'm more afraid of losing the chance that it could be something more. So yes, let's go on a date."

Liam's smile grew slowly, and Hannah's heart started to thump faster. Had she taken the step that everyone had been urging? Had she truly committed to going out with him?

"How about Monday, since it's your day off?"

Nerves kicked in, but so did enthusiasm. "This Monday?" She gulped. "Okay. Monday is fine. It's good."

"I'll pick you up at ten that morning. Dress casually."

"You already know where we're going?"

"I do. It's a surprise. And I'd like it to remain that way, so kindly don't let your curiosity run away with you." He grinned at her.

"You got it. I have more than enough mysteries to solve right now anyway."

Chapter Twenty-Three

Hannah's head spun as she left Liam at the door of the Hot Spot. She had a sudden urge to ring the old fire bell and announce to the world that she and Liam were going on a date. Instead, she quietly closed the door and reached for her phone. She had promised Lacy she'd be the first to know.

"Hannah! Where have you been? I've called and texted you a hundred times. Why haven't you responded to me or Sylvia?"

Perhaps shock value was best, she decided. "I've been planning a date with Liam."

Lacy's shriek nearly blew out Hannah's eardrum. "I want all the details!"

"You'll have to wait until after the date for them. He said it's a surprise. Now, what's all this about you and Sylvia? I know, I should have returned her call, but—"

"Hannah Prentiss, don't you dare change the subject."

"I'm not, Lacy. I promise. There's nothing to tell. He asked me out. I said yes."

The groan through the phone made it clear that her reply was unsatisfactory.

"I'll make a deal. If you tell me what our arrangements are with Sylvia tomorrow, I'll let you ask all the questions you want about our date."

"Why do you care more about going to the farm than telling me about your future?"

Hannah heaved a sigh at Lacy's exaggeration. Then she prepared to drop another bombshell. "Because I solved part of the mystery and need to go back to the farm to check something out about our jockey. I really have so much to catch you up on from the last twenty-four hours. I went out to talk to a detective who worked on the case years ago. He didn't really know much, but something he said started nagging at me."

"And that was?"

"He was talking about the jockey disappearing and how no one seemed to care much about that compared to the missing racehorse. He said, 'It was almost as if he hadn't existed.' And *he* didn't. Lacy, Mickey Dawes was a girl."

Hannah thought she might have heard a crash of something dropping, but otherwise there was complete silence through the phone.

"Lacy? Are you there? Liam and I went back to see Jamie Chadwick today, and all the pieces fell into place. He confirmed that Kentucky's Angel was ridden by a female jockey."

"But, but…*who*?"

"I don't know. Jamie wouldn't tell me. He said it wasn't his story to share."

"But he confirmed it?"

"He did, but it's too much to explain at this time of night. I'll fill you in tomorrow on the way out to the farm, if you're coming."

"Wild horses couldn't keep me away now. Pun intended. Sylvia's flight gets in at eight. She said she would meet us at the farm."

"Okay, then I need to get to bed. We'll have to get an early start to be there in time. I'll swing by for you—"

"Oh no. You're not getting off that easy. I'm your best friend. You owe me all the date details."

Since she knew there was not a chance of sleeping, the way her brain hummed with excitement, Hannah sank into one of the booths and filled Lacy in. Half an hour later, when she had finally fulfilled all best friend obligations, she said good night and headed upstairs. She was just closing her apartment door behind her when her phone chimed with a text.

Looking forward to Monday.

Hannah leaned back against the door and closed her eyes, hugging herself to contain the butterflies. After all this time, she and Liam were officially going on a date. And she'd solved part of the mystery. Not bad for one day.

Tomorrow they would go back to the farm where it had all begun. Was it possible that she could find out who Mickey really was?

Despite her doubts, Hannah slept soundly and rose early to pick up Lacy. The drive to the farm passed quickly as Hannah told Lacy everything she'd discovered.

Between the updates and teasing about Liam, Lacy regaled Hannah with stories of the dog she'd taken in, and his nightly wanderings. "He always shows up at some point, and he loves to visit with my horses. I'm almost as curious about his owner as you are about Mickey's identity. But I guess until someone identifies him, Bluegrass Hollow Farm has a part-time herd dog."

The stories were repeated once they met up with Sylvia, who was astounded to hear of Hannah's discoveries and shared her frustration at still not having discovered exactly what happened to Mickey or Kentucky's Angel.

"When I didn't hear back from you right away, I lured Lacy out here with the promise of books," she told Hannah. "I lost a packing day to my injured ankle, then I had to be back in Atlanta for another job, so I never got to deal with the last boxes of books I'd found hidden away in the attic. Some aren't in great shape, but my boss thought there might be some of value, so I was hoping Lacy's husband might have an interest in them for his bookstore. Hopefully, we'll have time to search around for more clues for you too."

"I have a good feeling about it," Hannah assured her.

The feeling had begun to wear thin by the time they'd spent two hours digging through boxes of musty books. Lacy set aside a few tomes that were in good condition, but the majority were not of resale quality.

"I'm so sorry," Sylvia said as she picked up a children's book that was covered in white powdery blotches. "There must have been a leak in the attic at some point, and no one noticed it had dripped on these boxes. I'd hoped more of them were salvageable."

As she moved to set the book in the discard pile, a piece of paper floated to the floor. Hannah reached over to retrieve it. She glanced down at words written in delicate script, and her breath caught. Her throat clogged with emotion, and she had to clear it before she spoke. "I think I found a clue."

Lacy jumped up and came over to where Hannah sat cross-legged on the floor. "What?"

Hannah held up the piece of cardstock with delicately scalloped edges. "I think it's a birth announcement. Someone must have been using it as a bookmark and stuck it in here. The writing is perfectly legible." She cleared her throat again. "It says 'John Randolph Chandler and Angelina Michaela Chandler joyfully announce the birth of their daughter, Helen Marie, this fifth day of August in the year 1975.'"

Hannah showed the card to Sylvia. "This is the estate owner's name, isn't it? Our librarian traced the property records. We couldn't figure out why a California businessman would have anything to do with a missing racehorse, but it wasn't him at all. It was her, Angelina Michaela—Mickey." She gaped at the card, unable to believe it. "Jamie Chadwick said they had an incredible bond from the moment the filly was born. They even shared a name. Angelina Michaela. Mickey, the girl who raised and rode her namesake, Kentucky's Angel."

"You did it," Sylvia exclaimed. "I didn't think it was possible, but you did it. You solved the mystery of who the box belongs to."

Hannah's body was still trembling, but her joy dampened as reality hit. "I know her name, but I still don't know what happened to her or why she and the horse disappeared. Or how they ended up here in Blackberry Valley of all places."

Sylvia stood and walked to the back window. She stared out in silence for a long moment, then turned to face Hannah and Lacy. "I'm not entirely sure I should be doing this, but I don't think there's anything unethical about it because you figured it out all on your own. Come with me. I have something to show you."

Hannah and Lacy exchanged glances.

Sylvia saw it. "I promise I wasn't holding out on you. What I'm going to show you—well, it never even occurred to me it was connected until you found the names and discovered that the jockey was a woman. Come look. Then we'll talk."

The trio donned their outerwear, and Sylvia led them out the rear door and into a field. After about ten minutes of pushing through muddy fields, they approached a wall of hedges. They followed the line of greenery to a small gate. As Sylvia pushed it open, Hannah could see they were in a small private burial ground.

"Does this belong to Angelina's family?" Hannah asked.

Sylvia stopped at the single headstone. It bore the name of Angelina's husband, John Randolph Chandler.

Hannah quickly scanned the cemetery, but there was no accompanying headstone for his wife. A sense of calm expectation fell over her. "Angelina is still alive?"

"The estate was portioned off," Sylvia said. "She is selling the house and old barn, but kept a section for herself and her daughter's family and the equine therapy center they run." She winced suddenly. "I guess technically we shouldn't be here, because obviously she is keeping the family burial plot."

Hannah noticed buildings visible through a gap in the trees. She pointed a shaking finger. "Is that her equine therapy center?"

Sylvia nodded, and it was all Hannah could do not to race through the trees. How could she have been so close all this time and yet had no idea? Questions flooded her mind, but having come this far, she couldn't bungle the situation by acting impulsively. She needed to consider how best to approach a woman who had remained hidden for decades. And then she had to come up with a plan to convince Angelina to see them.

Angelina. It felt so odd to have a name at last.

Hannah glanced over at Lacy, but saw that her friend was distracted by something else. A brown-and-white streak raced across the grass and jumped on her. "Hey, buddy," Lacy said with a laugh.

The dog came up to Hannah, sniffed, and then nudged her leg before he dashed across the manicured cemetery lawn. As her gaze tracked him, Hannah noticed another set of headstones off to the side. She hurried after him—and immediately the now-familiar sensation of goose bumps raced over her skin.

Slowly, Hannah approached the largest headstone and gently rested her hand on the marble to trace the halo-shaped mark above the letters *KA* and the years of the horse's birth and death. Tears filled her eyes and rolled down her cheeks as emotion overwhelmed her.

She swiped at her tears with one hand and with the other lightly traced the numbers *1990*. She'd known she would never find Kentucky's Angel alive after sixty years, but this headstone was proof that the mare had gone on to live a long life, which Hannah knew included at least one colt. And Angelina had started an equine therapy center.

Lacy wrapped an arm around Hannah's shoulders while the dog sat at her feet and leaned against her leg. They stood like that for long minutes as Hannah let her mind play back the photos she'd seen of Kentucky's Angel racing. She inhaled deeply and then slowly let out her breath, along with all the tension that had built up in her body these weeks.

Angel had not been harmed. By all signs, she had lived a good life. The most important piece of the mystery was solved for

Hannah—although her detective's heart would not be satisfied until she talked to Angelina and found out what happened on the eve of the Derby so many years before.

As eager as Hannah was to speak with Angelina, there was one other person she wished she could call. She imagined that Jamie Chadwick would be as happy as she was to discover this news, but telling him would be unfair to the woman who'd stayed hidden from him for all these years. She owed it to Angelina to keep this secret at least until she got permission to share it, but in her heart, Hannah hoped she would be able to reunite them.

She stood by Angel's grave, lost in thought, until her phone beeped an alert reminding her that she had the final Gratitude Feast planning meeting starting in two hours. As reluctant as she was to leave, duty called. As the three women began the trek back to the house, the dog ran circles around them before bounding off across the fields in the direction of the equine therapy center.

Hannah shook her head in amusement and smiled at Lacy. She had a feeling they'd finally figured out to whom the pup belonged. Confirmation of that, like her visit to Angelina, would have to wait, though. As impatient as she was, she knew the mystery had held for sixty years. It could wait one more day to be resolved.

Chapter Twenty-four

Lexington, Kentucky
May 1963

Chaddy leaned against the chain-link fence and soaked in the drama. Thousands of people were on their feet in the four-tier grandstand as Kentucky's Angel rounded the last turn of the Derby prep race and flew down the backstretch, opening her lead with each stride.

When she finished ten lengths ahead of her closest rival, the crowd couldn't be contained. They knew history had been made in front of their eyes, and more than a few whispers about a Triple Crown began to circulate. Angel had dominated the field from the first turn and never looked back. Would the filly be the first horse to win the Triple Crown since Citation in 1948?

Expectations were high as Jamie and Chaddy joined Mickey and Angel in the winner's circle for what had become a familiar routine. They had developed a protocol to keep Mickey from drawing too much attention. When track journalists asked questions, Jamie or Chaddy stepped forward to answer, leaving Mickey with Angel. By now, the reporters had accepted the jockey's shyness and focused instead on the horse and her trainers. As soon as the blanket of flowers was draped over Angel and the trophy awarded, Mickey slipped away.

It took longer than usual for the hullabaloo to die down, and Mickey was waiting in the barn when Jamie returned with Angel. They had their own routine here as well. Jamie always removed one of the victory flowers and presented it to Mickey. Chaddy usually left, allowing them their quiet time away from the crowds. Today he was distracted, and when he looked up, he realized he was intruding on a private moment.

Jamie had reached down to kiss Mickey's cheek as he presented the flower. They gazed deeply into each other's eyes for a long moment with hands linked. Chaddy blew out a breath as he quickly looked away, realizing he'd been wrong in his assessment to his boss.

Apparently there *was* someone Mickey loved as much as she loved horses—the boy she'd grown up with, the person who shared her love of horses. His grandson, Jamie.

Turning to leave, Chaddy's heart sank at the realization that he wasn't the only one who had seen the private exchange between Mickey and Jamie. In the doorway stood the one person who should never have witnessed the tender moment. What was he doing here?

Chaddy noted the intense emotion in the other man's eyes and knew his error in letting Mickey ride would exact a heavy price. The question now was who among them would pay it?

Chapter Twenty-Five

"Are you going to tell Mr. Chadwick that you found Angelina?" Lacy asked Hannah as they drove away. Sylvia had gone to her meeting, so they were alone in the car.

Hannah frowned as she mulled over her answer. "I don't think so. We don't know why she left yet. Maybe she doesn't want him to know. After all, she could have reached out to him at any time in the last sixty years, but she didn't. I would want to get her permission before I tell him anything."

"You don't think she was trying to escape *him*, do you?" Lacy sounded horrified. "He seems like such a nice man."

"That's my impression also. He seems honorable." Hannah thought back to how he wouldn't share "Mickey's" secret. Knowing what she did about the treatment of female jockeys, Hannah suspected that protecting Mickey's reputation might be connected somehow. "I think he was in love with her."

Lacy didn't seem surprised. "Maybe she didn't reciprocate his feelings. But isn't running away with a champion horse an extreme reaction?"

Hannah had to agree. "I guess the only way we'll find out for sure is to talk to her."

"But, Hannah, what if she won't see us?"

Lacy's question lingered in Hannah's mind as she drove home. They couldn't have come so far and made such progress unraveling the mystery, only to have Angelina refuse to speak to them—could they? She had to think carefully about how to approach the mysterious woman.

She recalled the reason she had first started on this quest. All she'd wanted was to return the box to the person who had left it behind. She should start with that. It was a simple explanation for her call, and it was the truth. Hannah decided to call as soon as she got home, before her meeting. She would spend the entire afternoon weighted by the fear of rejection if she didn't. For the rest of the drive, she was deep in thought.

As soon as she arrived at the Hot Spot, before she even went inside, Hannah picked up her phone and dialed the number Lacy had found for Angelina Chandler. Her heart thudded as she waited, but after a few seconds, a message announced that the number she had called was no longer in service.

Hannah realized it made sense for the number to be disconnected. It was probably the phone for the farm, and no one lived there now. She quickly looked up a number for the equine therapy center and called there instead.

"Hello, may I help you?"

The voice sounded slightly out of breath, but it certainly was not that of a woman in her seventies. "Hello, my name is Hannah Prentiss. I'm looking for Angelina Chandler."

The voice turned coldly formal. "Mrs. Chandler is not in at the moment, but I am her daughter. May I take a message?"

"How lovely. Please ask her to return my call." Hannah knew she'd made a mistake when she heard the daughter's crisp reply.

"I will take your number and relay the message, but I can't promise Mother will return the call. She doesn't talk to many people outside the center these days."

Knowing she had one last chance, Hannah rattled off her phone number and added, "Please tell her I have something of hers I would like to return."

"Okay, Ms.—What did you say your name is?"

"Hannah Prentiss. I own the Hot Spot in Blackberry Valley. Perhaps you know it."

The tension in the woman's voice eased. "I've eaten there. The food is delicious."

"Thank you." It was the most promising reply she could hope for, given the circumstances.

"Well, Hannah Prentiss, I don't know what a restaurateur could want to return to my mother, but I will pass along your message. Good day." The call ended.

All Hannah could do now was wait and pray that Angelina was curious enough to call. In the meantime, she had a committee meeting to finalize decorations for the Gratitude Feast.

"The restaurant is lovely with your autumn decor, Hannah. It really is." Miriam's tone was hesitant. "It's just that we usually decorate in a way symbolic of our gratitude."

Hannah pulled her thoughts away from Angelina and horses. "I'm sorry, but I'm not exactly sure what that would look like in decorations."

"What do you think about a cornucopia of local produce at the center?" Elaine suggested. "That would showcase our gratitude for our community of suppliers. We could add small labels with the farm names."

"That's a brilliant idea, Elaine," Connie chimed in.

Hannah agreed. "I love it."

The rest of the ladies chorused their approval.

"Great," Elaine said. "I'll put that together."

They continued brainstorming ways to tweak the restaurant's decor. Hannah was unpacking cranberry spice candles to use as centerpieces when her phone rang with an unfamiliar number. She answered at once. "Hello?"

"Good afternoon," said a woman's voice. "Am I speaking with Hannah Prentiss?"

Her heart rate ticking up, Hannah answered, "You are."

"Ms. Prentiss, this is Angelina Chandler. My daughter said you wanted to speak with me."

Hannah gestured to her friends to carry on without her as she ducked into the kitchen to have the conversation in private. She trusted her employees and friends implicitly, but as Jamie had said, it was Angelina's story to share.

"Thank you so much for returning my call. I told your daughter that I had something that belonged to you. I didn't give her the details because I wanted to be able to explain." Hannah quickly recounted the story of finding Sylvia and the box.

"Young lady, if you are looking to file a lawsuit over an injury, speak to my attorney. Good day."

"No, wait. That's not it at all. I only wanted to return the box to you."

"If it was for sale, I assure you we no longer need it."

Her tone was still clipped, and Hannah felt her opportunity slipping away, so she drew a deep breath and took a chance. "Even if it's a box of memorabilia from when you raced with Kentucky's Angel?"

The gasp on the other end of the line was audible, but then there was a tense silence before Angelina replied. "Whatever are you talking about?"

"Don't worry. No one spilled your secret. I figured it out on my own, and it is safe with me. I wanted to be sure the box wasn't sold in error. The things were so lovingly compiled that I couldn't imagine the owner parting with them willingly."

Angelina's silence was so palpable that Hannah could feel her weighing her response. She could only hope that the young woman who had loved her horse would win out.

Finally, Angelina replied, "I would like to see the box."

Her voice was tremulous, and Hannah felt what the admission cost her, but she also sensed the love and hope behind the response. "I would be happy to bring it by the center. When would be a good time?"

"As soon as possible, I suppose." Angelina's voice had warmed slightly, perhaps relieved at the decision having been made.

Hannah glanced at the clock. As much as she wanted to go immediately, she couldn't make it there and back in time for the dinner rush—not if she hoped to have enough time to hear Angelina's story.

"I don't know if your daughter explained, but I run a restaurant in town. We open soon, so I can't bring it by tonight. I can come tomorrow morning after church if that suits you."

"You not only run, but own the restaurant, according to my daughter. That's remarkable. Tomorrow morning will be fine. I trust you know how to find us since you managed to locate me—which no one has done in over sixty years."

Hannah hung up with her blood zinging through her veins. At long last, tomorrow she would meet the woman who had ridden Kentucky's Angel.

Chapter Twenty-Six

Hannah and Lacy were on the road to see Angelina shortly after the church service the following day. Though the two friends tried to talk about the upcoming Gratitude Feast, excitement battled with their nerves, making conversation difficult. Over and over, they found themselves discussing what Angelina would reveal, *if* she chose to reveal anything.

When they finally arrived at the equine center, a woman of around fifty met them at the door. "Hi there. One of you must be Hannah."

"That's me," Hannah piped up. "This is my friend, Lacy Minyard. She's been with me through this whole endeavor."

"I'm Angelina's daughter, Helen. It's nice to meet you both. If you have things to do today, I'd be happy to give my mother the box for you."

"I was hoping to deliver it to her myself," Hannah replied. "I have a few things I'd like to explain to her about it."

Helen grinned. "My mother thought that would be your response. She's in the stables. I'll take you there."

Hannah thought her heart might pound out of her chest with anticipation. She was to meet Angelina with her horses. Short of meeting her with Kentucky's Angel herself, it was the most perfect scenario she could think of. "That would be lovely. I've been reading about the work you do here."

Helen led her and Lacy down a gravel path through a wooded area that ended at a spacious barn.

As they entered the building, Hannah heard a sharp bark and welcomed the now familiar brown-and-white dog who came running and jumped on her in excitement.

"Rusty, down," a woman's voice commanded.

The dog behaved instantly, dropping to his haunches and thumping his tail against the floor.

A petite, gray-haired woman emerged from the nearest stall, her presence every bit as commanding as her voice had been.

"It's all right," Hannah assured the woman, who must be Angelina. "We're already friends, though we didn't know his name."

"How?" Angelina asked.

Lacy introduced herself and Hannah, and filled Angelina in on where they'd met the dog and how he'd led them to Sylvia and the box, which Hannah had bought hoping to return it to its rightful owner. She explained that Rusty had been visiting her farm almost daily and playing with her horses while she and Hannah tried to locate his owner. "Who knew finding you would solve both mysteries?"

Hannah chimed in from where she crouched on the straw, rubbing Rusty's ears. "It's taken us time and quite a bit of detective work to find you."

"I'm amazed you did, and I truly want to hear how, but let's tour the barn and therapy center. Then we can go back to my office and see what you found. Helen can put the box there to wait for us."

Hannah gave Rusty an extra rub before she rose to her feet. It felt like they were being tested before Angelina would speak about the box, but unless she'd missed her mark, the woman had warmed up to them instantly upon seeing Rusty's reaction. "Thanks, buddy," she whispered.

For the next half hour, Angelina walked them through her facility, showing off state-of-the-art treatment rooms and explaining the work they did. "My husband was nearly killed in a tragic skiing accident. I suddenly had a young baby and a husband who could no longer walk. He had run a successful sporting goods company, living the adventurous life that his business was built on. The accident crushed everything he had worked for. He was angry and scared, and I understood that. I, too, once had everything I could want and lost it. Our bond deepened over that shared loss of dreams and hopes, the understanding that things that had driven us our entire lives could be taken from us in an instant." She gestured to their surroundings. "From the ashes of those dreams rose something new—this equine therapy center."

Hannah was confused, feeling like she was missing a huge central part of this story, but she forced herself to be patient. Angelina would explain what she wanted to share in her own way and in her own time. But she could ask at least one question. "Your husband had equine therapy after his accident?"

Hannah's question was met with a smile of approval. "He did. I think he agreed so I would stop asking, but it turned out to be the first therapy that really helped his spirit." She cast them a sly grin. "Perhaps my love of horses was infectious."

More questions rose in Hannah's mind, but she bit her tongue and listened.

"Hippotherapy, as it is really called, wasn't practiced in the United States back then, but John's doctor heard of it from a Swedish friend. He had a journal article about it in his office waiting room. There was a horse on the cover, so naturally I picked it up to read. All else had failed in his treatment, so we had nothing to lose by trying it." Angelina stopped to catch her breath.

"My husband made very good progress. He would never be returned to his pre-accident health, but the therapy improved his quality of life. Helen witnessed that as she grew up, and she decided to devote her life to the study and practice of it." Angelina smiled proudly at her daughter. "She studied under some of the finest practitioners in Europe. It is her life's work. I guess you could say the love of horses is in her blood. Now, would you like to meet ours?"

Lacy laughed. "Would we ever!"

Angelina had been enthusiastic in describing equine therapy, but Hannah noted an extra spring in her step as they headed out to the pasture. Hannah pulled up short at the sight of the horses grazing and playing. Her hand involuntarily rose to her chest as she drank in the view. This was Angelina's life.

One filly broke from the pack and raced across the field toward them. Hannah slowly stepped up behind Angelina, who was letting the filly nuzzle her, and gasped softly. "She's descended from Kentucky's Angel." Goosebumps raced along Hannah's arms, and it was all she could do not to reach out and stroke the chestnut filly.

Staring at her in surprise, Angelina asked, "How do you know?"

Hannah let out a deep sigh. "I recognize that halo marking. Angel had it. So did Kentucky's Dawn, and last week I saw it on a horse named Kentucky's Future."

Angelina was trembling when she addressed Hannah. "Where did you see that horse?"

"At Camden Farms, when I was visiting with Jamie Chadwick."

For a moment, Hannah thought she would have to catch Angelina, as the color drained from the older woman's face. She visibly worked to pull herself together and told Hannah, "I think it is time to return to my office and hear the rest of your story."

Though Hannah was reluctant to leave the horses, she knew it was time. This was it—her chance to find what she had been searching for.

Angelina led them into a comfortable room, more like a rustic living room than an office in a barn. Helen had laid tea out for them, and they made small talk about the therapy center while Angelina poured and passed a tray of pastries. Rusty curled up with his chin on Lacy's feet, but his twitching tail kept swiping Hannah's ankle. She reached down and stroked his fur.

"I wish I had room for a dog." Hannah sighed. "It's like when I was a child and pestered my parents for a horse. Practicality must outweigh sentiment."

"You don't have room for even a small one?" Angelina asked absently. She was trying to play the proper hostess, but Hannah could see how distracted she was.

She answered anyway. "Not a horse or a dog. I live above my restaurant and work long hours. It wouldn't be fair to a dog to be alone so much."

"You have a kind heart, Hannah Prentiss. Rusty sensed it." Angelina sipped her tea and then changed the subject. She pointed at the box on the table. "And now, I need you to answer a burning question. I guess the box explains the why, but how did you find me after all these years?"

Lacy laughed. "If you knew my friend, you'd know that a lot of people ask questions like that. She has a knack for solving the unsolvable."

Hannah was happy to answer. "Initially, I was just curious, but it became more than that. Sorting through the box of memorabilia reawakened the horse-crazy adolescent in me. I guess I couldn't believe that anyone intended to sell something so personal. I was sure it was a mistake, so I was determined to return the collection."

Angelina's eyes glistened as she listened to Hannah. She had to clear her throat before she could respond. "It *is* terribly personal, and I thank you." Pausing again, she took a breath before continuing. "Selling off an estate is like selling off parts of your life. After my husband passed, I no longer had any use for most of what was in our house. I convinced myself they were just things, inanimate objects that carried memories. I could sell off the pieces and still cherish the memories. But I'd forgotten that I stuck that box up on the shelf in the tack room. It was so many years ago." Her expression grew distant, and her voice faded. "When I did it, I was shutting off a part of my life that no longer existed."

"Are you sure you want to reawaken the memories now?" Hannah asked gently. "I'm sorry if I stirred up pain."

Smiling bravely, Angelina said, "I am an old woman now. Maybe it is time I faced my past."

Hannah rose to slide the box in front of her.

Angelina slowly lifted the lid and removed the programs with an almost reverential grace. Tears trickled down her cheeks, but joy overrode the sadness as she thumbed through the booklets. She laughed at names, whispered stories about the other jockeys, and reminisced about races she had won with Angel. Hannah and Lacy listened, enthralled by this glimpse into the past.

Finally, Angelina reached into the box to remove the last item, the album. She laid a hand on the cover and closed her eyes. Hannah could only imagine what Angelina must be feeling. Gently she rested her palm over the older woman's soft hand. "I'm sorry if I upset you."

Angelina lifted shining eyes. "No, my dear. You've stirred up beautiful memories I have not allowed myself to think of in decades." She appeared lost in thought, but then, as she slowly turned the pages, she spoke. "It was not always the custom to have flowers placed on a victor after a race, but when it was, Jamie always made sure that I received a flower from the blanket. He would present it to me in the barns after everyone had left. Those flowers from him were more precious than the win."

Angelina turned the page and gently ran her finger over the circlet of flowers. She raised her other hand to cover her face. "Dear Jamie." She sighed. "I loved him so. Leaving him was the hardest thing I ever did in my life."

Hannah's heart clenched as Angelina confirmed what she and Lacy had believed. "So why did you do it?" She gasped and immediately apologized. "I'm so sorry. That's not my place to ask."

Angelina rubbed her hand where Hannah assumed she'd once worn a wedding ring. "It's a long story, but if you have the time, I think I would enjoy finally sharing it." She looked directly at them for a moment. "I can't swear you to secrecy, but there are people's reputations that could possibly be at stake if this story got out, even after all these years."

"We won't say anything you don't want us to. Right, Lacy?" Hannah promised.

"Absolutely," Lacy agreed. "We don't want to cause you any distress, so if telling us is too hard, you don't have to do it."

"You gave me back my precious memories. It's only fair I share some of them with you."

Chapter Twenty-Seven

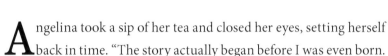

Angelina took a sip of her tea and closed her eyes, setting herself back in time. "The story actually began before I was even born. My mother was Helena Donahue."

Hannah gasped. "As in, the family that owns Camden Farms?"

Angelina smiled sadly. "The very same, though it's been held in a trust since my grandfather died. My father was a traveling salesman who stopped by the farm one day to try to convince my grandfather to purchase whatever he was selling that year." She paused, then continued in a resigned voice. "My father was not a very successful businessman. He always had some new get-rich-quick scheme. My mother was in the stables the day he stopped by. Apparently, I came by my love of horses quite naturally. To hear my father tell the story, it was love at first sight, but also forbidden. My grandfather had big plans for his only daughter, plans to build a dynasty by marrying her into another family of racing royalty. His plans certainly did not include his daughter eloping with the traveling salesman, but that is exactly what happened."

Angelina fiddled with her napkin, twisting it into minute folds as she resumed her tale. "My grandfather, God bless his soul, was a cantankerous and single-minded man who immediately disowned his daughter. I sometimes wonder if he softened a bit with age. Jamie's grandfather had a theory that I reminded him of his daughter, and though he couldn't relent enough to actually acknowledge me publicly, allowing me to ride his precious horses said more than words ever could. I would have appreciated the words, but I cherished my time with the horses, so maybe I was more like him than I care to accept."

She sat back in her chair and released a sigh. "I'm sorry. I'm sure you didn't need all that background. Shall I refresh your tea before I get to the part of the story you actually care about?"

Hannah held out her cup, but she had to contradict Angelina's statement. "You had me hanging on every word. It's such a tragic story, though. I suppose there is no hope your mother and grandfather ever reunited?"

Angelina shook her head. "Sadly, no. My mother died giving birth to me."

"Oh, how awful," Lacy cried. "I'm so sorry we are dredging up all these memories."

With a shrug, Angelina said, "That is a very old one. I always felt close to my mother when I was with the horses. Jamie's grandfather took me under his wing. He and Jamie were the only ones who knew who I was when I showed up at the farm. I disguised myself as a boy so no one would have the chance to turn me away."

"How did you ever keep such a secret?" Hannah asked.

"At first it wasn't so difficult. People saw what they expected to. I was dressed as a boy, Chaddy and Jamie called me Mickey, and no one raised a question. It went on that way for years. I suspect some guessed, especially as Jamie and I grew older and our friendship turned to love. But by that time, no one on the farm would have betrayed me. We were family to each other."

"So why did you leave? How could you do that to Jamie if you loved him?"

A tear slipped down Angelina's face, and she fumbled for a tissue before she answered. "*I* didn't do anything to him. *He* is the one who rejected me."

Lexington, Kentucky
May 1963

Her grandfather was standing by the floor-to-ceiling window overlooking the farm when Mickey knocked. He glanced over his shoulder and spoke gently. "Come in, my dear."

Mickey slowly entered the room, unsure where to go until he moved to sit behind his big oak desk and gestured that she should take the chair across from him.

He sat back in his chair, elbows on the armrests, fingers steepled under his chin, and studied her. Mickey grew uncomfortable and confused. Why had he called her here? Only the knowledge that this man controlled her access to Angel kept her seated as the silence stretched on.

He finally cleared his throat. "Some people have called me a hard man, among other things." He spoke slowly, as if the words were hard to expel. "I am not a man prone to admitting his mistakes, but I have made two grave ones in my life." He closed his eyes briefly, and when he opened them, Mickey saw intense sadness and regret.

"The first was sending your mother away. I thought I was doing what was right, that she would come to her senses and return. I was wrong, and I have had to live with the guilt of that decision ever since."

Mickey sat quietly, stunned by his unexpected revelation, but his next words cut her to the core.

"My second mistake was in letting you ride Kentucky's Angel."

She let out an involuntary gasp.

Her grandfather shook his head. "Let me finish." He leaned forward over the desk and met her angry gaze. "The first time I realized it was you riding Angel, something unlocked in my heart. You were the spitting image of your mother. I'm not a sentimental man, but I felt like God had given me a gift I didn't deserve, allowing me to see you here every day. A magnificent horse and a gifted rider who was my own granddaughter. My selfish joy blinded me to the realities we would face if you competed on Angel."

Mickey's heart thumped. "Did someone find out?"

"I suppose it was arrogant of Chaddy and me to think no one would take note of the jockey who was racing the surprise star of both her two- and three-year-old seasons. But if anyone had suspicions, they didn't voice them." He made a wry face. "Either out of respect for, or fear of, me."

"But now someone has?"

He closed his eyes again in a way that reminded Mickey of how she centered herself before beginning a race. "Both of my mistakes are tied to one man—your father. He came to see me a week ago."

"Wanting money again, I'll bet," she muttered.

"Yes, but this time the request was more of a threat. Either I give him a managing share in this farm—or he reveals the identity of Angel's mysterious jockey."

For a moment she thought she might faint. Only the rage that built inside kept her steady. That her father—the man who had ignored her for her entire life because he blamed her for her mother's death—would choose to ruin her because of his greed, did not surprise her. What destroyed her was the idea that he might succeed.

"I didn't say anything to you before because I needed time to think how best to proceed," her grandfather said.

Mickey dared to let hope blossom as she observed his resolute expression. "You have a plan?"

He nodded. "We have to create a scandal bigger than the one he's threatening."

Mickey gaped at her grandfather. She knew he had to be at least as angry as she was, probably more so because his entire operation was at stake. Yet he seemed so calm. And that scared her almost as much as her father's threat. "Chaddy once told me that you would never leave your horses for love of a man."

"You mean like my mother did."

Her grandfather cleared his throat. "I made the mistake of trying to force a decision on her." He waited until Mickey looked up, then he held her gaze. "This time, I am asking you to decide."

"I don't understand."

"Your father is a smart man despite his grievous faults. He is not threatening me alone. He is threatening you. He will expose you and prevent you from racing ever again."

Defiance built in Mickey. She'd long ago shielded herself from her father's meanness. She would not give in to this threat. So what if she couldn't race? No scandal could stop her from working in the barn. "I don't care."

Her grandfather's voice was soft and sad as he continued. "As I said, he is a smart man. He did not stop at that threat. He saw you with Jamie. He knows your feelings for him. If I don't give him what he wants, he will ruin Jamie as well as you and me."

"How can he do that? We've done nothing illegal."

"Not technically, but surely you have heard the talk at the track, the disgust the jockeys show at the idea of a woman riding with them. They will boycott any race we enter if we dare to show up with you astride

Angel. We will be ostracized if we do not give in to your father's demands."

Resignation suffused her grandfather's voice. "I am the one to blame for this decision. No one else. So I am the one who must fix it, because your father will gain control of this farm over my dead body." Barely suppressed rage replaced the resignation. "I will stop him, but I need your cooperation."

"What do you need me to do?"

He heaved an exaggerated sigh. "I may be an old fool, but I know what it is to love, and I know what it is to sacrifice. What I'm asking is simple. Do you love Jamie enough to leave him? If you do, I have a plan."

Mickey sagged back against her chair, shattered. Her grandfather's question had ripped open her heart. "Why would you ask that?"

Charles Donahue sat rigidly in his chair and the gaze he turned on her was fierce. "The only way to thwart your father is for you and Kentucky's Angel to disappear. Forever."

Mickey blinked, certain she could not be hearing correctly.

Her grandfather continued. "I'll send you to California. I own a small farm there where you can live. I'll arrange a small staff and give you Kentucky's Angel as compensation for everything you've lost."

"I won't do it."

"You have no choice in the matter."

Mickey couldn't find her voice. She'd thought women not being allowed to ride was bad, but her grandfather was proving how absolutely powerless she was. She could argue all she wanted, but, in the end, Camden Farms and the horses belonged to him.

But how could she leave Jamie? Her grandfather was making it sound like this was a sacrifice she had to make for loving him, but that was not what Jamie would want. She was certain of that. If she had to leave, then Jamie needed to come with her.

"I will do as you say." She watched her grandfather's expression ease. "But I have one condition."

"What is that, my dear?"

"I want Jamie to come with me."

For a moment she thought he would refuse. But then he swallowed and nodded. "I'll offer him that opportunity." He paused. "But you can't leave together. For this to work, it is only you and Angel who can disappear. I will allow Jamie to follow later, once the scandal has died down."

Mickey didn't like that arrangement, but she had to accept her small victory. She didn't care if she couldn't race. If she had Jamie and Angel, and her father's plan was thwarted, not racing would be a small price to pay. "Thank you."

Angelina shifted in her seat. "I didn't do anything to Jamie. I left because my father was a bitter man who would have ruined everything. My grandfather convinced me that leaving was the only way I could save Camden Farms from my father. He would have destroyed my grandfather and Jamie, and I couldn't allow him anywhere near the horses."

She sat quietly, twisting her fingers in her lap. "Perhaps there was another way, but I was young and frightened. I believed my grandfather when he said it was best if he sent me away. We had to deprive my father of his ammunition."

For the first time that day, there was bitterness in her words. "It's hard for a woman today to understand how different it was back then. In some ways I straddled a great societal change as much as I did any horse. Women weren't allowed to be jockeys. It would have raised a huge scandal if it had come out that Jamie and my grandfather knowingly let a woman ride Angel in those races. With my disappearance, nothing could ever be proven."

Hannah nodded sadly. "I think I understand what you mean. Before I put together who you were, I was doing some research. I read about the races that were boycotted to prevent women from racing, the comments that were thrown around."

"One jockey said we should be home doing dishes instead," Angelina said angrily. "Another said our spaghetti was burning at home to show we had no place there. I made my choice when I registered as Mickey Dawes, and I was ready to face any consequences." Angelina seemed to wilt before their eyes. "What I hadn't considered were the potential consequences to others. I couldn't let my stubborn determination cost my grandfather everything."

For the first time since Hannah had met her, Angelina seemed every one of her seventy-plus years. It broke Hannah's heart to have disrupted the peace she had obviously fought so hard to gain. But then she thought of Jamie.

Hannah leaned forward in her seat. "But what about Jamie Chadwick? If you loved him, how could you take Kentucky's Angel and leave him?"

"What do you mean?" Angelina seemed genuinely puzzled.

"As much as you loved Jamie, it was the filly you took with you. You left Jamie with no explanation."

Tears that looked like betrayal flashed in Angelina's eyes as she spoke. "No. I would never have done that."

Hannah glanced at Lacy, whose face mirrored her confusion. "But, Angelina, the horse went missing when you did. Jamie had no idea what happened," Lacy explained.

Angelina stared at Lacy as bewilderment flooded her face. "What are you talking about? We didn't go missing. It was all carefully planned out. My grandfather gave me Angel in exchange for having to start over. I didn't want to leave. I begged my grandfather to find another way, but he insisted. I guess I saw a flash of the man who had disowned my mother, and I was scared. I agreed, but only if he would let Jamie come with us. He wasn't happy about losing his trainer, but he conceded. He told me Kentucky's Angel would be scratched from the race, and I needed to leave, but Jamie would have to stay behind for appearances' sake, so as not to arouse any suspicion."

Angelina stopped talking and reached for a sip of her tea, but Hannah could see her struggling to compose herself. She took an automatic sip and set the cup back down with trembling hands, but as she stiffened her posture and faced them, Hannah had the sense she was trying to read their reaction.

"I don't want you to feel sorry for me, ladies. I had a good life. I made a sacrifice, and unfortunately, I lost the man I loved, but sometimes in life you have no choice. I have been blessed to know and love two wonderful men. Both were strong men, not intimidated by a woman who knew what she wanted. And I had my horses. Maybe not to race, but to ride and to love. And what more could I ask for than that?"

Hannah was struggling to take in what she said. "So what happened the night before the race? How did it all play out?"

Angelina stared at her in confusion. "Nothing. I did a training run with Angel at the track the morning before the Derby, sort of a farewell to that life. When we got back to the barns, I rubbed her down and spent some time with her. I kissed her goodbye and promised to see her soon."

"And what did you say to Jamie?"

Angelina glanced away. "I didn't. I was a coward. I knew if I saw him I would never have the courage to leave, so my grandfather promised to be the one to tell him after I was gone. He would explain that once the hubbub over the missing horse died down, Jamie could join me in California. Grandfather would gift us enough money to start our own breeding farm out west. Only it didn't work out that way."

Angelina's voice had weakened a bit at the end, but she took a deep breath and continued.

"That part of my story ends there. Jamie chose not to join me. I waited and waited until my grandfather finally came to see me. He said Jamie wasn't willing to give up his life in Kentucky. Grandfather was very apologetic, and for the first time in my life, he was affectionate and grandfatherly. He convinced me to go to college and to try to build a future for myself. He set me up on a small farm so I could keep Angel. I guess that was my reward for saving his beloved Camden Farms."

Angelina swiped at a stray tear running down her cheek. "I was too heartbroken to care, but Angel helped me. Her love was unconditional. I did go on to college to study to be a trainer. That's where I met John. We became friends, then fell in love and eventually married. We had Helen before his accident changed everything again."

Hannah sank back against the chair cushion. She didn't want to be the one to tell Angelina that her grandfather had not upheld his part of the bargain, but she should know. It was only fair to Jamie after all these years.

"Angelina, remember when I said Jamie didn't know what happened?" Hannah kept her tone gentle. "He wasn't faking. I don't think he ever heard anything about the plan."

In the wake of Hannah's words, Angelina's body crumpled. "My grandfather never asked Jamie, did he?"

Hannah gave the merest shake of her head, and the elderly woman started to tremble. It lasted only a moment. Then she nodded, more to herself than anyone else, and Hannah caught a glimpse of the inner steel, the core of strength that had enabled her to survive the tough times in her life.

"I should have known. A leopard doesn't change his spots." Angelina closed her eyes briefly. When she opened them, she faced

Hannah and Lacy with impressive dignity. "What did Jamie think happened? Did he tell you?"

Hannah gathered her thoughts before she answered, giving Angelina what Jamie had told them about how he'd found horse and rider missing and searched for them.

Tears streamed down Angelina's face unchecked, and Hannah wanted to stop, but Angelina motioned for her to keep going.

"Mr. Chadwick said he walked all over that park searching for you, but as the hours passed, he knew in his heart that you weren't there. He said he didn't know why you had left—whether willingly or because of foul play—but he knew you were gone."

Tears continued to roll down Angelina's cheeks. "Oh, Jamie. How he must hate me."

"I don't think he hates you." Hannah stopped there. She had no right to tell Angelina that Jamie still loved her after all these years. His words might have given her that impression, but how would he feel once he heard the truth? "I think you should talk to him. Explain everything."

Angelina seemed to age and shrink before their eyes. "I don't know if I could do that."

Hannah wanted to reassure her, but she was worried that her meddling had already caused too much harm. "I suppose you could leave it in the past. You did send Kentucky's Dawn to make amends."

"Is that what Jamie thinks?"

"I don't know what he thinks. He wouldn't really talk about it beyond saying that colt made his career. He said it wasn't his story to share. But he introduced us to Kentucky's Dawn's descendant. I knew him immediately because he had the same halo mark."

"Kentucky's Future." Angelina smiled. "That's a good name. It makes me happy to see Angel's descendants make their mark in the racing world, though I've long since lost interest in it myself. I just love being with horses. I learned that with Angel. I didn't need to race in the Derby to be happy. I just needed to ride her. And not racing gave her a better quality of life. That mattered more to me. She could run to her heart's content with no pressure."

Angelina was silent for a long time before she spoke again. "Jamie lost way more than I did, all because he tried to support me. From the time Dawn was born, I knew he was special just like I'd known with Angel. But I didn't want to make the same mistake twice and have Dawn bond too much with me. So I sent him as a gift. It wasn't to make amends. Nothing could ever do that. But I hoped with Dawn, Jamie could build the career that was derailed when I left with Angel."

Helen had been listening in silence the whole time, but now she stepped in. "I think it's time for a rest, Mama."

Hannah and Lacy immediately stood to leave. Hannah reached into her pocket and pulled out a pen, then she leaned over the box and wrote Jamie's name and number on the cardboard. "In case you decide to call," she said softly as she touched Angelina's hand and bade her goodbye.

Helen saw them out, and Hannah felt obligated to apologize. "I'm sorry if we tired your mother out."

Helen had her mother's kind eyes. "Yes, she is tired now, but I think this was good for her. She has told me some of the story in the past, but I think she kept most of it locked away. Just like we can't let a boil fester on a horse, we shouldn't let old wounds go unhealed. I will talk to her later. Maybe she will use that phone number. Thank you for leaving it."

As Hannah and Lacy returned to the car, Lacy tuned in to Hannah's mood. "You want to call Mr. Chadwick, don't you?"

"I do," Hannah admitted. "But I won't."

"Good. Now that your mystery is solved, you can focus on the Gratitude Feast—and your date!"

Nodding, Hannah said, "But what if…" Her voice trailed off as she felt Lacy's glare. "I'm not trying to meddle. I really hope she calls him, but it's her decision to make. I just want it to be fixed."

Lacy shook her head. "Hannah, you can't right every wrong in the world, and this one is over sixty years old."

Hannah pulled up at a stop sign and turned to her friend. "If Neil had disappeared sixty years ago and someone knew where he was, wouldn't you want them to tell you?"

Laughing merrily, Lacy said, "If Neil disappeared sixty years ago, I'd have bigger problems than where he went since he wasn't even born yet."

She chuckled despite herself. "You know what I mean."

Lacy swallowed her laughter. "I do. But I don't know the answer. Maybe you should talk to Liam about it on your date. Now, let's go back to your apartment and pick out date clothes."

Chapter Twenty-Eight

Lexington, Kentucky
May 1963

Chaddy stood in the entrance to the barn observing his brokenhearted grandson. Only two weeks ago, this stall had buzzed with the excitement of pre-Derby prep and anticipation of a victorious run for the roses. Now it was a somber, empty place.

A pall hung over Camden Farms. Workers went about their business, caring for the other horses, mucking out stalls, dispensing food, training the yearlings, and clocking the mares and stallions who had upcoming races, but a miasma of sadness cloaked them all—especially Jamie. The heart had gone out of the farm with the disappearance of Mickey and Kentucky's Angel.

After the first frantic days of searching, Jamie had retreated into himself. For the past week, he'd stayed in the stables, barely eating, sleeping less, apparently waiting in the hopes that Mickey and Angel would miraculously reappear.

He'd been interviewed by the sheriff, questioned by Donahue, and sought out by newsmen, but Jamie had no more answers than anyone else. Mickey and Angel had simply vanished into thin air.

Chaddy's heart ached as well, as much for his grieving grandson as for the missing duo. He knew Jamie couldn't go on like this, but he also understood the loss that devastated the young man. He and Mickey had been together pretty much every waking hour of every day for the past eight years. Since Kentucky's Angel had begun to show promise, they'd lived and breathed her training together. And suddenly Jamie was alone.

Chaddy also couldn't shake the memory of one evening a month ago, when he'd seen Mickey's father lurking in the barn after a race. He'd mentioned it to the police and discussed it with Charles Donahue, but his boss had dismissed Dawes as a threat. The man had an alibi for the days around the Derby.

Still, Chaddy couldn't shake the feeling. A champion racehorse would have made the money-grubbing man a small fortune. He'd pointed that out to Donahue, but his boss had reminded him that Angel was too well known in racing circles to have been of any use to him. He couldn't race or sell a stolen horse.

The scandal had continued to grow as the days passed. The missing jockey and champion horse captured massive attention and triggered endless speculation. Almost as distressing as Jamie's loss were the rumors that swirled around him—rumors that he'd been paid off to throw the race.

Ridiculous, all of them. Anyone could see that the man was broken.

When he'd seen Dawes in the barn that night, Chaddy had wondered who would pay the price for letting Mickey ride. Now he knew the answer was his grandson, and Jamie would pay with a broken heart.

Jamie had made the mistake of falling in love with a girl and a horse. Chaddy knew a little about that. And he knew that working with other horses was the best way to climb out of heartbreak. He pushed off the wall and walked over to the stall.

Jamie raised his head slowly, eyes bloodshot, his hair unkempt from all the times he'd run his fingers through it. "They're not coming back, are they?"

His voice was hoarse and tortured, and Chaddy wished with all his heart that he could disagree, but Jamie needed to move on, needed to face reality. "It doesn't look like it."

Jamie buried his head in his hands and asked for the millionth time, "What happened? Where is she?"

"I don't know. The police have found no evidence of foul play. No one at the track saw anything unusual that evening."

"But the security team?"

Chaddy answered patiently, as he always did. "All anyone saw was Mickey taking Angel for a walk and then grooming her and staying with her. There was nothing even remotely different from any other night."

"But there were all the other horses, all the other jockeys and trainers and everyone getting ready for the Derby."

"They've all been questioned."

Chaddy eased his old body down on the bale of hay beside Jamie. He couldn't voice the conclusion that most people had come to—that the jockey had run away with the horse for reasons unknown, though there was plenty of harsh speculation. Chaddy draped an arm around his grandson's shoulder. "As hard as it is to say, I think it's time you accept that they are never coming back."

Jamie pulled away and looked at him with a haunted expression. "Never. I'll wait for her for the rest of my life."

Chapter Twenty-Nine

"I think you should wear this." Lacy held out a hunter-green sweater from Hannah's closet. "You can wear it with jeans and your cute ankle boots. And you have that lovely suede jacket that matches your boots."

Hannah eyed her friend suspiciously. "Why are you so intent on dressing me for this date? Did Liam tell you where we're going?"

Lacy didn't answer, but buried her head in Hannah's closet. "If you don't like the green sweater—which is a mistake because it makes your hazel eyes pop—the blue cable-knit one is pretty too."

"I don't know." Hannah pushed past Lacy and unearthed a sparkly top and velvet pants that she'd worn to an event in LA last year. "I was thinking of this." She held the blouse up against herself. "The sequins make my eyes sparkle more than the sweater does."

"Don't you think that is a bit dressy for a morning date?" Lacy asked, trying to be tactful. "This is Blackberry Valley, after all. We're not that into sparkles on a Monday morning. And I believe Liam told you to dress casually."

"See, he did tell you!" Hannah crowed in triumph.

Lacy glared at her through narrowed eyes. "Admit it, you were never going to wear the velvet pants and sparkles, were you?"

Hannah fell back on the bed, laughing. "Of course not."

"I should have told you yes, and then you could have seen Liam's face when he arrived to pick you up in his Jeep."

Grinning wickedly, Hannah said, "It's not too late."

"Tell me you're not trying to sabotage this relationship before it even gets off the ground."

Hannah sat up, suddenly serious. "I promise I'm not. I really like him, Lacy. But what if it doesn't work out? This is such a small town. I'd see him everywhere. And everyone knows both of us, so I'd have to explain to everyone what went wrong."

"Don't go borrowing trouble. Half the town is rooting for the two of you. We can't all be wrong."

"Well, maybe the other half is right," Hannah muttered.

Lacy sat on the bed beside her. "What's this really about, Hannah?"

She shrugged. "I'm scared. I haven't had the best track record with relationships, but I want this one to work."

"Then be yourself. Liam already really likes you. Make a promise to yourself to enjoy your time with him, and then do it. Take that advice from an old married woman."

"You're not old."

"But I am wise," Lacy teased. "And I've been happily married for twelve years." She stood up and started to hang the rejected clothes back in Hannah's closet. "And on that note, I need to get home to Neil. He's been so busy lately that we've barely seen each other."

"You'll bring him to the Gratitude Feast, won't you?"

"The entire town is going to be there. Of course he's coming."

As Lacy headed for the door, Hannah called after her, "Oh, please thank Neil for the book and tell him it helped me solve the mystery."

Her friend waved and left.

The next morning, Hannah was ready early in the outfit Lacy had chosen. After assessing herself in the mirror, she added a pretty autumn scarf for color. She started pacing the restaurant, straightening napkins, rotating pumpkins, replacing candles, anything to avoid obsessively checking her phone. By the time Liam finally arrived, she'd worked herself into a state of nerves.

He waited for her at the Hot Spot entrance and when she stepped out, he smiled to see her and then frowned. "I don't deserve sparkles and velvet?"

Hannah swatted at him. "Been talking to Lacy about me, have you?"

Liam helped her into the Jeep. "Someone had to make sure you were attired properly for our day together."

"You could have just told me where we're going. Where *are* we going?"

"Nice try, but that would spoil the surprise." Liam hurried around the back and hopped in the driver's seat. He started the vehicle and headed out of town, which only increased Hannah's curiosity.

"It's a lovely day for a drive in the country," she commented.

"Yes it is," Liam responded, frustrating her with his lack of detail.

"Hardly any traffic."

"Which means there's nothing to distract me, so why don't you update me about your meeting with Angelina? I've been waiting to hear, but you didn't call."

Hannah went quiet and took a deep breath before she answered. "I was nervous."

"To tell me what you found out? Was it that bad?"

"About this date," she blurted.

Liam glanced over at her, then slowed the Jeep and pulled over onto the shoulder. He put the Jeep in park and faced her. "Hannah, we don't have to do this if you don't want to."

She looked up, startled, and made a small sound of surprise. "But I do. I really do. I'm just nervous."

Liam reached across the seat to take her hand. "Me too. But, Hannah, that's because you matter to me. And things that are important, things that matter—they make us nervous." He hesitated and drew in a long breath. "I really like you. I've been looking forward to spending a day with you for a long time."

"We did that when we explored the caves."

"That's true. But this is different."

"I know. That's why it scares me."

"Hannah, look at me."

She gazed solemnly into his brown eyes, and the concern and affection she saw there eased the knots deep within her. "Those things that matter and make us nervous? They also make us happy," she murmured. "I don't want to let the nerves ruin something wonderful." Her face relaxed into an easy smile that Liam returned.

"Ready to keep going?"

"That would be easier to answer if I knew where we were going," she joked.

Liam laughed and pulled back onto the empty road. "So, tell me what you found out this week. No more stalling."

Hannah laughed. "Was that a pun? Stalling? Horse stalls?"

Liam's deep laugh rumbled through the car. "Not intentional, but since it made you laugh, sure."

"If I tell you, will you tell me where we're going?"

"If you tell me, I'll show you where we're going."

Hannah sighed in resignation, and then began to relate everything she had learned. When she got to the end of her meeting with Angelina, they were just turning up a long farm lane.

"So that's it? You just left Jamie's phone number with Angelina and didn't tell him?"

"It was really hard, but, to quote Jamie Chadwick, 'It wasn't my story to tell.'"

Liam shot her a quick, knowing smile. "That must be killing you."

"It is, because I'm still not sure I did the right thing in telling her. Liam, what if I ruined two people's lives because I couldn't contain my curiosity?"

"That was the risk you took, but the alternative is you might have given them a chance to reunite after all these years. Angelina said it was time to face her past. Of course, I can't know this for sure, but that sounds like she had doubts or regrets about how she handled it."

"I could tell she was very torn. The decision literally changed her life—and Jamie's."

"It sounds like she went on to build a good life for herself despite the rough start."

"Yes, she clearly loved her husband and built a loving family and business with him. But you should have seen the way she reacted when I mentioned Jamie's name. I thought she was going to faint."

Liam's tone was thoughtful when he responded. "Hannah, we can't know the outcome of this. You did what you thought was right, and you did it with the best of intentions. I don't think you should regret telling her, and I think you were right not to tell Jamie. She was the one who left. She needs to be the one who returns—if she chooses to."

"Thank you, and I know you're right about that. It's just killing me that Jamie doesn't know how her grandfather manipulated her."

"I understand, but think about it. Angelina didn't know that until you told her, right?"

Hannah nodded.

"That's a pretty serious betrayal. Angelina just learned what her grandfather had done, decades later. She'll need time to process it all before she can make a decision about how to proceed."

The tension in Hannah's chest finally started to ease. "Thanks, Liam. I hadn't thought of it that way, but you're absolutely right."

"In the meantime, how about I distract you from thinking about it?" Liam gestured toward a huge red barn beside the road as he pulled into a parking lot. "Since the Hot Spot has a farm-to-table concept, I thought you would enjoy brunch here. An old friend of mine owns the farm, and his wife converted an unused barn into a restaurant. It's about as farm-to-table as you can get, since everything on the menu is produced either right here or on one of the neighboring farms."

Hannah was ecstatic. "Liam, this is incredible. I love visiting other restaurants and being inspired." She smiled as he came around to open her door.

They walked up a short path and entered through the renovated barn doors. Just inside, two old wheelbarrows overflowed with gold and burgundy mums. The walls featured antique farm implements, seed posters, and photos of family members working the fields through the years.

They entered a big country dining room lined with floor-to-ceiling windows, and a petite woman hurried over to greet them. She hugged Liam then took Hannah's hands. "You must be Hannah. I'm Sarah, and I'm so glad Liam brought you here. He's been telling me all about your Hot Spot and has me dying to visit. I hope you'll enjoy your meal with us."

Liam guided Hannah across the room to a table overlooking the fields. "You're always serving others, so I thought it might be nice for you to be served for a change."

Hannah was overcome. The warmth of Liam's hand on the small of her back, the care he had put into this choice of date, the adorable restaurant, the breathtaking view. "It's absolute perfection, Liam." She smiled at him as he pulled out a chair for her. "Thank you."

When Liam was seated across from her, Sarah returned. "You have the place to yourself for now. We don't usually open this early, but for you and Liam, we gladly made an exception. I have menus, or I can offer the chef's sampler."

"Oh, I'd love the sampler," Hannah said. "I'm so curious about what you serve."

Liam agreed, so Sarah hustled off to put in the order.

"I can admit when I'm wrong," Hannah told Liam. "You were right to keep our destination a secret. There is no way I could have possibly imagined how special this place is."

For the next hour, Hannah and Liam tasted samples and shared conversation.

"The other night, you asked me why I left Blackberry Valley. Have you always known you'd stay?" Hannah asked when they were deep into their meal.

Liam set his fork aside. "From the time I was a little boy, I knew I wanted to follow in my grandfather's and father's footsteps and be a fire chief. But there have definitely been times in the last few years that I questioned my decision to stay."

Hannah's heart sank at the comment. "Why?"

"It can be lonely when your family is gone and your friends are starting families of their own."

Hannah understood. "Family is the thing I missed the most when I lived in California. Now I love being near my father and uncle, my brother and cousins, and all the kids."

"I haven't had that since my parents moved to Florida and my grandfather went to Clarkston Commons. That's why I considered leaving. But that changed when you arrived."

Liam's honesty left Hannah breathless. She recovered in the only way she knew how, by offering to help. "We often have a huge family dinner on Sundays. This time of year it usually revolves around football. You're welcome to join us anytime—as long as you don't mind the noise."

"Noisy family is a good thing. I've taken to working longer hours to compensate, but balance is important. I'd love to hang out with your family some Sunday."

"Since it's all about family, you should bring your grandfather too."

"That would be great, Hannah. He's happy at Clarkston Commons, but I know Gramps misses his friends in Blackberry Valley. He'll love to visit with your dad and uncle."

Sarah came over to check on them. When Hannah finished gushing about the meal, she said, "I'd offer to take you in to meet the chef, but I know you have an appointment to get to. You'll have to come back." She turned to Liam. "Your packages are in your Jeep."

Liam stood and held Hannah's jacket out for her. As they crossed the sun-dappled parking lot, Hannah asked, "We have an appointment? Our date isn't done?"

"Only having brunch wouldn't be a very original first date, would it?" Liam grinned.

"Brunch at this place would be." Hannah had noted his emphasis on *first* and studied him. "It was a lovely first date. Is it presumptuous to hope for a second one?"

"Not presumptuous, but definitely premature since this one's not done yet." He held open the Jeep door. "Hop in. We need to make tracks. I don't want to be late."

They left the restaurant lot, and Liam turned onto the road heading away from Blackberry Valley. Hannah was beside herself with curiosity, but this time, she bit her tongue. She'd learned her lesson.

After about half an hour driving through open country, Liam turned down another farm lane. Ahead lay a field of horses. Some were grazing, some playing, and others raced along the rail with manes and tails streaming out behind them. Hannah's jaw dropped in delight when Liam turned in to the farm lot. "You brought me to see horses."

He grinned at her. "Nope. I brought you to *ride* horses."

"Liam!" Hannah couldn't contain her squeal. "I think this even tops Sarah's restaurant."

For the next hour Hannah was beside herself with joy as they took refresher lessons and then were able to ride across the field. If she imagined it was Kentucky's Angel she was riding—well, there was nothing wrong with that. Finally, happily exhausted, they relinquished the horses and returned to the Jeep.

As Liam opened the door for her, Hannah tried to thank him. "My ten-year-old self is overwhelmed at having had this chance to ride, and my adult self is speechless at how much thought and effort went into planning this date. You really went out of your way to make sure it was something I would enjoy and remember. Thank you."

After Liam helped her into the front seat, he left the door open while he retrieved a package from the back. "I have something for you. A memento if you will." With a flourish, he presented Hannah with a bouquet of red roses. As she buried her face in them, trying to hide the tears that had suddenly sprung up, he handed her his second present—a brand-new photo album. "I hope it's not too presumptuous to think you might want to save them."

Hannah burst into laughter, but after a moment she took his hand, her heart full. "Thank you, Liam. This day, this time with you. This has been the best day of my entire life."

"I hope there'll be many more fun days we can measure this one against."

She couldn't wait to find out.

Chapter Thirty

The next week passed in a flurry of regular restaurant business, last-minute preparations for the Gratitude Feast, and moments where Hannah paused to soak in the memories of her perfect date with Liam.

And then it was the day of the Gratitude Feast. Sunday after church, Pastor Bob and Hannah welcomed what seemed like the entirety of the town gathered outside the Hot Spot.

The pastor raised his hand, and slowly silence descended on the crowd. When he had everyone's attention, he addressed them. "This Thursday, we will celebrate a national day of Thanksgiving, but today is our own Gratitude Feast, a time for us to reflect on what we mean to one another and to celebrate the incredible community we share. Through good times and bad, we come together, and nowhere is that more evident than here today. We weathered a storm, and Hannah has graciously welcomed us to her restaurant. Let us give thanks to our Lord for His bountiful blessings as we celebrate together."

A chorus of "Amens" followed.

Hannah addressed the crowd. "It's so good to be back home and part of this amazing community. I loved growing up here, but I don't think I fully appreciated how special it is until I moved away. Thank you all for welcoming me home and for making the Hot Spot the community hub I always wanted to create. I speak for Jacob,

Elaine, Raquel, and Dylan, as well as myself, when I say we are so grateful for all of you."

The crowd applauded.

"Speaking of Jacob," she continued, "I know many of you have eaten his food in the Hot Spot, but I have to give him a special shout-out for all the time, effort, and love he's poured into creating an amazing menu for today's celebration. If you see Jacob, please be sure to let him know how much you're enjoying his food. And finally, I would be remiss if I didn't give credit to our outstanding committee and to our chairwoman, Lorelai, who worked so hard to make this our best Gratitude Feast ever."

Amid the cheers, Hannah beckoned to Liam. He came up beside her and grabbed the rope, and together they tugged the bell that had once been used to summon firefighters but now welcomed the community.

Hannah flung open the Hot Spot doors and invited her friends and neighbors inside.

Lorelai's committee had been hard at work since the wee hours of the morning, taking a break only for the church service, and they had transformed the old firehouse into a festive celebration of autumn, with cornucopias and pumpkins and mums decorating the tables and the traditional *Gratitude* banner draped across the wall above the buffet.

Jacob had filled the tables to overflowing with a variety of appetizers, and the aromas wafting from the kitchen promised even more goodness to come.

Once again, Hannah felt herself completely overwhelmed by all the blessings in her life.

Pastor Bob came to stand beside her, and Lorelai linked her arm with Hannah's. "Hannah, we can't thank you enough for this."

Hannah shook her head. "As I said outside, Jacob is the one who deserves most of the credit. He threw himself into this project, working long hours and perfecting the recipes for us to enjoy. Lorelai, you and your committee took care of everything else. I only provided the space."

Lorelai smiled. "It was truly a community effort."

The afternoon rolled on, with friends and family wandering in, dropping off additional food, and sharing in the fun. Liam, Archer, and Colt kept the children entertained with outside games and tours of the fire truck and sheriff's cars. Every once in a while, Hannah would hear a fire engine horn followed by shrieks of laughter.

Hannah's friends from the church group had pushed a table over to a booth and were enjoying themselves together, while their husbands and other football fans gathered around a screen Colin Steele had set up for watching the games. Hannah was happy to see Liam had brought his grandfather from Clarkston Commons. Patrick was laughing and talking with longtime friends. In fact, everyone seemed to be having a wonderful time.

Lacy and Neil wandered over to say hello.

"Hannah, this is so fabulous. I think you've started a whole new tradition," Lacy gushed. "We may never go back to the church hall."

A week ago the idea would have thrown Hannah into a panic, but now she welcomed it. Only one thing dampened her spirits. "You haven't heard anything from Angelina, have you?"

Lacy shook her head. "I was hoping you had."

"Nothing."

Jacob was laying out an array of desserts when Hannah heard Liam call her name. She glanced over to see him approaching the front door. When had he gone outside?

"I have some visitors I think you'll be happy to see." He stepped inside, and suddenly Hannah could see Angelina on his arm. Beside her, with a hand cupping her elbow, was none other than Jamie Chadwick. Joy filled her at the sight, and she rushed over.

"You're here. Together." Tears formed in Hannah's eyes as she struggled for words.

It was Jamie who replied. "We are indeed, thanks to you."

Hannah hadn't thought the day could get any better, but as she sat with Angelina and Jamie, listening to the story of their reunion, she thought her heart might burst.

"I'm sorry I kept silent so long," Angelina said. "At first I had a lot to reconcile about my grandfather, and then I had to gather my courage. I wasn't sure Jamie could ever forgive me."

"Of course I did," Jamie added. "I've loved Angelina my entire life. I'd be a fool to throw away a chance like this. We debated calling, but then we decided to surprise you here at the feast instead, so we could share our gratitude with you and the whole community. Because of your persistence, you have given two old people a chance to love again. We wanted you to know how much we appreciate that, so we brought a gift in your honor."

Angelina handed her an envelope. "We heard about the storm damage to the church, and how you had to change the venue. We hope this gift will help defray the costs of repair and still provide for the library."

Hannah stared at the check in awe. "I didn't do it for any reward."

"No," Angelina said. "You did it because of your kind heart and a penchant for solving mysteries, and that is enough for us."

Later, as the party was winding down, Liam came to tell Hannah he had to leave to drive his grandfather back home. "I don't suppose you could sneak away and come with us."

Lorelai overheard and urged Hannah to go. "You've done so much. Go, enjoy yourself. I'll make sure everything gets cleaned up."

Patrick was in his element to be with his grandson and Hannah, and he happily reminisced about past Gratitude Feasts while praising Hannah for the success of today's celebration.

The ride passed quickly, and once they had Patrick settled back at Clarkston Commons with friends who had already begun singing Christmas carols, Liam and Hannah headed home.

The Jeep was warm, and though she was sleepy, Hannah wanted to cherish every minute with Liam. She asked a question to stay awake. "How did you find Angelina and Jamie?" Hannah heard his warm chuckle before he replied.

"They came up to the fire truck and asked if I knew how to find you."

"I'm so glad they came."

"I hope you're feeling good about what you did. I know you had doubts, but the gift you gave them is precious beyond measure."

"I'm glad they have a chance to be together now. Angelina made a very difficult sacrifice in the name of family, but lost the man she loved in the process. I think he understood that."

"People often talk about God's perfect timing, and I think we saw it tonight," Liam said. "Speaking of timing, I know our schedules are incredibly busy and will probably conflict at times, but I really enjoyed our date, Hannah. I'd like to go out with you again if you're interested."

It wasn't until that moment, when she heard him utter those words, that Hannah realized how much she'd worried that he wouldn't ask. "I would really like that too, Liam."

They chatted companionably for the rest of the drive, and when they arrived at the Hot Spot, Liam came around to help her out. He walked her to the door. "Of all the things I am grateful for today, what tops my list is that you decided to come home to Blackberry Valley, and that I'm lucky enough to have you in my life." He leaned over and gave her a light kiss on the cheek. "I'll call you later to set up another date, okay?"

"I look forward to it. Good night, Liam."

"Good night, Hannah." He smiled as she slipped through the door.

She closed it behind her and, leaning against it, let the emotions of the day wash over her.

There was so much to be grateful for this Thanksgiving. She was home with family, finally owned her own successful restaurant, and had a strong community that she truly felt a part of. As she glanced around the dining room, she could see the table where Angelina and Jamie had sat earlier. Getting to be a part of their story and helping give them a happy ending went on her list as well.

And finally, she added the one person her heart was so grateful for that she was almost afraid to acknowledge it. Hannah smiled, thinking of Liam. She released a happy sigh. God had been so good to her. She could only wonder what would be next as she thought ahead to the holidays, a new year, and hopefully more intriguing mysteries to solve.

From the Author

Dear Reader,

I feel so blessed to be part of the Mysteries of Blackberry Valley series. I don't think I've ever had as much fun writing a book as I did writing about Hannah, Lacy, Liam, and all their family and friends in Blackberry Valley. One of my favorite things about reading has always been the way characters become so alive to me that I feel like I could easily recognize them if I met them on the street. I hope you feel that way as you read our stories.

Maybe you can identify with the horse-obsessed girl that Hannah once was. I certainly can. My father used to enlist the help of his school librarian to hunt for more of the horse books his young daughter devoured. Writing Angelina's story was like reliving a part of my childhood. Until I was nine, I grew up in the shadow of Belmont Racetrack in Queens, New York. Dad used to take my sisters and me to breakfast at the track so we could watch the horses train. What exciting memories were brought back to me as I wrote this book.

Whether you are a horse lover or not, I hope you enjoyed coming along for the ride as Hannah and her friends worked to find the missing horse and jockey!

Signed,
Cate Nolan

About the Author

Once upon a time, there was a girl who loved to read more than anything, and she especially loved mysteries. That girl, Cate Nolan, grew up to write her own stories. Today she is a Publishers' Weekly bestselling author of suspense and mystery novels.

Although Cate spent most of her life in New York, she now lives by the sea in Maine where the rolling waves and foggy mornings inspire her. When she's not writing, Cate is a Middle School English Language Arts teacher who encourages her students to develop their own reading and writing talents.

The Hot Spotlight

Many a horse-loving young girl has dreams of growing up to be a jockey and riding a champion mount in the Kentucky Derby, the Preakness, or the Belmont Stakes. All too often in the history of thoroughbred racing, those hopes and dreams were dashed by a dose of reality. Horse racing had long been considered a "gentleman's sport," and nowhere was that more obvious than in the struggle women faced if they wanted to be licensed as jockeys.

In *Run for the Roses*, Hannah learns what it was like to be a pioneering woman jockey in the 1960s from a book Neil gives her. The lessons she learned were based on my research in writing this book. As someone who had thought my main obstacle to becoming a jockey was being too tall—and not having access to any horses—I was shocked to learn about the treatment women jockeys faced.

Kathryn Kusner, the first woman to apply for a jockey's license in 1967, was denied because she was a woman. Her lawyer had to sue under civil rights laws so that the jockey licensing board was forced to issue her a license.

When Penny Ann Early attempted to ride at Churchill Downs in 1968, most people thought it was a joke. The male jockeys objected so strongly that they threatened to boycott the race.

Despite facing many of the same obstacles, including boycotts and ridicule, Diane Crump became the first woman to compete as a jockey when she rode in a race at Hialeah. Although she had previously been told to stay out of Kentucky racing to avoid controversy, she was the first woman to race at Churchill Downs, and in 1970 she became the first woman to ride in the Kentucky Derby. She went on to win more than 200 races in her career.

Crump was followed by other brave women such as Rosie Napravnik, who registered under her initials to avoid controversy, but who won the Kentucky Oaks twice, and Julie Krone, who became the first woman to win a Triple Crown Race when she won the Belmont Stakes in 1993.

Thanks to the efforts of these women, who endured cruel insults and even physical threats but would not be denied their dreams, today roughly a quarter of all jockeys are women. Like Angelina and Hannah, they had dreams and believed in themselves—a good lesson for us all.

From the Hot Spot Kitchen

JACOB'S THANKSGIVING FIREMAN'S PIE

Ingredients:

3–4 large sweet potatoes

½ cup dried cranberries

½ small onion, chopped (optional)

½ clove garlic, mashed (optional)

1 pound ground turkey or leftover shredded turkey

Water or broth as necessary

¾ teaspoon poultry seasoning

Additional rosemary or thyme as desired

1–1½ cups frozen mixed vegetables to taste

Drizzle of maple syrup

Olive oil

Lorelai's addition—corn bread crust if desired

Pie tin

Directions:

Bake sweet potatoes until soft. Scoop and mash with a fork. Add dried cranberries and mix.

Sauté onion and garlic in 1 teaspoon olive oil if including them. Otherwise, proceed to next step.

When onions are translucent, add ground turkey and stir until browned.

Start with ½ cup broth or water and add more as necessary. Cover to simmer until turkey is thoroughly cooked.

Add poultry seasoning to taste. You may prefer to add additional rosemary or thyme, but adding extra poultry seasoning can make it too dominant.

Once turkey is cooked, combine with frozen vegetables and ladle mixture into pie tin. Scoop sweet potato mixture on top and smooth to cover entire pie.

Drizzle with maple syrup and garnish with additional cranberries if desired.

Bake in 400-degree oven until all ingredients are heated through and sweet potatoes get a bit crispy, about 20 to 25 minutes depending on oven. Watch so they don't burn!

If you like Lorelai's idea of a corn bread bottom crust, you can use any corn bread recipe or mix and spread a thin layer. Bake before filling with turkey mixture.

If you have leftovers, refrigerate immediately. The pie tastes even better the second day!

Read on for a sneak peek of another exciting book in the *Mysteries of Blackberry Valley* series!

Crooks and Christmas Cookies

BY STEPHANIE COLEMAN

Hannah Prentiss was already five minutes late for her meeting with Amelia Jacobsen, and she hadn't even left her restaurant yet. But as she hurried to the door, head chef Jacob Forrest flagged her down.

"I watched an online video on dry-aging meat," he said, his eyes alight with excitement. "It looks time-consuming but not hard."

"I would love to hear more about this later." Hannah took another step toward the dining room of the Hot Spot. "Can we talk when I get back?"

By then maybe she would have thought of a way to break it to him that they'd probably have to charge more for dry-aged meat than the people of Blackberry Valley would want to pay. Jacob was endlessly creative with food but often oblivious to the realities of the food budget.

As Hannah swept past the hostess stand, Elaine Wilby frowned at her. "I thought your meeting was at three."

"Think I'll be on time?" Hannah quipped. "Call if you need me."

Inside her car, Hannah took the time to send Amelia a quick text. Sorry I'm late! I should be there in five minutes. What had she been thinking when she arranged this meeting for a Friday afternoon, one of her busiest times of the week?

She tucked her phone into her purse before pulling away from her usual parking spot outside the restaurant. When she saw one of the Holt twins had their patrol car parked outside Blackberry Market, she was grateful that she hadn't tried to speed on the way to Sally's Bed and Breakfast.

Or what would be Sally's Bed and Breakfast when it opened.

When Hannah first met Amelia a few months ago, Amelia had just moved to Blackberry Valley to help take care of her mother, Sally, who had owned a house on the edge of town for several years, a big place brimming with Southern charm. Hannah had never been inside, but she'd always admired its wide wraparound porch and the ornate trim work that rarely appeared in newly constructed homes.

For years, Sally had wanted to turn her childhood home into a bed and breakfast where she could serve guests all the foods that she was famous for among her friends. But Sally's husband had passed away not long after they purchased the property. Losing him so suddenly had aged Sally faster than anyone anticipated, and Amelia had moved in to help.

Like everyone else, Hannah had expected that Sally's death would lead to the big house going back on the market, but instead Amelia had fallen in love with the town and wanted to see her mother's dream come to fruition. While Amelia was older than Hannah's mother had been when she died, she reminded Hannah strongly of Frieda Prentiss. Hannah's mom had fought with grace until the end of her battle with cancer, and Amelia struck Hannah as the kind of woman with that same quiet strength. It would serve her well in her business endeavor.

Today, Hannah was meeting with Amelia to go over her menus and make suggestions before final orders were placed. Amelia, much like Jacob, had strong ideas about how the food at Sally's should look and taste but didn't yet know how to factor in the cost of ingredients or design a menu that eliminated food waste or stayed within budget.

A new sign had been put near the end of the drive. SALLY'S, it read in a tasteful, loopy font. The circular drive held two trucks and a work van. Converting the house to a bed and breakfast was a big job, and it looked like everyone was on task today. Hannah parked alongside a shiny Jeep Cherokee that seemed out of place then grabbed her purse and rushed up the steps of the wraparound porch.

She knocked on the door. Inside were sounds of drilling and hammering, so it was probably okay to simply walk inside, but it still felt strange.

"Are you here to see Amelia?" asked a male voice from behind her.

She turned and found herself sharing the porch with Isaac Jacobsen, Amelia's nephew. Isaac was from Nashville, and Hannah always felt awkward and unpolished in his presence. He was about her age, maybe a couple years younger, and wore his clothes more tailored, his hair sleeker, and his shoes shinier than other men she knew in town.

"Yes, I am," Hannah said with a smile. "I'm afraid I'm a bit late."

"Come on in." Isaac pushed the door open, and the cacophony of construction noises became even louder. "Your name is Hannah, right? You own the Hot Spot?" He grinned, showcasing a mouthful of gleaming white teeth. "I had an excellent dinner there several nights ago. Fried smoked chicken, mashed potatoes, and roasted vegetables." He formed a chef's kiss with his fingers. "Amazing."

Hannah swelled with pride. "All locally sourced too. Our eggs come from my best friend, Lacy's, chickens, and they're incredible. And most of our vegetables are from—"

"No, you listen to me!" screeched a female voice.

"Excuse me," Isaac murmured. He headed toward the sound.

Hannah lingered in the entry, feeling increasingly awkward as every loud word reached her ears.

"I have lost everything because of you and your stupid delays!" The same woman continued to rant. "I should've been getting married tomorrow, and now I'm not, and it's all because of you!"

Hannah heard the low timbre of Isaac's voice as he entered the conversation, but she couldn't make out any actual words.

"I've had enough of your fake apologies," the woman snapped. "This isn't over. I will make you pay for what you did to me!"

Seconds later, the woman appeared in the hallway. Considering how loud she'd been, she was much smaller and younger than Hannah had anticipated. She appeared to be in her twenties, maybe even right out of college. She couldn't have been more than five feet tall, with beautiful dark hair that fell to her shoulders, a striking olive complexion, and cheekbones like a runway model's.

The woman's dark eyes landed on Hannah. "Whatever you do, do not trust either of them." Her voice was low and hot with anger. She jabbed a finger in the direction she'd come from. "They're liars."

With that, the woman marched to the front door, flung it open, and slammed it shut behind her. She stormed across the patio and stomped to the Jeep Cherokee.

Upstairs, a drill whirred, drawing Hannah back to the activity inside the house. Once again, she could hear the low rumble of Isaac's voice, only this time she could also hear the soft sounds of someone crying. Probably Amelia.

Feeling like an intruder, Hannah ventured several steps down the hall. "Amelia?" she called tentatively.

But it was Isaac who answered, "Come on back, Hannah. We're in the kitchen."

Hannah followed the hall around a bend and stepped into a huge kitchen that took her breath away. Renovations were completed in here, apparently.

Isaac gave her a tight smile. "My aunt has gone to the restroom to wash her face and collect herself. I'm sorry you had to hear that."

"I'm sorry it happened," Hannah said. "Would it be better for me to come another time?"

"No, now's fine." Isaac waved away her suggestion. "Aunt Amelia will be back in a moment. Coffee?"

"Sure. Thank you."

Hannah's hand rested on the cool, quartz countertop, and she took in the splendor of the kitchen. The professional range, the stainless-steel prep area, the espresso machine, the enormous refrigerator. She'd been in many impressive kitchens over the course of her career, but not many brand-new ones. Hannah felt an irrational desire to move in.

A pocket door slid open, and Amelia stepped out. "Sorry to keep you waiting, Hannah," she said in her soft voice. Her face was blotchy, and her eyes were red.

"No apology necessary. I'm sorry for your trouble." Hannah smiled at Isaac as he handed her a mug of coffee. "Thank you. This smells divine."

He grinned at her. "Coffee is kind of my thing."

His grin looked strange alongside Amelia's frown.

Amelia took in a shuddering breath. "Violet is understandably angry with me. She was supposed to have her wedding ceremony here tomorrow, but that was before the whole…incident with my first contractor. When everything got delayed, we tried to make different arrangements with Violet, but it didn't go well."

Isaac snorted. "That's putting it mildly. Violet took the news so poorly that her husband-to-be got spooked and called the whole thing off."

While Isaac seemed unfazed by Violet's visit, Amelia looked as though she might burst into tears again.

"I feel terrible about what happened." Amelia took a towel from its hook and wiped the kitchen faucet, which already appeared to be perfectly clean. "I refunded her deposit. I offered to find a different date of her choosing at no cost. I tried to get her booked at Blackberry Inn, but Sabrina didn't have any availability."

Hannah wasn't too surprised that Amelia had gone to such lengths to make the situation right, and it only made her more upset that Violet had been so unpleasant to Amelia.

"You did your best," Isaac said as Amelia scrubbed the already-clean counter. "Let it go."

He wasn't being unkind, exactly, but he was behaving as though his aunt was overreacting. Hannah had been shouted at more than a few times in her line of work—such was life in the restaurant business—and more than once had cried afterward. Being told to "let it go" was never helpful.

"It sounds like you did everything you could," Hannah said, making her voice as warm as possible. "And you certainly can't help that her fiancé broke off the engagement when he saw how she reacted."

"I suppose not." Amelia bit her lower lip. "She'll probably say horrid things to all her friends though. This won't be good for business, and we're not even open yet."

"Does she live in town?" Hannah asked, after sipping her coffee. "I don't recognize her."

"No," Amelia said. "Cave City, I think."

"I don't think we need to worry about her." Isaac handed a steaming mug of coffee to his aunt. "Sure, she might say some bad things to friends, but she strikes me as the type who's overly critical. People will probably shrug it off as Violet being Violet."

"Maybe," Amelia murmured.

"And as soon as people taste Grandma's legendary rosemary lemon shortbread, they really won't care what Violet's saying," he added.

This coaxed the slightest of smiles onto Amelia's face, so Hannah chimed in. "Absolutely. I would drive clear to Louisville for one of Sally's shortbread cookies. Or a piece of her chocolate tart."

Amelia's face brightened considerably.

"I assume you know to not bother asking for the recipes," Isaac said with a grin.

"Oh, I know." Hannah returned the smile. "We've all tried. 'Family secrets.'"

"More like Grandma-and-Aunt-Amelia secrets." Isaac leaned against the counter and sipped from his own cup. "I'm family, and I'm still not privy to the recipes. Maybe we should call this place 'Secret Sally's.'"

Amelia glanced at the clock and yelped. "How is it almost three thirty already? I'm sorry I've kept you waiting so long, Hannah. Don't you open soon?"

Hannah waved away Amelia's concerns. "No need to apologize. Do you feel like going over your menus, or would you rather hold off?"

"Let's do it now. With our estimated opening in less than three weeks, I really can't afford to put it off any longer." Amelia gestured to an area that would normally hold a small kitchen table but contained a desk instead. A tin of candy was open on it. "Would you like some toffee?"

Hannah eagerly reached for a square. "You don't have to ask me twice."

Sally's desserts were legendary in these parts. She had been known for her bristly, abrupt manner, but the more time Hannah had spent with her, the more she'd liked her. She'd been sad to hear about Sally's death.

While interacting with Sally was an acquired taste, her baked goods were not. Unlike most cooks, Sally had refused to share her recipes, saying they were her intellectual property and would someday draw throngs of visitors to Blackberry Valley.

Hannah hummed as the candy melted on her tongue. Sally's toffees were the perfect blend of buttery, salty, and sweet. How many pieces would a polite woman take? And how much value did Hannah place on being viewed as a polite woman?

"I just wonder what she'll do now," Amelia said as she settled behind her desk. The regret and sorrow in her tone signaled to Hannah that the conversation had returned to the bitter bride.

"I think you handled it well, given the circumstances," Hannah insisted. "You even called Blackberry Inn to offer your competition the chance to make it right with her. That's above and beyond."

Amelia nodded slowly. "Yes, but I don't think Violet Presley sees it that way." She sighed. "I don't know what she'll do or say, of course, but I can feel in my bones that what happened with Violet will come back to haunt me somehow."

Hannah didn't want to say it aloud, but recalling the fire in Violet's eyes as she'd stormed out the front door, she had to agree.

Printed in the United States
by Baker & Taylor Publisher Services